Zach's mind raced with all sorts of possibilities that had nothing to do with police work but everything to do with the discovery phase—starting with what Raissa was wearing under her silk nightie. She smiled down at him, sexy, hot, and so clearly issuing a challenge. Zach rose from the chair and locked his lips on hers in a single fluid motion that made her gasp. He pushed her back against the wall, enjoying the momentary surprise that crossed her face before she grabbed his head and lowered his lips to hers once more. He brought his hands up to cup her face as their mouths parted and their tongues met.

Then something struck him on his neck and he dropped to the ground, certain he'd been hit by lightning.

"Got him!" a woman shouted. "Cover me, Mildred."

"Wait!" He heard Raissa yell in the frenzy.

His entire body screamed in pain, and when he turned to see what had happened, he got a blast of spray right in his face. He felt the burning of Mace and hoped to God that the woman who had attacked him had a bigger weapon to use, because as soon as he could see again, he was going to shoot her.

"Are you all right, Raissa?" the woman asked. "We saw him strangling you."

Zach managed to get one eye partially open and saw Raissa staring down at him, her face a mixture of amazement and amusement. Two other women stood in front of her—an older woman with the Mace, and a younger one with a stun gun. Jesus, what kind of hotel was this?

Other books by Jana DeLeon:

MISCHIEF IN MUDBUG
TROUBLE IN MUDBUG
UNLUCKY
RUMBLE ON THE BAYOU

PRAISE FOR JANA DeLEON!

MISCHIEF IN MUDBUG

"*Mischief in Mudbug* is full of fun, action, and enough twists and turns to keep the pages turning. All of the characters are well written and drive the story, but Helena's ghost gets me every time. Ms. DeLeon does a great job keeping you wondering what's going to happen next. If you're looking for some giggles and surprises mixed with some romance this one's for you."

—Night Owl Romance

". . . a delight to read. By combining realistic, rich characters with an attention-holding plotline, Jana DeLeon has created a book that will satisfy any palate."

—Once Upon a Romance

"Lighthearted and very funny at times, *Mischief in Mudbug* moves along at a breakneck pace . . . A breezy mystery with romance overtones that will keep you turning the pages."

—Fresh Fiction

TROUBLE IN MUDBUG

"DeLeon brings her spunky style to a novel that's plenty of fun to read. The characters are easy to indentify with and demonstrate their multifaceted personalities in their actions and words. DeLeon is excellent at weaving comedy, suspense, and spicy romance into one compelling story."

—RT Book Reviews

"Funny and exciting, DeLeon manages to keep you guessing and laughing from start to finish . . . I would recommend this to anyone."

—Night Owl Romance

"Interesting characters and a fun and entertaining mystery make *Trouble in Mudbug* a novel I highly recommend."

—Romance Reviews Today

Showdown in Mudbug

JANA DeLeon

LOVE SPELL  NEW YORK CITY

pbk
D

*To my parents, Jimmie and Bobbie Morris, for raising me
to be fearless and hardheaded, and for always making me
feel like the smartest person in the world. You've given me
the confidence to succeed.*

LOVE SPELL®

July 2010

Published by

Dorchester Publishing Co., Inc.
200 Madison Avenue
New York, NY 10016

ISBN 10: 0-505-52849-5
ISBN 13: 978-0-505-52849-0
E-ISBN: 978-1-4285-0901-6

The name "Love Spell" and its logo are trademarks of Dorchester
Publishing Co., Inc.

Printed in the United States of America.

10 9 8 7 6 5 4 3 2 1

Visit us online at www.dorchesterpub.com.

ACKNOWLEDGMENTS

Thanks to my critique partners Cari Manderscheid, Cindy Taylor, and Colleen Gleason for your sound advice and for just listening to me complain. Thanks to my daily chat buddy, Leslie Langtry, who can make even the worst things funny. Thanks to Jimmie, Donna, and Katianne Morris, for your continued support and for pushing my books. Thanks to my unofficial assistant, Tracey Stanley, for making sure I eat breakfast and get to work on time and for talking about my books to anyone who will listen. Thanks to RWA and DARA for the education you provide and always looking out for a writer's best interest. Thanks to the cover artist—this cover blows me away! Thanks to my editor, Leah Hultenschmidt, for always making my books better and working to get the perfect cover. And special thanks to my agent, Kristin Nelson, for always pushing me to extend myself and believing that I can.

Showdown in Mudbug

Chapter One

Raissa Bourdeaux went through the uses of the different-colored candles for what had to be the hundredth time. She knew Mrs. Angelieu was more interested in gossiping than actually buying anything, so there was really nothing more to do but continue to point to items and wait her out. She glanced at her watch and was dismayed to find it was hours before closing. Monday had been a very long day.

"And then," Mrs. Angelieu said, her face animated, "I told Lucille that I just couldn't believe she'd bring that casserole dish to the church. Why, it belonged to her mother, and everyone knew what a harlot her mother was. It's a wonder God didn't send lightning down right there in the middle of her potato salad." She gave Raissa a single nod and waited for confirmation.

"Well," Raissa said, struggling for something that wasn't rude, "that certainly would have been a show. But God hasn't really been that obvious since the Old Testament. I mean, I haven't heard of a burning bush in a long time."

Mrs. Angelieu laughed. "You always know how to put things in perspective, Raissa. That's why I love talking to you. I consider it my weekly dose of reality."

"Oh, you don't have to come to me for that. Just turn on any news channel."

Mrs. Angelieu sobered. "It's just horrible about that missing child, isn't it? My Lord, I can't imagine what those parents are going through."

"What missing child?"

"Why, it's been all over the news today. That sweet little six-year-old girl who went missing from her bedroom last night. Just vanished."

Raissa frowned. "I haven't had the TV on all day, so I didn't know. That's very sad."

Mrs. Angelieu nodded. "Well, I'm going to take one of these pretty blue candles and get out of here. Maybe you can have a nice glass of wine and relax a little. I don't mean to offend you, Raissa, but you look a little tired."

"It's been busy lately," Raissa said as she rang up Mrs. Angelieu's purchase and wrapped the candle.

"Well, that's better than being bored, I suppose," Mrs. Angelieu said as she took her bag. "I'll see you next week." She waved to Raissa as she exited the shop.

Raissa locked the front door and put the CLOSED sign in the window. She had no other appointments and simply wasn't in the mood to deal with another Mrs. Angelieu. The old woman couldn't have been more wrong about being bored. A couple of weeks before, Raissa's close friends had found themselves in a mess of trouble. After a harrowing week of bombs, poisonings, a disgruntled ghost, and too many lies to count, Raissa would have welcomed a day with nothing better to think about than whether God should send lightning into the potato salad of a former harlot bowl owner.

She turned off the lights for the shop and headed up the back staircase to her apartment above the store. It was small, but it suited her perfectly. Raissa had learned long ago to economize. At any given time, she might need to put everything important into her car and disappear. It had been a long time—more than nine years—since the last time she'd had to change everything in her life but the clothes on her back, but she knew that possibility was always there. Long-term plans were not part of her life.

She poured a glass of wine and turned on the television. The news had preempted local programming to feature more about the missing girl. As soon as the picture flashed on the screen along with the girl's name, Raissa clunked her wine down on the coffee table, the liquid sloshing onto the carved wood surface. Melissa Franco, the abducted child, had been in Raissa's store many times with her mother, Susannah. They didn't necessarily believe in the paranormal, but every month the little girl convinced her mother to stop in after their visit to the doctor across the street. The pretty candles and stones in the front display were apparently too much for the child to resist, and her mother always bought at least one more item for Melissa's growing collection of pink and purple.

The reporter suggested the girl had run away, but Raissa didn't buy that for a moment. Melissa was always happy and very inquisitive, asking Raissa endless questions about her shop, the candles, and ghosts. She was obviously doted on by her mother and didn't even cross the street without first grabbing her mother's hand. Not the kind of girl who would have run away from home. And certainly not the kind of girl with the street smarts to remain hidden in the midst of a city-wide manhunt.

As the report began going over the details of the case, Raissa's pulse began to race. Melissa had been asleep in her bedroom the night before, and there was no sign of forced entry. She'd simply vanished. Raissa took a big gulp of her wine, her hand shaking as she sat the glass back on the table.

Not again. Not after all these years.

Her head began to pound and she pressed her fingertips to her temples. Everything flooded back to her in a rush. The unanswered questions about entry into the house—every case the same. The seemingly identical victims, although she could never make a connection between the families. The girls, returned a week later, but with absolutely no memory of the abduction or anything that had happened to them while they were missing. Two years of undercover work blown by her trying to solve those cases. The man she knew was guilty, but couldn't find evidence against.

The reason Raissa had fled protective custody nine years ago.

Detective Zach Blanchard stood in front of his captain's desk and waited for the ass-chewing that was most certainly coming. The captain had already gnawed off one side this morning, but apparently someone had noticed Blanchard still had a little ass left and thought he could do with losing the rest.

"What the hell were you thinking?" Captain Saucier's face was beet red. "You interrupted the mayor in the middle of a city-planning meeting to ask him to provide an alibi for his son, whose daughter is missing. It's official, Blanchard. You've lost your fucking mind!"

Zach took a deep breath and started to explain. "According to Mr. Franco, he was with his father at the time of Melissa's disappearance. I needed to have that corroboration, and that meeting was scheduled to run all day. I didn't want to waste any more time investigating someone I don't think is guilty while the real kidnapper gets away."

Captain Saucier stared. "Statistics have shown time and again that a parent is often involved in the disappearance of a child, yet somehow you know *this* father can't possibly be guilty. Fine. Problem is, you've now indicated that he's a suspect to the entire city commission."

Zach bit back a response, certain that the fact that he'd been on the receiving end of a gross miscommunication, which had led to the unfortunate city-planning meeting interruption, wasn't going to matter one bit to the captain. "You're right, sir. That was a miscalculation on my part, and I hope it hasn't caused the mayor or his family any inconvenience."

"Inconvenience . . . You mean like being called a suspected kiddie killer on the evening news? No, they're used to that kind of thing. After all, they're in the public eye." The captain slammed one hand down on the desk. "From now on you don't so much as shit without clearing it with me first. Do you understand me, Blanchard? I've got the entire city up my ass with a microscope. Do you have any idea how uncomfortable that is?"

"No, sir. I don't."

"Damned right you don't, and with that kind of police work, you never will." He pointed a finger at Zach. "You *will* do everything on this case by the book. No hunches, no running off on rabbit trails, no funny business."

"Yes, sir."

"I mean it. Screw this up, and you'll still be writing parking tickets when you're walking with a cane."

"Everything will be by the book. I promise." The captain didn't look convinced, but he didn't start yelling again, either. Zach figured that was his opportunity to give the captain a nod and clear the room before his boss found out Zach had questioned the mother again that afternoon and the woman had collapsed in a faint just before he left.

By the book.

Just hearing the captain say those words rubbed him all wrong. He always did things by the book—except for that one time—and apparently he was never going to live that down. It was the damned book that said he should interview and alibi every member of the household as close to the disappearance as possible. Panic, stress, and unfortunately in some cases, guilt, tended to set in quickly and sometimes clouded people's minds to information that could lead to a break in the case.

So the mayor's assistant hadn't exactly told him that the entire city council was in that conference room. Matter of fact, she hadn't told him it was the conference room he was barging into. If he'd known that, he might have figured out the mayor wasn't alone. He *was* a detective, after all.

He was concentrating so hard on being aggravated that he almost walked right past the woman seated in front of his desk.

"Can I help you?" he asked. She was a looker, without question.

The woman met his gaze, and he felt his breath catch in his throat. Her eyes were a bright green, like the color of well-cut emeralds. He'd never seen anything quite so gorgeous on someone's face. She rose from her chair and extended her hand. "Detective Blanchard? My name is Raissa Bordeaux. Detective Morrow said I should speak with you."

Zach shook her hand, momentarily surprised by the firmness of her grip, then glanced across the room at Detective Morrow, usually a first-rate asshole. Morrow smirked, then shot out of the building. Great. Zach slid into his chair across the desk from the woman, certain this was going to be a waste of time. "How can I help you, Ms. Bordeaux?"

"I have information on the kidnapping of the Franco child."

"Okay," Zach said, and picked up a pen. "What kind of information?"

"This isn't his first time. That child is one of many who have been taken."

Zach stared. "Melissa Franco is the first child abduction this city has seen in a while that wasn't a custodial issue. I think you're mistaken, Ms. Bordeaux."

"The others didn't live in New Orleans. There were girls in Baton Rouge, in Florida, Mississippi, and New York. Surely there's a way you can compare this case with other kidnappings."

"The FBI keeps a database that we can use for such things, but what I'd like is a damned good reason why I should query that database. My boss isn't big on notifying the feds of anything going on in his precinct. He likes control."

"This is far bigger than your boss knows. If this is like the other cases, we're on a short clock. All of those other girls were returned a week later."

"With no memory of what happened, right? I've heard this tale before, Ms. Bordeaux, when I was a kid and my parents were trying to scare me into staying in the backyard."

Raissa raised one eyebrow. "Oh, they all remembered something, but probably not anything you'd want to hear. You have a narrow window of opportunity to catch this person, and I'm guessing, since the victim is the mayor's granddaughter, you don't want to mess this up."

Zach narrowed his eyes at the woman. "And how exactly do you know about these other kidnappings?"

She hesitated—rarely a good sign—then sighed. "I'm a psychic, Detective Blanchard. I saw the other girls in a vision."

Zach felt his jaw clench. "I see. Well, thank you for your information, Ms. Bordeaux. I'll be sure to add your name to the reward list in case of an arrest."

Raissa's face flushed with red and her eyes flashed with anger. "I debated a long time whether to come here, and it certainly wasn't because I care about extorting money from a frantic family. Do yourself a favor and check the database. Unless, of course, you're not interested in getting the best of your friend, the helpful Detective Morrow."

"I can't access that database without a direct order from my captain, which I'm not likely to get off the vision of a so-called psychic. There's a little girl missing out there and you're wasting our time."

Raissa leaned across the desk and lowered her voice. "The house had a security system that was armed, but the alarm never went off and it was still engaged the following morning. There is no trace evidence, and unlike most public kidnappings, you haven't received a ransom request."

Zach straightened in his chair. "We haven't released that information."

Raissa rose from her chair. "One of us is wasting time, Detective, but it's not me." That said, she walked out of the precinct without so much as a backward glance.

Zach leaned back in his chair and shook his head. A psychic. Yeah, right. No wonder Morrow had been so tickled to send her over to Zach. "By-the-book Blanchard" had limited-to-no patience for anything remotely screwy. Psychics were definitely screwy. Likely, Morrow had fed her the information about the security system and ransom note just to make the practical joke more believable.

He watched as she passed on the sidewalk in front of the big window at the front of the station, and couldn't help admiring her long lean legs, or the way she filled out a pair of jeans. What a shame. She was probably the best-looking woman he'd seen in forever.

Unfortunately, nut or no, the woman was right. He should run the case through the FBI database even though the captain hadn't quite gotten to that point. Time *was* of the essence, and the case had strange components that would send up an immediate red flag if there were others with the same MO. He sat up straight and logged on to his computer, hoping like hell that the mayor's granddaughter didn't fit the profile of the other missing girls. If that was the case, the captain might have a heart attack, and with the way things stood now, Morrow was next in line for his job.

Raissa stopped at the corner of the block, angry at herself. *You should have left it alone, but noooooo, you had to go taunting him with what you knew.* She punched the button for the crossing light and jammed her hands in her pockets, trying to control the urge to slug someone. *But it's a child, just like the others, and maybe this is the time he'll be caught.* She watched the screen on the other side of the street and tapped her foot. *It's not your problem anymore. You risked everything before and got less than nothing. Why risk it again?*

She heard running steps behind her, but before she could turn around, someone hit her from behind, launching her into the street—and directly into the path of an oncoming bus. Before she'd even tensed the muscles in her legs to move, an older woman yanked her by the arm, darn near pulling it from her shoulder, and she leaped up from the street just as the bus came to a screeching halt a good five feet beyond the spot where she'd been lying. Raissa clutched her shoulder with one hand and spun around.

But the street was empty.

She figured whoever had pushed her had kept running and was long gone by now, but where was the woman who had pulled her out of the street? The bus driver rushed off the bus, his face white as a sheet.

"Are you all right? I saw that guy push you, but I couldn't stop. I don't know how you managed to move that fast, but I'm glad of it."

"Did you see the guy who pushed me?"

"Yeah, but he was wearing one of those hooded shirts and sunglasses. Coulda been anyone."

"And the woman?"

The bus driver shook his head. "Didn't see no one but you."

Raissa motioned to the street. "You had to have seen her. The woman who pulled me out of the street."

The bus driver studied her for a moment. "Ma'am, I don't know how to tell you this, but there weren't no other woman anywhere on this street. I gotta have perfect vision to drive this bus, and that's what I got." He looked around the street, then back at Raissa. "Maybe you should pay a visit to the Lord's house sometime soon. That's the only explanation I got."

Raissa nodded. "Thank you, Mr. . . ."

"Cormier. Been driving for going on thirty years and ain't killed no one yet. I'm glad that didn't change today. You going to be all right? I can call nine-one-one or something."

"No, thank you, Mr. Cormier. I'll be fine."

The bus driver nodded. "Well, if you need anything, you can find me through the bus company. Like I say, I didn't get a good look at that man or nothing, but I'd be happy to talk to the police, if they was asking."

"I appreciate it, Mr. Cormier, but at this point, I think there's little the police could do."

"You're probably right. You be careful, miss." He climbed back onto the bus and gave her a wave as he pulled away from the corner.

Raissa lifted a hand in response, then hurried across the street to her car. She slid into the driver's seat and looked over at her uninvited passenger. "I'm going to die, right?"

The ghost in her passenger seat frowned at Raissa. "Crap."

Raissa stared at Helena Henry, feeling her pulse race. Of course, she'd known the ghost was around. Maryse and Sabine could both see her and had told Raissa about her. But knowing her friends were telling the truth and seeing the truth in her car were two totally different things. Then there was that small matter of Maryse's theory on Helena's appearances.

"This isn't good, is it?" Raissa finally asked. "Maryse says every time you're visible to someone, their life is in danger."

Helena sighed. "I wish I could argue, but I'm afraid my track record speaks for itself."

"It was you who pulled me out of the street, wasn't it?"

Helena nodded.

"But why are you here? At the street corner? In my car?"

"Well, I was. . . . I thought . . . you see . . . Oh, hell, I just had this feeling that you were in trouble, so I've been following you around."

"A feeling?"

Helena waved one hand in dismissal. "I know. Now

I sound like all the rest of you nutbags with your spirits and tarot cards and psychic visions, but damn it, I don't know how else to explain it. You were on my mind for days and no matter what I did, I couldn't shake it, so finally I got Maryse to drop me off at your shop."

"Maryse knew about this and didn't tell me?"

"She didn't want to worry you. She said if you saw me, then we'd rally the troops. Otherwise, she was putting it down to my overactive imagination. Well, that and the fact that I started a diet last week."

Raissa's head began to spin. "This is too much to process right now. I'd love nothing better than to drive home and pour myself a glass of the strongest thing I have in my apartment and mull this over, but I've got something urgent to do."

Helena shrugged. "Unless you plan on drinking the Drano under your sink, I don't think you're going to figure it out today anyway. But I wouldn't mind a glass of wine, and maybe a slice of that cheesecake you bought today at lunch. Just don't tell Maryse. She's picking me up in an hour."

Raissa started the car and pulled out of the parking lot. "I thought you were on a diet."

"Hey, I just saved your life. Are you going to deny me a little piece of pie?"

"Helena, I'll buy you pies for the rest of your life if I manage to stay alive like the others."

"Cool!" Helena smiled. "That will show that skinny bitch Maryse. She keeps harping on me about my diet, but I think she's just jealous that I don't gain weight."

"Then why are you on a diet?"

"Maryse and Sabine refuse to keep feeding someone they can't take as a tax deduction, especially as I don't need to eat in the first place. And it's not like I can walk into a grocery store or diner and load up. It was getting a bit exhausting trying to steal when it has to be in my pockets or it's visible to everyone, and I feel guilty about the stealing part, unless it's someone I really don't like." Helena looked down the street at the police station, then back at Raissa. "Hey, you went to the police about that little girl that's missing, didn't you? Did you get a vision or something?"

"I got something."

Helena stared at her for a couple of seconds. "You're not really psychic, are you?"

Chapter Two

Raissa strolled into the Internet café across town, her laptop tucked under her arm. Her normally casual look had been replaced with a loud pink blouse, skintight black pants, and a wig with long red curls. As she waited in line for a latte, she pulled a mirror from her purse and studied the ceiling edge around the room while pretending to check her lipstick. She closed the mirror and tucked it back into a huge silver bag. She'd been right—no security cameras.

She placed her order and received a compliment from the clerk on her long turquoise nails with purple dolphins, then collected her coffee and took a table on the patio outside that offered her the best view of the street corner. Placing the laptop on the table, she gave the street the once-over, her eyes safely hidden behind the polarized lenses of her sunglasses. After a quick glance back inside the shop, she peeled the dolphin nails off her fingertips, satisfied that no one would ever think that the dolphin-nail-wearing woman and Raissa Bordeaux were the same person.

When her fingers were free of the long nails, she opened her laptop and started working. It took only minutes to get to the files she'd come for, even with the added time of diverting the FBI firewall security, but then she hadn't been known as the best hacker at the bureau for nothing. She inserted a flash drive and began the download of every case file she could think of that might be relevant, every possible angle she could come up with that might keep her alive. Her fingers flew across the keyboard, and the screen scrolled with page after page of downloading data. She looked at the time and checked the street again. A minute, maybe two, was all she had left before they closed in on her.

She opened the last log she wanted to check and scanned the list. The second-to-last entry was the one she expected to find. Mission completed, she pocketed the flash drive and deposited the laptop in the trashcan before she left the cafe. A block from the café, she slipped into the alley and pulled a large trash bag from her purse. She shoved the sunglasses, wig, and purse inside, along with the fake nails she'd removed earlier, then buried the bag in a Dumpster behind a Chinese restaurant. As she exited the alley, she peeled the wax off her fingertips, scattering the remains on the sidewalk as she went.

She had a moment of regret at the thought of the laptop crushed alongside latte remnants, but the reality was, it was marked. If she used it to access the Internet again, the trace would begin automatically. Still, it always killed her to sacrifice good computer equipment, which is why she always picked up old systems at garage sales and secondhand stores. With minimal tinkering she could upgrade them to suit her purposes.

She glanced at her watch as she hopped into her car. Despite his obvious disdain and disbelief of her profession and the "evidence" she'd given him, Detective Blanchard had run the case through the bureau—just ten minutes before. She knew it would take at least forty-five minutes for him to get clearance approval and for the information to queue. She figured that gave her about an hour to double-check that everything was in order at her shop before the surly detective paid her an "unofficial" visit.

That meant an hour to ensure that the outside of every door and window of her shop was free of fingerprints, just in case she'd properly read the serious and quick-thinking Detective Blanchard. Once he realized Raissa was right on all counts, the logical thing to do would be to scrutinize the source. And since the source in this case didn't want her fingerprints run through a national database, at least not until she'd had an opportunity to come up with plan B, an unscheduled date with Windex was in order. She smiled. How unlucky for Detective Blanchard that Raissa had nine years of experience in remaining out of sight.

Zach scrolled down the screen, scanning the result of the FBI database search he'd done earlier. His pulse quickened as the screen scrolled, child after child. All six years old. All blonde with blue eyes. All missing from a locked house with frantic parents who had been cleared of any involvement. All had been returned a week later, and medical examinations had revealed no injury or abuse. None of the cases had ever yielded a decent set of clues, much less been solved.

And every single child had claimed she'd been abducted by aliens.

Shit.

He scrolled back to the top of the page and checked the cities—Tallahassee, Orlando, Gulfport, Jackson, Baton Rouge, Brooklyn. Son of a bitch. That psychic had nailed it.

Damn it! How in the world was he supposed to explain to his captain that a psychic had tipped him off? And that the chief suspect was apparently a character from *The X-Files*. He shook his head. The answer was simple—he didn't explain. They would have run the case through the FBI database eventually. Zach could just claim that the odd aspects of the crime made him decide to do it sooner rather than later. He wouldn't even mention the alien thing. The captain could just read that himself.

But there was also a whole other issue to deal with.

Zach didn't believe for one second that the woman he'd met was really psychic. Zach didn't believe in psychics at all. Which meant that Raissa Bordeaux had come about that information some other way than through spirits or tea leaves. And the only way that came to mind was that she knew who had kidnapped those girls.

Or had done it herself.

Zach combed the printouts of everything he could find on Raissa Bordeaux, which was next to nothing. A mere two pages. A ten-year-old would have a file bigger than this woman. Raissa—no middle name—Bordeaux had appeared in New Orleans nine years ago. She'd worked as a waitress at a bar downtown for about a year, and then she'd opened her little shop of paranormal tricks. Her driver's license was nine years old, and as far as he could tell, she hadn't been issued one prior to then. Her Social Security number showed only her waitress income and the business, and beyond that, Raissa Bordeaux didn't exist.

No arrests, no credit history, not even a parking ticket. It was as if the woman had appeared out of thin air nine years ago.

Zach frowned and tapped his pencil on the desk. Women who abducted children usually did so because they wanted their own, or they were involved in a baby-selling ring. But these missing girls had been too old to sell to couples wanting an infant. It was more likely Raissa Bordeaux knew so much because she was somehow involved with the man who had taken the girls.

Zach wasn't buying that "vision" nonsense for a moment, but fronting for some guy running drugs, prostitution, kiddie porn, whatever—*that* he'd buy.

It was a shame that all the real lookers hooked up with piece-of-shit men. As long as he lived, Zach was certain he'd never understand the attraction. But there was really no other explanation. Either Raissa Bordeaux liked little girls and was playing a game with the police, or she knew a man who liked little girls and she wanted out of whatever she'd gotten herself into.

Zach was banking on the latter.

He rose from his chair and grabbed his keys off the desktop. It was time to pay Ms. Bordeaux a visit. And maybe try to pick up a random fingerprint while he was there. She might be able to change her driver's license and Social Security card, but fingerprints are forever.

When the buzzer to her apartment sounded, Raissa glanced at her watch and smiled. One hour, ten minutes. She walked over to the window and saw the unmarked police car parked at the curb across the street from her shop, just as she'd expected. She pressed the intercom button in her kitchen. "Can I help you?"

"Ms. Bordeaux?" Zach's voice boomed over the intercom. "It's Detective Blanchard. I need to talk to you."

Raissa smiled at the formal yet agitated tone of his voice. "Certainly. I'll be right down."

Detective Blanchard stood just outside the shop door, staring at the items in her display window, a look of consternation on his face. "You're working late, Detective," Raissa said.

"Yes, well, given the circumstances, we all are."

Raissa nodded and stared at him. He stared back for a moment, obviously waiting for a question or an invitation, but Raissa wasn't about to make it that easy. Keeping Detective Blanchard off balance was a must. She couldn't afford for him to figure out her angle. Better he decide she was a weirdo who tracked child-kidnapping cases than know the truth.

Finally, he cleared his throat. "I had a couple of questions for you, if you have the time."

"Sure. Like what?"

"I checked on similar cases, and you were right. In fact, you were too right. Every single city had a matching case file. I want to know how you got that information, Ms. Bordeaux."

"I already told you, Detective Blanchard. I'm psychic. It came to me in a vision."

Zach's jaw clenched. "We both know that's a load of horseshit. Now, you can either give me the answer I want here, or you can give it to me back at the station."

"I know nothing of the sort, and it's particularly bad manners, even for a police officer, to refer to someone else's livelihood as horseshit. Especially when that horseshit is most likely going to put you ahead of Detective Morrow on the captain's list, right?"

"This has nothing to do with Morrow or the captain." Zach's face began to redden. "This has to do with a child abductor that I'd damned well like to find."

Raissa nodded. "I'd like that, too, but I'm afraid there's nothing else I can tell you. I don't have any more information than what I've already given you."

"You're lying. Either you took those girls yourself, or you know who did." Zach blew out a breath. "Look, Ms. Bordeaux, it's obvious to me you're hiding from someone. There's no record of your existence before age twenty-four. I know you're not who you say you are, and if you push me, I'll dig into your background until I get what I'm looking for."

Raissa cocked her head to one side and studied him. "You know, I believe you would. The only problem with that is then you'd be spending all your time and energy on me, which will get you no closer to finding that little girl or her abductor. You're going to have to trust me on this, Detective. I don't kidnap children, and if I knew who did, I would give you that information."

"You're walking a thin line, Ms. Bordeaux."

"Aren't we all?"

"No. My past is an open book. I suggest that unless you want me to finger you for this kidnapping, you open up your own."

"I wish you'd concentrate on the facts you have and the things you can control. I'm not your problem, I assure you."

Zach shook his head. "You're a problem all right. And your assurance means nothing. I don't even know who you are. How am I supposed to trust anything you say?"

Raissa shrugged. "Then don't trust me. Waste time chasing rabbits, and he gets away with it again. I'm sure I don't have to tell you that none of those cases yielded any clues, except the extraterrestrial kind. Do you really want the mayor's grandchild on Channel Four saying she was abducted by ET?"

Zach's eyes narrowed. "How did you know they all claimed aliens took them?"

"Because I could read their thoughts at the time. How do you think I knew about them at all?" Raissa stepped inside the shop. "If we're done, I'd like to get ready for dinner."

"We're done for now, but don't get too comfortable with that. I'll be back."

"I look forward to it, Detective," Raissa said and

closed the door behind her. She sneaked over to the far corner of the shop and waited a couple of seconds, then peeked through the blinds. Sure enough, the detective was trying to pull a fingerprint off the front door to her shop. What a shame she'd wiped that door handle clean just thirty minutes before.

She watched as he bent over and studied the handle. An even bigger shame was that such a nice butt was wasted on such an uptight man. She dropped the blinds slat and sighed. Not that she had any business admiring butts, anyway. Men were a luxury she couldn't afford. She'd tried the occasional fling, but too many times the man wanted to get serious, and Raissa couldn't go there. She had been safe for a lot of years. No man was worth risking her life for   not even if the sex was absolutely fabulous.

She grabbed her purse from behind the counter and slipped on a pair of lacy black gloves. The dead bolt on the door didn't so much as squeak, and she thanked God again for whoever had invented WD-40. In a flash, she twisted the doorknob and flung the front door open, practically yanking the handle out of Zach's hand.

He jumped back as if he'd been shot, and it was all Raissa could do not to laugh. His expression went from horrified to guilty to aggravated faster than a race car shifting gears. Raissa stepped outside and stared at him, her eyes wide with faked surprise. "Why Detective! I didn't know you were still here." She glanced at the handle, covered with fingerprint powder, then back at Zach, who slipped his hand with the brush behind his back.

"I appreciate the care of my door handle, but it only requires a good moisturizer. Powder really isn't necessary." She locked the door behind her and gave him a big smile, waving one gloved hand as she walked out into the hot summer evening.

It was almost eleven P.M. before Raissa finished her business and headed back to her apartment. The street from the parking lot to her shop was dimly lit, and Raissa stayed alert, knowing that anything was possible on a dark New Orleans street. Normally, she tried to limit her nightly excursions, but the people she needed to see didn't do daytime. Unfortunately, her investigative trip hadn't yielded her the information she'd hoped for.

She was certain she knew who had taken those girls but had never been able to prove it. She'd been close, so close, to the answer—or so she believed—when everything had fallen apart. She'd tried for years to shut those bright blue eyes from her mind, but in her dreams they still haunted her. Why were they taken, and what horrible things had happened to them that they couldn't remember?

But even though Melissa Franco's disappearance was exactly the same as the others, no one had seen the man she suspected. Not for at least six months, best she could figure, which troubled Raissa more than she wanted to admit. Granted, New Orleans wasn't his territory, but he had family here and was the lead man in Baton Rouge for Louisiana's most notorious mobster. Sonny Hebert valued trust above everything else. If no one had seen Monk in six months, then what did that mean? She could think of only one possibility, and it involved a trash bag, rocks, and the Mississippi River.

She was half a block from her shop when she saw a shadow move in front of the alley. She stopped for a moment and studied the street, looking for another sign of movement in the shadows, listening for a sound that might tell her whether it had been animal or human.

There was nothing but silence.

You're overly alert. But even thinking it didn't alleviate the uneasy feeling she had as she studied the alley. And since that uneasy feeling had saved her butt more times than she could count, she wasn't about to start ignoring it now.

She slipped her pistol from the holster on her ankle and edged closer to the building, silently creeping toward the alley. It seemed even her breathing echoed in the stale night air, and she paused just long enough to control her breaths. Five more steps.

She eased up to the corner and studied the shadows that stretched out onto the sidewalk in front of the opening. No movement. Then she focused all her attention on listening, trying to decipher any noise that might indicate the threat her body so clearly felt was there. She waited five seconds, six seconds, seven and then she heard it. The tiny shuffle of feet on the cement. Barely a whisper. But unmistakable.

She gripped her pistol with both hands and lifted it to her shoulder. Taking one deep, silent breath, she whirled around the corner and came pistol to face with a man.

He threw his hands in the air as soon as he saw her gun, and the sheer terror on his face made Raissa wonder if she'd mistaken a simple bum for a professional killer. But a quick glance disqualified the bum theory. Blue jeans, T-shirt, and tennis shoes weren't exactly a tuxedo, but they were clean and the man's hair was short, his face completely shaven. This was no bum.

He stared at her, his eyes wide, and finally tried to speak. "Raissa? Raissa Bordeaux . . . right?"

She studied him for a moment. Something about him looked familiar, but she was certain she'd never met him before. She never forgot a face. "Who are you and how do you know my name?"

The man's eyes widened even more and he swallowed. "My name's Hank. Hank Henry."

And suddenly Raissa realized that she'd seen a picture of him in the Mudbug newspaper. Hank Henry—the disappearing ex-husband of her friend Maryse and son of the recently risen Helena Henry—was a legend in Mudbug. Mostly for being a coward and an idiot, not exactly the sort of legacy most people wanted to leave behind. Good-looking, smooth talking, and utterly useless was exactly how Maryse had described her ex, and taking a closer look at him, Raissa decided she'd probably agree with the "good-looking" assessment, but the smooth talking was nowhere in sight.

Apparently pistols pointed at his head gave Hank stage fright.

But then, given his propensity for activities that were not necessarily legal and his never-ending shortage of cash, Raissa wasn't convinced that his lurking in the alley was benign. After all, he'd been hiding out for years, and his mother's death had only profited charities and not her wayward son. Why show up now? "What do you want?"

"I need to talk to you. It's important. I . . . well, I . . . I think you might be in danger."

Raissa narrowed her eyes at him. "From who?"

Hank's gaze darted between the gun and Raissa. He swallowed again and looked at her. "Sonny Hebert," he whispered.

Raissa sucked in a breath, her heart pounding in her chest. She glanced behind her, then back at Hank.

Whatever else Hank Henry might be, the one thing Raissa was certain about was that he wasn't a killer. "I think you better come with me." She tucked the gun in her waistband and motioned for Hank to follow. He gave her a nod and fell in behind her.

A couple of minutes later, Hank was seated at her tiny kitchen table, and she set two glasses of scotch on the table with the rest of the bottle between them. "I figured this wasn't the sort of conversation that called for coffee or tea."

Hank looked grateful but not the least bit relieved. Whatever had him hiding in a dark alley waiting to accost a woman he didn't really know must be heavy, which was worrisome at best. The Hank Henry she'd always heard about was usually in minor trouble, but nothing of the sort that had him stalking women and looking as jumpy as a cat. "How do you know Sonny Hebert?"

Hank froze for a second, then stared down at the table. "Look, I did some stupid things in the past. Really stupid. I had a gambling problem, and I owed the wrong people money."

"You borrowed money from the Hebert family to gamble? That's not a problem—that's a death wish."

"Don't you think I know that? But I swear, when I made the deal, I had no idea the Heberts were behind it. It was one of their cousins, different last name, and I didn't make the connection until it was too late."

"So all this hiding out you've been doing isn't from the Mudbug police."

"Heck, no. Spending some time in the Mudbug jail would be a relief compared to this, but I can't get caught staying anywhere too long, especially in places I can't walk out of. Know what I mean?"

Raissa nodded. Oh yeah, she knew exactly what Hank meant. Anyone could get caught—and in jail, you were a sitting duck.

"Another month and I'll have all my fines in Mudbug paid, so it won't be an issue." Hank leaned forward a bit in his chair and looked directly at Raissa. "Ms. Bordeaux, you don't have to believe a word I say, but I want you to know that I'm clean. Been clean for over a year. I did some time in rehab—different name, of course, and nowhere near New Orleans. I'm a changed man, and I want to live a different life, but I can't do that with the Heberts looking for me under every cypress tree in Louisiana."

"How much do you owe them?"

Hank raised both hands in the air. "Nothing! I swear I don't owe them a dime. We had a deal, and I worked off my debt. Working off that debt is what sent me to rehab. I'm not a great man, and I know my morals are lacking, but I don't have the stomach for the way those men live. I had to get clean. There wasn't any other choice."

Raissa frowned. "So if you don't owe them, what do they want?"

"They keep asking me to do stuff . . . jobs, you know? I've told 'em I'm straight and I don't want any trouble, but seems like whenever I go to one of my old haunts, there's always one of the family hanging around."

"There's plenty of people who'd be happy to do Hebert's bidding and take the paycheck. So why keep bothering you?"

Hank blew out a breath. "I think it's because they think I know something."

"Know what?"

"That's just it. I don't know. But they keep asking

these strange questions about people in Mudbug and stuff."

Raissa mentally counted to five. "So they're asking you questions, trying to get you to admit to something they think you know, but you don't know what that something is?

Hank nodded. "Yeah. I mean, I guess I saw or heard something I wasn't supposed to, but hell, how am I supposed to know which thing it was? These people didn't do picnics and bowling league. It could be anything."

Raissa tapped one finger on the table and stared at the wall behind Hank. "No, it couldn't be anything. You were privy to the inner workings of a mob family for a while and, I'm sure, saw plenty. But whatever they're afraid you know, I'll bet it doesn't have anything to do with extortion, or loan-sharking, or even murder."

"What then?"

"Something worse, much worse."

Hank's eyes widened, and Raissa knew exactly what he was wondering—what's worse than murder? If only she had an answer. "So," Raissa continued, "you said you thought I was in danger from the Heberts. What makes you think that?"

Hank lifted his glass and downed the rest of the contents. Hand shaking, he placed the glass back down on the table. "Because they asked me to kill you."

Chapter Three

Raissa slammed her scotch glass onto the table. "They asked you to kill me?"

Hank nodded, clearly frightened. "Not you by name, exactly, but they said that friend of my ex-wife's that was a psychic . . . but they were clear that it wasn't Sabine. I told 'em no, straight out. I ain't never killed no one, and I ain't about to start."

Raissa narrowed her eyes at Hank. "How did you find me?"

"I remembered Sabine saying your shop name before, so I looked it up." His eyes widened. "Oh, shit. I led them right to you, didn't I?" He jumped up from the table. "Jesus, I didn't even think—How could I be so stupid?"

Raissa rose from her chair and placed her hand on Hank's arm. "Don't worry about it. They know about your connection to me, so they already know how to find me, I'm sure."

Hank stared at her for a moment, still not quite buying it. Finally, he blew out a breath and sank back into the chair. "Then why come to me at all? If the Heberts want you gone, and they know who you are and where to find you, they could have already handled this. Why ask me when they already knew I wasn't going to do it?"

Raissa sat back down and thought for a minute. "I think, given my connection to Maryse, they figured you would warn me."

Hank still looked doubtful. "You're saying they're sending you a message? What message?"

Raissa's jaw involuntarily clenched. "That if I don't disappear on my own, they're going to help me."

Zach sat low in his car just down the road from Raissa's shop. He'd seen her coming down the block and wondered why she stopped before reaching her building. When she slipped the pistol from her ankle holster, he'd been ready to bolt from the car, but something had stopped him. The ankle holster for one. Sure, plenty of people carried in New Orleans, and a single woman living in a downtown apartment would be remiss not to have some form of protection, but an ankle holster was definitely not the most common place for a woman to carry a gun.

And it was the way she moved—as if she'd been trained for exactly what she was doing.

Against his better judgment, he'd waited as she entered the alley, giving her ten seconds before he hurried to assist. When the seconds had passed and she hadn't appeared, he cursed himself and his stupidity and eased out of the car and across the street. He crouched behind a mailbox and listened. For a moment, all he heard was the regular noises of the street—paper rustling on the sidewalk, the sound of car engines in the distance—but then it trickled down to him. The sound of voices.

So Raissa's instincts had been right. There had been someone in the alley, but apparently that someone was more interested in talking than in something more insidious. He was just about to move closer when Raissa and a man stepped out of the alley and hurried to her building. Her pistol was tucked in the waistband of her jeans, and she didn't seem the least bit concerned about protecting herself from the man who followed her.

She glanced his way as she unlocked the door to her shop, and he ducked behind the mailbox, hoping she hadn't seen him. A couple of seconds later, he heard the door click shut. He watched until he saw the light in the upstairs apartment come on. Deciding Raissa was done with whatever she was up to that night, he crept back across the street and climbed into his car.

Zach hadn't recognized the man who had been hiding in the alley, but Raissa must have known him well enough to let him in her apartment. Which made him wonder why the man hadn't called or simply rung her doorbell. Why lurk around the corner, running the risk of being shot?

Zach looked up at the apartment again. The light was on in the front room, and Zach could make out a silhouette of the man sitting at a table. A minute later, Raissa set glasses on the table and joined him. Surely, if the guy was a friend or boyfriend he wouldn't have been hiding in an alley. Which left business.

He looked down at his watch.

Kinda late for a business meeting. He watched another thirty minutes and finally saw them rise from the table. A minute later, the man slipped out the front door, scanned the street, then took off in the direction of a lone truck parked at the other corner. Zach hunched down in his seat so the man wouldn't notice him as he drove past.

He watched the rearview mirror until the man had turned the corner, then started his car and took off after him. The truck turned again at the end of the next block, and Zach pressed the accelerator. His quarry was entering the highway, which gave Zach the perfect chance to get his license plate without being made.

He followed the truck onto the highway and eased beside it in the next lane. Zach gave brief thanks that the license plate was clean and easily readable and jotted the number down before continuing on the highway past him. Two exits later, he merged right and exited the highway, heading for the police station. It should be almost empty this time of night. A great time to run a plate without someone looking over his shoulder and asking questions.

Only one cop manned the front desk when he walked into the station. Zach gave him a nod and went to his own desk. It only took a minute to open the database and plug in the truck's license plate. Another minute and he was looking at pages of information on one Hank Henry. He scanned the pages, shaking his head. This Hank was a piece of work, and stupid.

He seemed to have the uncanny ability to be involved with the wrong thing at the wrong time.

But for over a year, his record was clean as a whistle. Interesting.

He checked another database, but no prison system had a Hank Henry listed as a recent resident. So the question remained: what was a man of questionable background and character doing hiding outside Raissa's store? And why did she invite him inside for drinks?

Questions he couldn't answer. Not yet. But Raissa Bordeaux definitely required more looking into.

It was a bright and sunny morning in Mudbug when Raissa pushed open the door to the Mudbug Hotel. Little bells tinkled above, alerting anyone inside to her entrance. No one was at the front counter, but she'd barely stepped inside before she heard Mildred, the hotel owner, yell, "Raissa, we're in the office. Come on back."

Raissa stepped down the hall, wondering who "we" was. For whatever absurd reason, Helena had insisted Raissa meet her at the hotel to "discuss an action plan."

Since Hank's visit last night, Raissa figured she had much bigger things to deal with than forming an "action plan" with a ghost, but on second thought, she decided an invisible partner *did* come with some advantages. Raissa had assumed the ghost intended to meet her outside the hotel, but after several minutes of waiting, she decided to try inside, even though she had no good explanation for Mildred as to why she'd be visiting her hotel in Mudbug when Raissa should have been preparing to open her shop in New Orleans.

Based on Mildred's greeting, an explanation wasn't necessary. Which meant that Helena must have talked to Sabine or Maryse, or both, and they were waiting at the hotel to come up with a plan. At the end of the hall, she stepped through an open doorway and into Mildred's office. The hotel owner was perched in a huge office chair behind her desk, eating a muffin and playing cards. Even more disturbing was her opponent.

Helena Henry sat across the desk from Mildred, grumbling about her hand. "I see you three doughnut holes and raise you one muffin." Helena was dressed in a long, flowing, pink gown made of some type of gauzy material. On her head sat a wide floppy hat in the same shade of pink as the dress, with a ring of white and red roses around the top.

Mildred looked up at Raissa and smiled. "I'm making Helena earn her breakfast."

Raissa stared for a couple of seconds, not sure what to even think—*way* beyond having anything to say. "You can see Helena?" she asked Mildred.

"Oh, yeah. She turned up like a bad penny right after my car wreck." Mildred motioned to Raissa to take the seat next to Helena. "Already poured you a cup of coffee. Might as well have a seat and drink a bit."

Raissa slid into the chair, still a bit numb. "And you're okay with this? I mean, I always got the impression you didn't go in for anything remotely out of this world."

"Absolutely right, but what the heck was I supposed to do? You can't exactly refute the evidence, especially when it's loud and eating you out of hotel and home." She disposed of two cards and pushed some doughnut holes and a minimuffin into the stack of food in the middle of the desk. "Call."

Raissa looked over at Helena, who studied Mildred's face, most certainly trying to determine if her doughnut holes and muffin were now at risk. "What in the world are you wearing, Helena? Yesterday you just had on jeans and a T-shirt."

Helena waved a hand in dismissal. "I take Mondays off."

"Off from what?"

"From my wardrobe-through-the-ages adventures. Oh, it sounds like fun when you start, but it's actually a lot harder than you think to come up with something creative every day. Last month, I did music through the ages MTV-style. This month is classic movies through the ages."

Raissa started to understand, and wasn't sure whether that made her feel better or more confused. "So this is . . ."

"*Gone with the Wind*," Mildred supplied. "My suggestion. I wasn't about to allow her in my hotel with what she had on before. I don't care if no one else can see her. I can, and that's enough."

Raissa looked over at Helena. "What movie were you dressed like before?"

"*Boogie Nights*," Helena replied.

Raissa laughed. "*Boogie Nights* is a classic?"

Helena huffed. "It is if you've watched the last scene."

Raissa grinned and looked over at Mildred, who was frowning at Helena. "I can see where the problem might have come in."

"So," Helena went on, "that's why I'm wearing the pink flying-nun dress. I wouldn't want to offend Mildred's delicate sensibilities, even though those traveling salesmen she rents rooms to watch stuff that make *Boogie Nights* look like *Scooby-Doo*."

Mildred shook her head. "Well, since I'm not walking through walls and spying on customers when they darned well think they're alone, I don't have issues with what they do in their rooms, as long as I don't know about it. Sophia bleaches the sheets when people leave anyway."

"Gross," Raissa said. "I think I'd rather talk about my impending doom."

Mildred laid down her cards and nodded. "That's why we asked you here. I've spoken to Sabine and Maryse. They both had other obligations that kept them from being here this morning, but we all agree—you've got trouble coming. No one sees Helena who doesn't live to regret it, but the good news is, so far, everyone's *lived*."

Raissa sat back in her chair and sighed. "Only by the skin of their teeth. You were all very lucky."

"Yes, that's true, but we also heeded the warning— the Helena kind—and we took care to know that something serious was in the making, even if none of us could understand it all at the time."

"I know you took precautions," Raissa agreed, "but the reality is, if someone wants to kill you, they most likely will. The only way to stop that train is to either eliminate the killer or the reason he wants you dead."

Mildred nodded. "Exactly. So that's what we're gonna do. With Sabine and Maryse, it was harder to pin down because they weren't even aware of some of the things they'd gotten into. So we were off looking for an enemy without a clear view of the situation from the beginning."

Raissa looked at Mildred. "And you think somehow that's different with me?"

"Well, yeah. At least that's what we're hoping. I mean, after everything that happened last month and your involvement with it all, Maryse, Sabine, and I thought maybe Helena should shadow you for a bit and make sure you couldn't see her. We were just starting to think we'd gotten it all wrong when someone shoved you in front of a bus."

"And then I could see Helena," Raissa finished.

"Right," Mildred said. "But the only thing in your life that changed from that moment to an hour before was you talking to the police about that missing girl. Helena was there when you talked to that detective, but you couldn't see her then. So we know it has something to do with the missing girl and your talking to the police. We just need you to tell us what."

"What makes you think I know?" Raissa asked.

Mildred glanced over at Helena, then back at Raissa. "I've always known you were hiding from something. I figured it was an abusive husband or the like, which is why I never pressed you for answers. But after knowing you as long as I have, I've decided you're too strong to have been abused. Which means that whatever you're hiding from is a lot worse than one angry, vindictive man."

Raissa nodded. "You're right. It's not one man."

Mildred narrowed her eyes at Raissa. "You were a cop, weren't you?"

Raissa felt a wave of anxiety pass over her. She shifted in her chair and looked down at the floor, millions of denials already forming in her mind. Finally, she looked back up at Mildred and in an instant, she knew.

It was time.

Time to stop running. Stop hiding from her past. From the truth.

"I was an FBI agent."

Helena sucked in a breath and stared at her, wide-eyed. "Holy shit! You were a supercop. No wonder nothing fazes you. You've got balls of steel."

"Ha!" Raissa spit out that single word. "If I had balls of steel, I wouldn't have spent the last nine years hiding behind scented candles and tarot cards. If I had balls of steel, I'd have taken out the entire Hebert family so I could have my life back."

Mildred put one hand over her mouth. "The Hebert family . . . as in Sonny Hebert, the Don Corleone of southern Louisiana?"

"Yeah. As in, not one man—but a 'family.'"

"Holy shit," Mildred repeated Helena's words, then downed her entire cup of coffee. "Okay, this is far worse than I had imagined."

Helena nodded. "That's not the kind of family that does barbecues and beer."

"No," Raissa agreed. "They're more into extortion, and money laundering, and God knows what else."

Mildred refilled her coffee cup, pulled a bottle of scotch from the bottom drawer of her desk, and poured a generous amount into her coffee. She handed the bottle to Helena, who took a huge gulp straight from the bottle, then doctored her own coffee and passed the bottle to Raissa. Raissa, who had never been one to drink after another person, wasn't quite sure the ghost counted, but it still bothered her on too many levels, so she passed on the whiskey altogether.

"Okay," Mildred said, "so there's a bit of a setback in our original thinking, but there's no cause to panic."

"Are you fucking kidding me?" Helena said. "Hell, I'm panicked, and I'm already dead."

Mildred frowned. "Well, at least they can't kill you twice."

"That's not entirely true," Raissa said. "I died nine and a half years ago when one of the Hebert clan put a bullet through my chest. They resuscitated me in the ambulance. On paper, I've been dead ever since. So in this case, if the Heberts get me, then technically they have killed me twice."

"We're not going to let that happen," Mildred said, her voice growing strong again. "I promise you, Raissa, we will see you through this. The first thing we have to do is find you someplace safe."

Raissa laughed. "I know you mean well, and I love you for it, but I'm trained to hide, and they still found me."

"I didn't say you should hide, since you're right, that's obviously not going to work. But I *do* think relocating to a more defensible location would help."

"You mean move? No, I can't move. I have a business to run—"

"*Which*," Mildred interrupted, "you've already offered to cut down to part time to cover Sabine's store for her honeymoon. Sabine will be at Beau's place in New Orleans tonight, and they fly out tomorrow. There's no reason for you not to move here temporarily."

"I don't know," Raissa said, her mind racing with all

the reasons that involving more people in her mess was a really bad idea.

"You should do it," Helena urged. "It's not like just anyone can come and go in Mudbug without being noticed. And you could stay at the hotel."

Raissa struggled to come up with a good argument, but had to admit that the idea wasn't the worst one she'd heard. In fact, it came with the advantages Mildred had mentioned and a few that she hadn't thought about. Finally, she nodded. "Okay. I'll move, but just for the rest of the week, and I'll still have to commute to my store a couple of times. I can reschedule my readings, but I don't want to cancel on my regular customers."

Mildred frowned, and Raissa knew she'd wanted a full-time commitment, but it was something that Raissa just couldn't offer without lying. One, because remaining in Mudbug wouldn't allow her to do the investigating she needed to do in New Orleans, and two, because if her situation even came remotely close to putting her friends in danger, then Raissa was out of Mudbug like a gunshot.

"What about your family, Raissa?" Mildred asked. "Do they know where you are?"

"My parents are both dead, and we weren't really tight with any relatives. So there's no one missing me, if that's what you're asking."

Mildred nodded and studied her for a couple of seconds. Finally, she sighed. "You're not going to bow out until you find that missing girl, are you? It's somehow tied in to your past and the Heberts'."

"I think so," Raissa said, "but I've never had any proof."

Helena's eyes widened. "There have been others . . . other little girls that were taken?"

"There were others before Melissa."

Mildred swallowed, then cleared her throat. "What happened to them?"

"They were returned a week later without a mark on them and no memory of what happened to them after their abduction. There's a very narrow window of opportunity to catch this guy and stop this from happening again." Raissa rose from her chair, already mentally packing a bag of necessities for her stay in Mudbug. "I have to go home and get some things. One of my conditions for staying here is that you let me rig the hotel with security. It can all be done with fingernail-size lenses and infrared. I won't install anything in the guest rooms, except for my own, but I insist on rigging at least the outside of your quarters, Mildred, or I won't stay here at all."

Mildred nodded. "Whatever you think is best."

"Good," Raissa said, "because as much as I want to find out what happened to those girls, I'd prefer it not be firsthand. Abduction is not on my list of things to do, and it's doubtful I'd come back without a mark on me . . . if I came back at all."

Mildred narrowed her eyes at Raissa. "I don't suppose you really are psychic, right? I mean, not that I wouldn't find that a bit creepy, but, well, we already have a ghost. I guess I'm willing to consider any edge we might have, even the strange ones."

"I wish I were," Raissa said, "but it's all a very clever front. Or at least, I used to think it was."

"But all those things you knew . . . How did you guess all those things and get them right? No one's that lucky."

Raissa smiled. "It was never luck. I'm a highly skilled computer hacker and an expert at surveillance. Someone asks me what's wrong with their marriage, I follow the husband and find the girlfriend, or the doctor's office. Then I hack the girlfriend's computer, since usually women don't destroy the evidence, like mushy e-mails, that the cheating husband asks them to. Or I hack the doctor's office and find out what he's being treated for. I feed them enough information to sound like a vision but send them off on the right track for exposing whatever is going on."

"No shit." Helena stared at Raissa in admiration. "That whole psychic gig is a genius way to use those skills. I take back every time I called you a nutbag."

Raissa laughed. "Thanks, Helena. Coming from you that means . . . well, damned near nothing, but I'll take it anyway." Raissa rose from her chair. "Are we done here? Everyone satisfied with the master plan?"

Mildred looked over at Helena who nodded. "I'm as satisfied as I'm getting," Mildred said. "But I really wish you'd reconsider staying here full-time."

"No can do, Mildred. I'm not trying to upset anyone, but this whole thing is far bigger than just me."

Mildred straightened up in her chair and stared at Raissa, her eyes wide. "You're going to try to catch that guy, aren't you? You have no intention of lying low or leaving this to the cops."

"This may be my last chance," Raissa said. "Think about those girls. Think about their mothers. And then tell me what I should do."

Mildred was silent for a couple of seconds, and Raissa knew her mind was racing to find an argument, anything that would hold up to Raissa's logic. Raissa also knew that Maryse and Sabine, Mildred's surrogate daughters, would be lodged in her mind, too. Finally, Mildred slumped back in her chair and nodded. "I don't like it, but I shouldn't expect anything less from you." She rose from her chair and surprised Raissa by giving her a hug.

"I don't even know if you have any family or if they even know you're alive," Mildred said as she released her, "but I want you to know that I consider you my family, another one of my girls. I'm not going to ask you to promise not to do anything dangerous, but I *am* going to make you promise not to die on us."

Raissa's eyes moistened and she rubbed her nose with one finger, sniffling. "That's a promise I'll be happy to make." She gave Mildred's hand a squeeze, then hurried out of the hotel before she embarrassed herself by becoming just another weepy woman.

Chapter Four

At two thirty P.M., Raissa closed the door to her shop after her last appointment and put the CLOSED sign in the window. There were a million things that had to be done before she could commence her part-time-living adventures in the Mudbug Hotel, but one absolutely couldn't wait.

She entered her upstairs apartment and opened the closet, scrutinizing her choices. This excursion wasn't exactly a jeans-and-T-shirt sort of call, not unless she wanted to stick out by a mile. She made her selections, then began a midafternoon transformation.

Twenty minutes later, she peeked through her shop blinds, scanning the street for Detective Blanchard's unmarked police car. Clear. Thank God. She left her shop and drove to a corner bar on a seedy side of town. Unlike most bars, this one was always open and always had clientele. It tended to cater to people who didn't keep regular business hours—drug dealers, hookers, petty thieves, and not-so-petty thieves—just the kind of people she was looking to see.

She was certain she made quite a picture walking down the sidewalk to the bar. The whistles and cat-calls confirmed her choice of the short, tight, black leather skirt and blue sparkly top with a plunging neckline. Her six-inch stilettos put her right at six foot two, and the platinum wig put the finishing touches on the entire getup.

Satisfied that she looked like any other working girl, she opened the door and walked into the bar. The man she was looking for was sitting at the counter and he gave her a mental undressing as she walked in. She gave him the ole come-hither smile and walked to the back of the empty bar, shaking her hips as she strolled. She slid into a high-backed booth in the corner and waited for her prey to take the bait.

It didn't take long.

Spider, as he was called by the Hebert family, was predictable, if anything. And creepy, hence the nickname. A minute later—just enough time for her to slide her 9-millimeter from her handbag—he rounded the corner and peeked into her booth. Raissa was ready.

She reached up with one hand and pulled him into the booth by his hair. Spider screeched a bit but then leered over at her. "You like to play rough, do you? I can get into that."

Under the table, Raissa shoved her weapon into Spider's crotch. "Rough is my favorite," she whispered, "but I don't think we're talking about the same thing."

Spider's eyes widened with shock or fright, or both. He had always been a coward. "Wha—what do you want? I ain't done nothing to you."

"I want information, Spider," Raissa said in her normal voice and had the pleasure of watching the blood drain from the man's face.

"Taylor?" The man stared at her. "No fucking way. You're supposed to be dead. They told me you was dead."

"I'm sure they did, and likely things would be much more convenient if that were true, especially for you. But I'm sorry to tell you that I'm very much alive and still have a bullet scar on my chest from your nine."

She pressed the gun a bit harder into his crotch. "I owe you, you know."

"C'mon now," Spider begged, sweat forming on his brow. "We can work something out. What do you need? ID, passport? I can get you a new life."

Raissa laughed. "You think I've been walking around for the last nine years as Taylor Lane? I had a new identity the moment I got released from the hospital." She smiled at him. "We're going to work something out, though. I want information."

"What kind of information?"

"Where can I find Monk?"

Spider swallowed. "Ain't nobody seen Monk in at least six months."

"Bullshit." Maurice Marsella, aka Monk, was Sonny's right hand. "Is he in the joint?"

"No. I swear, ain't nobody seen him. I pay Lenny now. He said I wasn't gonna ask no questions about the change, and I ain't gonna."

"You must have heard something." She pressed the gun harder against his jeans until he flinched. "What's the word on the street?"

Spider leaned in and whispered. "You gotta promise you won't say this came from me."

"I'm hardly going to pay Sonny a visit. I think your secret is safe with me."

Spider looked around the empty bar, then back at Raissa. "Word is that Sonny had him offed, that Monk's at the bottom of the Mississippi."

Raissa frowned. This didn't fit into her suspicions at all. "You're sure?"

"All I know is, Lenny's taken over all of Monk's territory. Ain't nobody seen Monk in half a year, and ain't no one mentions his name in front of Sonny."

"So who's got his stuff—you know, from his house?"

Spider shrugged. "Sonny, I guess. What didn't burn. Whole place went up in flames . . . well, I guess it's been about six months ago."

Raissa looked Spider directly in the eyes. "You wouldn't lie to me, would you?"

"Hell, no. I ain't heard exactly what happened to Monk, and I ain't likely to. Nothing to lie about." Spider licked his lips and glanced over at the entrance to the bar. "Does Sonny know you're back?"

Raissa nodded.

Spider let out his breath in a whoosh. "Thank God. I mean, I wouldn't want to be the one carrying that news. As far as I'm concerned, I never seen you, okay?"

"Not exactly. I still have enough on you to put you away for a long time. I can pull that evidence out if I want to."

"What do you want from me? I already told you I didn't know nothin'."

Raissa reached into her bra with her free hand and pulled out a card with her cell number on it. She handed it to Spider. "You don't know anything *yet*. But if you hear anything at all about Monk or that little girl that's missing, you'll call me. Right?"

The blood rushed from Spider's face. "You don't think Sonny has anything to do with that little girl . . . Oh shit, you do. I ain't got nothing to do with hurting kids, and I never would. I got some standards, even if you don't believe it."

"Just keep your eyes and ears open. If you come across anything out of the ordinary, then you give me a call. The phone's unregistered, so no one will ever track it back to me."

"Out of the ordinary?"

"Anything that's not business as usual. And I mean *anything*. If Sonny wears a white suit or calls his mother on any day other than Sunday, I want to know."

Spider nodded but still looked confused. Raissa could hardly blame him. The last time she'd seen Spider, he'd put a single bullet through her chest. Raissa had still threatened to kill him while she was standing there bleeding.

"Go on," Raissa said and nodded toward the door. "I need to leave, and it's probably better for you if we're not seen together." Spider jumped up as if he'd been shot, and Raissa realized she'd never removed the gun from his crotch. What a shame.

She slipped the gun back into her bag and had started to slide out of the booth when Zach Blanchard slid in beside her.

He gave her the once-over, and Raissa could feel a blush starting on her very-exposed chest. "Ms. Bordeaux," he said with a smile. "That's an interesting outfit for a psychic."

"Well, psychics are rarely boring."

"It was even more interesting when you threatened that man with castration by Glock."

Shit!

"He owed me for a tarot reading." She shrugged. "I have this *thing* about old debts."

Zach raised his eyebrows. "I bet."

"Well, if you don't mind, I've got a ton of things to do."

Zach studied her for a couple of seconds. "You know, I could haul you in for assault on that man."

"Well, now, that would be your word against mine, and I'm not going to admit to being that close to Spider's crotch any more than you're going to admit looking at it."

Zach blanched. "You really know how to hurt a man." He glanced at her hands, then the empty table. "Bare-handed, and there's not a thing I can take with me to run a print. You're sharp, but you're not going to be able to avoid me forever."

An idea flashed through Raissa's mind, and before rational thought took over she ran her index finger along her lips, coating the tip with bright red lipstick. Zach's eyes widened as he followed her finger along the sexy pout of her mouth and sweat began to form on his brow. She leaned close to him and rolled her finger on his cheek, leaving a perfect print.

She slipped up from the booth seat and perched on the edge of the table, looking down at him. Giving him a wink, she spun around on the table and slid her long legs onto the floor. She pulled her skirt down to a barely legal level and leaned over the booth, placing her lips next to his ear.

"When you come to question me later," she whispered, "wear a uniform, and definitely bring hand-cuffs."

Unable to speak, Zach watched Raissa walk out of the bar, her curves swaying with every step in the sexy, spiked heels. His body had responded to her in all inappropriate manners, especially considering he was on duty. Especially considering she was a suspect.

His face still tingled where she'd left her print, and he tried to block his mind from recalling the way she'd run that finger across her lips and the look in her eyes as she'd done it.

Too late.

He groaned and waved a hand at a waitress at the far end of the bar. What he wanted was a scotch. What he was going to settle for was a piece of Scotch tape to remove the fingerprint from his cheek. No way was he walking into the CSI unit sporting a lipstick print on his face. There were some things a man could never live down.

He wondered briefly where he'd stashed his old patrolman's uniforms and if they still fit.

She's a suspect.

He blew out a breath. The sooner he ran that print, the better. God forbid he came up with nothing, because he was certain his spare handcuffs were in his glove box.

Hank Henry pulled the business card from his pocket and checked the address once more. This was the place. He parked his truck and walked across the street to the construction site, scanning the workers for the owner, a guy named Chuck. He finally located the man on the side of the building and introduced himself.

Chuck gave him the once-over, then lit a cigarette. "Pauley says you do some damned fine cabinet work."

Hank nodded. "I'm glad Pauley's happy with his cabinets."

"Pauley also said you do some damned fine drugs and some not-so-fine petty crimes."

Hank gritted his teeth and counted to three. *You have to expect this given your past. Don't take the bait.* "Well, sir, that would have been absolutely correct if you'd spoke to me a year ago."

The foreman blew out a puff of smoke and squinted at Hank. "Got clean, huh? I can respect that." He crushed out his cigarette on the side of the building and motioned Hank inside. "Place is gonna be some sort of clinic. Every room in the place is going to need cabinets, and they didn't want those cheap white prefab jobs. Said it was 'too clinical,' whatever the hell that's supposed to mean. The place *is* a clinic, after all."

Hank nodded and poked his head into a couple of different rooms. After rehab, Hank understood exactly what *too clinical* meant. The center he'd been in was a restored Colonial mansion, and the people running it had taken a "home" approach to getting clean and their counseling. For the first time in his life, Hank had felt like a member of a family, right down to the chore list and sharing dinner every evening.

"Looks nice," Hank said, wishing he had the clout to actually score the job.

"Think it's something you can handle?"

Surprised, Hank looked at the foreman. "You're serious?"

"Of course, I'm serious. Did you think I had you come all the way down here just for me to smoke a cigarette and run my mouth?"

"Yes . . . no . . . I mean, I figured you were talking to me as a favor to Pauley. I guess I didn't figure you were serious about hiring me."

"Hell, I like Pauley, but not enough to hire any excon or reformed druggie he tosses out to me. My reputation's good in this town, and I want it to stay that way. Truth is, I saw the work you did at Pauley's bar, and it's some of the best I've seen in years. I like that you took the time to customize those cabinets particularly for the same feel as the bar, but higher scale. Really classed the place up, but without making the rest of it look shabby in comparison."

Hank smiled, pleased that Chuck had latched on to the very thing Hank had been attempting to do with Pauley's bar. "Thank you, sir. I really appreciate that, especially coming from you. Pauley says you're pretty well sought after for this sort of work."

Chuck nodded. "Stay pretty much booked." He pointed his finger at Hank. "If you're serious about being straight, I can help you make a name for yourself. You got the talent. If you have the discipline, you could have a hell of a career."

Hank stared at Chuck, feeling almost dizzy over his words. A second chance at life. And not just any life—a great life, doing something he loved to do. It was almost too good to be true, and before he could stop himself, he started mentally calculating all the ways he could screw it up.

Stop it.

He forced his whirling mind to a stop. This was a golden opportunity. Some people never got one at all. He'd been given plenty and pissed them all away. If he didn't make this one work, then he'd have to put a hit out with the Heberts on himself. "You really think I could make a living doing this?"

Chuck laughed. "Are you kidding me? With your talent, you could get rich doing this. So what do you say? You interested in this job?"

Hank smiled until his jaw ached. "Damn straight."

Chuck stuck his hand out, and Hank shook it. "Be here tomorrow morning around nine, and we can go over the plans and the owner's 'vision' for the clinic. The owner will want to be here for that. She's nice, though—doesn't pick things apart and ask a lot of questions like most women." He elbowed Hank in the ribs. "She's cute, too."

Hank shook his head. "I just got divorced from a great woman who I wasn't even married to for a month before I ran out on her. I'm not looking to ruin anyone else's life."

Chuck laughed. "Sounds like what I told my wife twenty years ago, but she did okay."

"I'll see you tomorrow at nine."

Chuck gave him a nod and walked off through the building, calling for one of the workers. Hank took one final look around and exited the building, doing his best to contain his excitement. His new boss might fire him if he looked outside and saw Hank skipping. Men probably didn't skip unless they were high, so no use giving the man any reason to worry. But still, his step was lighter as he crossed the street.

He'd already slid into the driver's seat before he realized he had a passenger. The blood drained from his face as he looked over and saw Rico Hebert cleaning his fingernails with a razor blade.

"What's up with the construction?" Rico asked, still focused on his fingernails. "You know this is my territory. If you're hitting them up for anything, you gotta cut me in."

"I'm not hitting them up for anything. The man hired me to build some cabinets."

Rico looked up at Hank. "Straight work? Why would you want to go and do something like that? Work a shitload of hours for pennies. Break your fucking back and put stress on your heart. A workingman's life ain't no picnic, Henry."

But being a Hebert was. Right. "I told you I was straight now," Hank said, trying to keep his voice strong and steady. "I meant it. I'll work all the hours in the world if it means I'm not looking over my shoulder for cops all the time. *That's* stress on your heart."

Rico shot him an amused look. "It's stressful if you're a pussy, but then I guess that's where this conversation is over, right?" He laughed at his own incredible humor. "So what about the job I asked you to do with the magic lady?"

Hank felt sweat begin to form on his brow. "I already

told you no, and the answer's still no. Get someone else."

"But no one else knows the broad."

"Hell, I don't know her, either! I've only seen her a time or two and that was at a distance."

"Hmmmmm. That's a shame. Sonny was really hoping you'd have the inside track on her. Sonny's real interested in knowing what she's up to. And you know how Sonny can be when he's really interested."

"She's my ex-wife's friend, not mine. And in case you've forgotten, I haven't lived anywhere near Maryse in over two years. I don't even know what *she's* up to, much less her friends."

Rico nodded. "Yeah, I guess I can see that. But you see, Sonny's real interested, and you know how he can be. So what do you say you do a little asking around, maybe to that pretty little ex-wife of yours, and find out what the magic lady is up to."

"And if I don't?"

"It wouldn't be that hard to put some drugs in your toolbox, make a call to that new boss of yours. Or maybe in your truck. Maybe even somewhere on the job site. Hard to know what I might come up with. I'm a creative motherfucker when I want to be."

Hank felt despair wash over him. He knew Rico was capable of everything he'd just threatened to do and much, much more. "I'll make a phone call, but I'm not promising anything. My ex may not know the woman's personal business."

"Let's just hope for your sake, she does." Rico opened the door and stepped out of the truck, then leaned back in the passenger-side window. "I'll be here tomorrow to see what you found out. And every day after that until Sonny's satisfied. Understand?"

Hank clenched his teeth and nodded. The last thing

he needed was Rico Hebert at his job site every day. Chuck would immediately know that something was up, and it wouldn't take much to find out who Rico was and what business he was in.

He was royally fucked.

Chapter Five

Raissa pulled into the dimly lit parking garage and slipped through the shadows to the back door of her store building. Her mind raced with all sorts of things, none of them good. What Spider had told her was the absolute opposite of what she'd expected to hear. If Monk Marsella was really at the bottom of the Mississippi and had been for six months, then there was no way he could have kidnapped Melissa Franco. Which meant either that she'd been wrong nine years ago when she'd pegged Monk for the kidnapper, or someone had picked up his work with the exact same MO nine years after the fact.

Neither were very plausible explanations.

She gave the alley and garage a quick scan, an old habit but a practical one, and was relieved to see that neither Zach or any of Sonny's guys were lurking around corners or trash bins. She unlocked the back door and hurried up the stairs to her apartment. No way had she been wrong about Monk. She'd seen the evidence firsthand in Monk's house, and the only person besides her with a key to that closet was Monk. If only she'd been able to get the evidence out before he came back and caught her snooping.

That proof that she'd pursued but not collected had cost her two years of undercover work and nine years of her old life. But if Monk hadn't kidnapped Melissa Franco, then who had? It couldn't possibly be a coincidence that the MO was exactly the same. Certain details of the case had never been released, so an unrelated copycat wasn't likely. The only other answer was that Monk had a partner. Someone who'd been in from the beginning and knew how to create the same setup.

But who, and why wait nine years between kidnappings? It made no sense.

Neither did hitting on Detective Blanchard.

Raissa unlocked the door to her apartment, trying to block her mind from the earlier scene at the bar. The fingerprint wasn't an issue. Sonny was well aware of where she was, so hiding was no longer a concern. The FBI would likely perk up considerably when Zach ran the print through the database, especially as Raissa knew the bureau had presumed her dead years ago when she'd fled protective custody and they'd been unable to find her.

I told him to bring handcuffs.

Raissa groaned and stepped into her apartment, a cold drink and a cold shower the first two items on her to-do list. She stopped short when she realized she had company. Maryse and Sabine sat at her kitchen table, staring at her as if they were waiting for her to pull a rabbit from a hat. Or maybe her cleavage.

"Do you give tarot readings in that outfit?" Maryse asked. "Or do you have *another* occupation you forgot to mention to your best friends?"

Her friends' obvious disapproval at her less-than-forthcoming behavior washed over her as if she'd been doused with a bucket of cold water. The good part was, she didn't need the shower any longer. The bad news was, it looked like the drink was going to have to be a triple. She tossed her keys on the kitchen counter, pulled a bottle of scotch from her refrigerator, and set three glasses on the table. Maryse raised her eyebrows at Sabine, but neither of them said a word.

Raissa poured a splash of scotch into each glass and added a couple of ice cubes, then slid into a chair at the table with her friends. She pushed a glass across the table to each of them and downed a good portion of her own. "I was a bartender in college," she said finally. "Got big tips for pulling the caps off beer bottles with my teeth. Took me two years of working at the FBI to pay for all the dental work I needed."

"You know that's not what we mean," Maryse said.

Raissa shrugged. "I might also do a little security work for corporations."

"What kind of security work?" Sabine asked.

"Companies hire me to test their system's security."

Sabine's eyes widened. "Companies pay you to hack their computer network? How do they even know how to find you?"

"Word of mouth on the Internet. Word goes out that a company is looking for me. I contact them on a secure computer with a new e-mail address, so I can remain anonymous. I get the particulars, hack their system, and point out where the weaknesses are."

Maryse leaned forward. "That is too cool, but how do you get paid if you have to remain anonymous?"

"Wire transfer to an offshore account."

Maryse stared. "You're kidding."

"I never joke about money."

"Just how much money are we talking about?" Sabine asked. "I mean, if I'm not being entirely too nosy."

Raissa smiled. "Anywhere from ten to fifty grand a job. Don't worry—I pay taxes on all of it. God knows, I don't need any more trouble with the government."

"So what happens if they don't pay?" Sabine asked, clearly fascinated with the entire thing.

Raissa laughed.

"Oh," Sabine said, her face clearing with understanding. "I guess if you just hacked their system, that wouldn't be a good idea, right? Talk about guaranteed payment."

"Holy crap." Maryse sighed. "Nine years, Raissa. In nine years of knowing us, you never once thought you could trust us with all this?"

"Hell, yeah. Jesus, all of this had nothing to do with trust. I didn't want to get people involved—especially with something that might put them in danger. Why do you think I keep my security testing anonymous? Even corporations can be convinced to provide information if the right person is asking. Surely, the two of you can understand that." Raissa frowned, knowing she was hitting below the belt a little. Well, a lot.

Maryse and Sabine had both recently gone through their own life-threatening crises and had tried in the beginning to get through it without involving anyone they cared about. In the end, it had taken everyone to make things right, but both still carried the guilt of how badly things could have turned out.

Maryse lowered her eyes to the table, and Sabine's face flashed with a look of guilt, then sympathy. "When you put it like that . . ." Sabine said.

"Bitch," Maryse said, and gave Raissa a small smile.

Sabine swatted at Maryse. "That's not polite. My God, you are never going to learn manners, are you?"

Maryse put on an innocent look. "Hey, for all I know, that could be her real name."

Sabine frowned and looked at Raissa. "Did Beau know who you really were?"

Oh shit. Raissa's mind raced for a way out of this one. Beau, ex–FBI agent and Sabine's new husband, had finally remembered seeing Raissa talking with an FBI assistant director in Washington, D.C. Despite the plastic surgery she had to change her appearance, he'd still recognized her, but promised to keep her secret. Apparently, he was a man of his word, but that might not score him many points with the woman he'd just married.

"Raissa?" Sabine prompted.

"Uh-oh," Maryse said, and scooted her chair away from Sabine's.

"Well," Raissa began, "he didn't remember me at all . . . at first."

Sabine narrowed her eyes at Raissa. "But then he did?"

"Yeah. That night at the hospital with Mildred, something made him remember, but I made him promise not to tell."

Maryse laughed at Sabine's frown. "Kind of a catch-22, huh? Your man has honor and integrity, but since he was FBI, that means he'll always be keeping things from you. Welcome to my world. Could be worse. At least you knew what Beau was when you met him."

Sabine's frown relaxed. "That's true." Maryse's husband, Luc, an agent for the Department of Environmental Quality, had been working undercover when Maryse met him. In fact, he was undercover investigating Maryse. Not the smoothest way to start a relationship, for sure.

"So," Maryse said and grinned at Raissa, "is that your official FBI undercover investigating sort of outfit? Because I have to say, it's kinda hot."

Raissa smiled. "Actually, I was at a confession."

Maryse hooted. "And what did they confess to?"

"Nothing I was hoping to hear, unfortunately."

Maryse sobered and nodded. "You're looking for that little girl, right? Have the police been giving you trouble since you handed them information you shouldn't have?"

"Just one," Raissa replied, and felt a blush creep across her chest and up her neck.

"Oh, no," Maryse said and poked Sabine in the side with her elbow. "I've seen that look. What exactly does Just One look like?"

Raissa sighed. "Hot enough to melt rubber."

"That sucks."

"You're doomed." Maryse and Sabine spoke at the same time, shaking their heads in sympathy. After all, they'd already been there, done that.

"You can't let him find out who you really are, right?" Maryse asked.

"Well . . . since Sonny knows who I am, there's really no use hiding any longer." Her mind flashed back to the bar—her fingertip pressed against Zach's face and every square inch of her body screaming for her to make it more.

Maryse snapped her fingers in front of Raissa's face and brought her back to reality. "Earth to Raissa," Maryse said. "Where did you fade off to exactly? Oh, no, you like him."

"I barely know him."

Maryse and Sabine gave each other knowing looks. "But you'd like to jump him," Maryse said.

"Jeez," Raissa said, "you're not long on meaningless conversation, are you?"

Sabine laughed. "Especially not when she happens to be right."

Raissa groaned. "Nine years of avoiding men because I can't afford to get anyone involved with my situation—for my sake and theirs—and my body's in overdrive for a man I should be avoiding like the plague. Not to mention, I find out that the very people I thought I was hiding from know exactly who I am and probably have for a while, which adds to my general confusion in about a million different ways."

Maryse nodded and wrinkled her brow. "It *is* strange. I mean, if the Heberts know who you are and where to find you, I'd figure you for keeping Helena company, you know?"

"I know. That's the part that confuses me the most. There is no love lost between me and Sonny Hebert, and as soon as the FBI gets a line on me, they'll rush him to trial and have me testify. There's a ten-year statute of limitations on racketeering, which is the biggie. The limit runs out on what I know in six months."

"Wow!" Maryse said. "So do you think them asking Hank to kill you was your cue to get the hell out of Dodge? Why bother now?"

Raissa frowned. "I'm just guessing, but there's only six months left that my word is any good in court, unless I turn up dead. If the government can prove conspiracy, then the statute would start on the date of the last conspiracy act. I put the police on my track when I told them about the girls. The FBI won't be far behind, applying pressure as only the FBI can do."

"I get it. No statute of limitations on murder, and they might crawl all the way up Sonny's butt, especially over an agent."

"Exactly."

"Still, that's not going to stop the feds from coming to collect you as soon as they know where you are. How much time do you have before Just One sets off the alarms?"

"My fingerprint is going to hit the national database—

it's probably going in as we speak—and before you know it, this building will be surrounded by local FBI, all wanting to lock me up or spirit me off to Kansas to be a chicken farmer."

"Is that such a bad thing?" Sabine asked.

"It is if I want to catch Melissa Franco's kidnapper," Raissa said. "I know I'm close. I can feel it, just like last time. If Sonny hadn't made me as an agent when he did, this would all be over already. The FBI can't force me to do anything, but I'm sure they'll send someone to try anyway."

Maryse looked over at Sabine, who nodded. "All the more reason to get you out of here and hidden in Mudbug," Maryse said. "I don't suppose it will take the FBI long to track you down there, but it might buy you a day or two."

Raissa downed the rest of her scotch. "I'm hoping the presence of more FBI in New Orleans, especially around my shop, will spark whoever took Melissa Franco to make a move they hadn't planned. I'm sure someone will be checking there. I just have to hope that they report to Sonny, and that Sonny is somehow involved, and that he gets word to whoever . . . What a mess."

"And you didn't even mention the part where you can see Helena. Not sure which is worse, her or Sonny Hebert."

Raissa sighed. "Thank you for reminding me. I guess the least of my worries is a sexy detective?"

Sabine shook her head. "The understatement of the century. But the first thing we're going to do is get you out of here and into the Mudbug Hotel, where at least you'll have people around looking out for you, and hopefully it will take the feds a while to catch on."

"And your choice of many, many hotel beds, just in

case the sexy detective finds you first," Maryse said and winked at Raissa. "You'd better get to packing. Throw in something slinky, just in case."

Sabine wagged her finger at Maryse. "You are supposed to keep her out of trouble, not get her in more." Sabine looked over at Raissa. "Give me a hug and wish me well. I'll be going straight to Beau's place from here, so this is the last time you'll see me before I get back."

Raissa rose from the table and gave Sabine a hug. "Have a wonderful time. And don't worry about anything here. I've got it handled."

Sabine released Raissa and nodded, but didn't look convinced. She gave Maryse a hug and left the apartment.

Raissa headed to her room to pack a bag. This might be her last chance to catch the kidnapper. Her last chance to stop another family from going through the agony and grief of losing their child, then the hundreds of unanswered questions that had followed every return. Hiding in Mudbug wasn't her first choice, but Maryse and Sabine were right. She wasn't going to get much done with the FBI—or Zach Blanchard—hounding her.

Maryse's comment about beds flashed through her mind. Who was she kidding? If anyone was going to hunt her down in Mudbug, she couldn't help hoping it was Zach.

Maybe it would be easier if Sonny Hebert just killed her.

Zach paced impatiently behind the computer, and the tech, Casey, glared at him for at least the hundredth time. "This isn't going to go any faster with you pacing," Casey said. "Don't you have someone to arrest . . . a doughnut to eat?"

Zach stopped pacing and shot Casey a dirty look. "I'm trying to avoid processed carbs, and I *might* have someone to arrest, if I had the results from that fingerprint trace."

"It's a national database, Detective, not internal."

"Damn it, I know what it is. Do you think I don't know? This is important, is all, and there's a lot of pressure right now."

Casey's expression changed to one of sympathy. "You working the kidnapping?"

Zach sank into a chair next to Casey, watching data whirl by on the monitor in front of them. "Yeah."

"I think the captain's got the whole department on overtime." Casey shook his head. "That case sucks all the way around. Little kid missing. Mayor's granddaughter. Makes me glad I'm a technogeek. If I did your job, I might just shoot someone who kidnaps little girls."

Zach nodded. "Don't think it doesn't cross our minds, especially on the kid cases. But if we did, then we'd be no better than the criminals."

Casey didn't look convinced. "I got a five-year-old, and I'll tell you here and now, someone hurts her, and the judge won't even be able to give me bail."

"I hear ya," Zach agreed, and rose from his chair. "I guess I'll get some coffee. You want anything?"

"Nah, I drink coffee after seven P.M., and I've got a night of no sleep ahead."

"That's the point," Zach said, but just as he was about to leave, there was an audible click, and the data on the monitor stopped moving. In the center of the screen was a link with the words *100% match*.

"Hey," Casey said, "we got something here." He reached for the mouse and clicked on the link. The screen flashed for a couple of seconds, then brought up a picture of a woman that resembled Raissa, except that wasn't the name on the screen. There was only one other line of text on the screen: *Wanted for questioning by the FBI.*

Zach bit the inside of his lip. As if he needed any more trouble, and he'd likely just brought the feds down on the department by running that print. Damn it to hell. Casey looked up at Zach, the look on his face mirroring the way Zach felt.

"FBI?" Casey said. "The captain's going to shit."

"You think?" Zach ran one hand through his hair and paced the tiny office a couple of times. "Send me that link," he said finally. "I better get upstairs. I'm sure it won't be long before the bureau is knocking on the captain's door."

Zach hurried out of the office and down the stairs to his department. Of all the things he'd been expecting to find, this one hadn't been on the list. What in the world was Raissa mixed up in? He knew little more about her now than he did before he'd run the print, and the last people he expected a straight answer from were the feds. He fought the urge to drive over to her apartment and question her immediately, but he knew better. Department policy was clear. When the feds wanted someone, they had to be contacted first. Local PD could not get involved with a federal case unless asked.

And the chances of the feds asking for favors was slim to none.

Which meant Zach was back to zero on Raissa Bordeaux and her magical, mystical visions. He sat down at his desk and opened his e-mail. Casey had already sent the link, so he clicked on it and opened the page again. It was definitely her, he decided as he studied the picture more closely. Her hair was different, and she'd obviously had some surgery done, because the nose and cheekbones were different. But he had no doubt it was the same woman. He leaned back in his chair, remembering the scene at the bar.

There was something about the man Raissa had talked to that was familiar, but he couldn't place it exactly. He leaned forward and accessed recent arrest records. Maybe the guy was someone he'd seen being processed in the precinct. Thirty minutes later, his eyes were watering and he still hadn't located the man from the bar. He was just about to try another tactic when his captain stuck his head out of his office and yelled at him, his angry voice booming across the office.

"Blanchard, get your ass in here now!"

Detective Morrow looked over at him, eyebrows raised. "Uh-oh. Looks like someone's in trouble."

Zach clenched his jaw and managed to walk past Morrow without saying a word. He stepped into the captain's office, expecting a spectacular reaming, but was surprised to find that the captain wasn't alone. One look at the man and Zach knew exactly what he was—the dark suit, starched white shirt, perfectly knotted tie, sunglasses (worn inside), and the fact that he stood in front of the captain's desk rather than sitting in one of the chairs. Definitely a fed.

"That was fast," Zach said. "What did she do, steal your personality?"

"Zip it, Blanchard." The captain shot him a warning look. "This is Special Agent Fields with the local office of the FBI. He wants to know where you got the print you ran. And so do I."

Zach hesitated for a moment, not wanting to give away his information, but he couldn't think of a single way around it that didn't involve his going to jail. Which wouldn't exactly help his quest for a promotion. "I got it off a suspect."

"What suspect?" the captain asked. "The only case you better be working is the kidnapping, and I haven't been made aware of any suspects."

"Maybe *suspect* is too strong a word. *Person of interest* is probably better."

"And just how did you come up with this person of interest, and why haven't I been informed?"

"She came into the station yesterday and claimed to have psychically received information on the kidnapping."

"And you believed her?" The captain stared at him as if he'd lost his mind.

"Of course not. But when I ran the case through the national database, I realized that she was right. She'd given me information on all the previous kidnappings with a similar MO. Things that were never released to the papers."

The captain's face turned red. "Jesus H. Christ, Blanchard! And you didn't think that was something the rest of us should know? That woman either took those kids or knows who did." The captain looked over at Agent Fields. "Someone better start explaining. Why does the FBI want this woman?"

"That information is confidential," Agent Fields replied.

"Confidential, my ass!" The captain rose from his chair and glared at Fields. "If that woman was involved with kidnapping the mayor's granddaughter, I want to know why."

"She wasn't involved with the kidnapping," Agent Fields said.

"Says who?" the captain asked.

"Says the Federal Bureau of Investigation," Agent Fields replied, a bored look on his face. "Now, if Detective Blanchard would provide me with this woman's alias and her address, you'll be free to go about your business."

"And if I don't?" Zach challenged.

Agent Fields smiled. "It wouldn't be very good for your career to refuse. Federal prison is generally not a pleasant place for cops."

Zach clenched his fists and fought the urge to clock the condescending butthole. "Her alias is Raissa Bordeaux. She owns a shop on Landry Street."

Agent Fields removed a BlackBerry from his front pocket and tapped the keys. "Address?"

"I don't have it memorized, but you can't miss it. It's the only shop on the street with tarot cards and a crystal ball painted on the window."

"Great," Agent Fields said. "This department is under orders not to contact Ms. Bordeaux in any way. Is that clear?"

"Now, hold it one minute," the captain argued. "This woman is the only lead we have in a kidnapping, and you're telling us to step off but giving us no good reason why?"

"Exactly," Agent Fields said. "I'm so glad you understand." He slipped the BlackBerry back in his pocket and walked out of the office without another word.

Zach stared at the captain. "He can just leave like that?"

The captain stared after Fields and muttered something that sounded like "worthless motherfucker," but since Zach wasn't completely sure whether the captain was referring to Agent Fields or himself, he didn't comment.

"Yeah," the captain said, "he can leave just like that." He pointed at Zach. "You are going to sit down and tell me everything you know about this Bordeaux woman."

Zach sighed. "I could tell you everything I know before I even finished sitting."

Five minutes later, the captain was convinced that whatever Raissa was into, it probably wasn't going to help their case. Or he just didn't want to admit that they would be in deep shit if they talked to her again. Either way, Zach had his walking orders from the FBI and his captain: no contact with Raissa Bordeaux.

It was a shame he had no intention of listening to either of them.

Chapter Six

Maryse looked over at Raissa, tapping away on her laptop, and bit her lip. "Are you sure this is a good idea?"

Raissa opened the glove compartment of Maryse's car and tucked a black box with a wire inside, hoping her hastily rigged equipment worked as planned. "Of course it's not a good idea. Why do you think we're here at midnight?"

Maryse stared out the driver's window at the mansion across the street. Sonny Hebert's mansion. "Trying to get ourselves killed?"

"God, you're such a whiner," Helena bitched from the backseat. "All that shit you went through in the last couple of months, and you're getting all worried about sitting in a car on a public street."

Maryse turned around and glared at Helena. "Do I need to remind you that all the 'shit' I went through the last couple of months was *your* fault, and I never did anything to put myself in the middle of it? And that I'm still taking antacids?"

"When you put it that way . . ." Helena grumbled. "Maybe you should double your dose, just for tonight."

"I'd love to, but the pharmacy was out . . . again."

"The pharmacy is always out of medicine. Call Dr. Breaux and ask for samples. I don't think I paid for medicine the last three years." Helena looked over at Raissa. "You want to help me out here? I'm sorta getting killed on this one."

Raissa smiled. "Don't worry about your stomach, Maryse. We're not getting any closer than this, and his security cameras don't scan farther than the curb in front of his house. Besides, it's not like we're going to walk up to the door and ring the bell."

Maryse turned in her seat to face Raissa. "Do you honestly believe sending Helena in there is a better option? The Harbinger of Death? The Master of Disaster?"

Raissa laughed and handed Helena a little round piece of plastic. "All she has to do is hide this somewhere in Sonny's office, preferably not a plant, as they are prone to being watered, and take a peek in a storage closet. Piece of cake."

Helena tucked the plastic piece in the front pocket of her black leather jacket, then took the second piece Raissa handed her and popped it in her ear. "Are we ready to go?"

"One second." Raissa tapped more keys on her laptop. "Say something, Helena."

"Something."

"Smart-ass," Maryse mumbled as Helena's voice screeched from the laptop.

Raissa adjusted the volume and gave Helena a thumbs-up. "All set. When you get inside, turn right, then let me know when you're in the big hallway. I'll guide you from there. And everyone pray that Sonny hasn't rearranged his house since last time I was there, or it's going to be a long night."

Raissa gave Helena the once-over. "So what's with the outfit? You still doing the classic-movie thing?"

"Yep," Helena said and climbed out of the car, tugging her spandex pants out of the crack of her butt as soon as she hit the sidewalk.

Raissa grimaced. "Should I even ask?"

Helena rolled her eyes. *"Grease 2."* She crossed in front of the car, the neon blue of the pants creating a glare from the streetlight.

Raissa studied her for a minute. "She's wearing a T-Birds jacket and motorcycle boots. Is she supposed to be a guy or a girl?"

Maryse shook her head. "I don't even want to know. Just be glad that lately her outfits cover most of her body. The MTV years were far less kind on the rest of us."

"Yuck." Raissa fitted a microphone around her ear and positioned it to the side of her mouth as Helena walked through the front wall of the house. "Helena, can you hear me?"

"Loud and clear," Helena replied. "I'm in the hallway. There's five doors on the right and three on the left. Jesus, this guy's house is bigger than mine."

"Try the third door on the right. That should be the office."

"Hold on . . . yeah, office furniture, computer. This is it."

"Great. Now find somewhere you can slip the device. A central location is better." There was a second of silence, then rustling.

"Let's see . . . plant, no that's real. . . . might need the paper clips. . . . crystal bowl of bullets—What the hell? Why can't he keep mints like the rest of us?"

"Just find a place. And not the bullet bowl. It's probably used a lot."

Maryse paled and made the sign of the cross.

"Yeah, yeah . . . there's a little flowerpot with a sad, fake flower in it. Looks like something a kid made. Will that work?"

"Perfect," Raissa said. "I remember that vase. Sonny's daughter made it."

"Well, he really ought to pay for some lessons. Kid can't even spell correctly."

"I'm sure he'd be happy to, but she died when she was five. Leukemia."

There was a pause on the other end. Then Helena said, "Oh shit, now I'm really going to hell, with that statement. Making fun of a dead kid's spelling. You could warn me about these things before I go putting my eternal soul at risk, you know?"

"I'm pretty sure God will overlook your anal-retentive spelling issues. Just stick the device in there and check that closet. Sonny's guys walk the grounds several times a night. I don't want them to see us sitting here for very long."

Maryse shot Raissa a dirty look. "That's information that might have been good to know. I could have borrowed someone else's car or something."

"And put someone else at risk instead?" Raissa asked.

Maryse crossed her arms and slumped down in her seat, looking warily across the street at the house. "I would have picked someone I didn't like."

Raissa grinned. "Well, that would narrow down your selection to human beings as a species. We can always drive around the block and pick someone at random."

"You know, you were a lot less scary when I thought you talked to spirits."

"Helena," Raissa directed, "check the closet."

"Yeah, yeah, I've got my head stuck in there. There's a bunch of file boxes and a trunk with a padlock on it. Has letters on the front . . . hold on . . . says 'Monk.' Hey, you ain't got me breaking into some preacher's shit, do you?"

Raissa felt her pulse quicken. "The trunk. Can you look inside? I mean, through the side or something?"

"I can try. It's awfully small and dark, so no guarantees on what I can see. I can pull the whole thing out—"

"No! Sonny is beyond anal-retentive. If anything is out of place, he'll sweep the office and find the bug."

"Okay, okay . . . hold on . . . It's dark in the closet and even darker in the trunk. I'm going to have to open the closet door and get some light in somewhere. I'm no vampire."

"Be careful."

"Yeah . . . okay, I got some light in here and I'm peeking through the top of the trunk. What the hell . . . I don't know . . . Are you sure I can't pull this stuff out for a better look?"

Raissa bit her lip, wondering if it was worth the risk, when Maryse grabbed her sleeve and pointed. "Lights! Someone is awake and coming down the stairs."

"Shit! Helena, close the closet door and make sure everything is perfect. Someone's coming downstairs."

Raissa heard the squeak of the closet door and held her breath, hoping the lights in the house continued in the direction of the kitchen and not the office. Seconds later, a light beamed on at the opposite end of the house, and Raissa let her breath out in a whoosh. "They're in the kitchen. It's probably Sonny. He has problems sleeping."

"You think?" Maryse grumbled.

"Helena, I think you should get out of there. Unless things have changed enormously, Sonny will grab something to eat and go to his office. I know he can't see you, but I'd really feel better if you were out of there before he gets in."

"No problem. I'm leaving now. Okay, I'm in the hall. Holy shit, Sonny Hebert is walking down the hall toward me. Crap, crap, crap."

"Don't panic. He can't see you."

"But it's Sonny Hebert. How the hell can I not panic?"

"Breathe in and out and ease by him."

"This is not good," Maryse said. "When Helena panics, things tend to go very wrong. Maybe I should start the car. Hey, maybe we should just leave now. She can find her way home."

"Sit tight," Raissa said, trying not to let Maryse and Helena's nerves affect her own. "Everything will be fine."

And that's when a crash echoed through the laptop.

"What the fuck!" Sonny Hebert's voice boomed.

"Damn it to hell," Helena said. "I hit that table and the vase and oh, shit, here he comes. Think fast, something to do, think fast, the cat—" There was a piercing wail, and more cussing from Sonny, but no clear indication of what was happening in the house.

Maryse sat frozen in her seat, and the thought flashed through Raissa's mind that her friend might have had a heart attack right where she sat. "Get the hell out of there," Raissa said to Helena, and grabbed Maryse's shoulder with her hand and shook her friend.

Maryse seemed to leap into consciousness and started the car just as Helena burst through the front wall of the house and ran across the lawn as fast as hot pants, motorcycle boots, and sixty pounds of excess, ghostly flesh allowed. Lights flashed on all over the mansion, and Raissa knew it was only a matter of minutes before the house, grounds, and street were covered with Sonny's men.

Helena jumped through the car door and crashed into the backseat as Maryse pulled away from the curb. "Don't speed," Raissa cautioned. "Make it look like we were just passing by. Don't draw attention."

Maryse's knuckles were white on the steering wheel

as she eased the car down the block and around the corner. When she'd made it another block away, she took a hard left and floored the accelerator, pushing the car onto the freeway as fast as she could possibly go.

"What happened?" Raissa asked.

Helena huffed and wheezed in the backseat, far more than someone who was already dead should. "When I get nervous, sometimes I touch things when I don't mean to. It's a pain in the ass, I tell you. Normally I have to concentrate to touch stuff, but when I need to be transparent, it just happens."

"I tried to tell you," Maryse said. "When it comes to being a ghost, Helena is an amateur."

Raissa shook her head, trying to absorb the concept of a ghost having to learn how to be a ghost. "Okay. That's weird and something I'll definitely remember going forward, but it will have to wait. What happened, Helena?"

"I hit a table in the hallway and it had a vase on it. The whole thing crashed to the ground, and Sonny was getting closer. Then I saw a cat in the bedroom next to the table, so I grabbed the cat and threw it at Sonny."

A clear mental picture of what had happened flashed through Raissa's mind and she began to laugh. "Oh, my God. You threw a *cat* at him? The biggest mob boss in the state, and you attacked him with his own cat. Priceless."

"Well, I figured he'd think the cat did it all," Helena defended as Maryse began to chuckle along with Raissa.

"Oh, it was a brilliant move," Raissa agreed, "but just not the normal plan of attack for someone like Sonny."

Helena pouted for a couple seconds more, then started to grin. "Okay, so it might have been a little funny. Well, a lot funny. If you could have seen the look on his face."

Raissa tapped on her laptop. "We can at least hear it."

She hit a key and Sonny's voice resounded through the speakers, "That fucking cat! I swear to God, if my wife didn't love that animal, I'd kill it now."

"You're sure it was the cat?" one of Sonny's men asked.

"Yeah, the alarm is on, and nothing's out of place, except the vasc, which I never liked anyway."

"So maybe the cat did you a favor."

"Yeah, maybe. But still. Damn cat usually spends all its time sleeping. I can't imagine what got into it."

"Maybe something spooked it. We'll take a look around, okay?"

"Yeah, yeah. That's a good idea."

Raissa clicked on the laptop and the voices stopped. "Cool. It's coming through great."

Maryse glanced over at her. "How are you getting a signal this far away?"

"I put a receiver in the abandoned building across the street this afternoon. It's recording everything and I can stream the audio anywhere I can get a decent satellite connection."

Maryse shook her head. "I'm not sure if I was more impressed with your alleged psychic ability or your computer genius."

"Ultimately, it's all the same thing." Raissa turned in her seat to look at Helena. "Were you able to see anything in the trunk?"

Helena shrugged. "Yeah, sorta. I mean, I guess. Hell, I saw something, but I don't think I saw it right. It doesn't make sense."

Raissa's skin began to tingle. "Tell me."

Helena frowned. "That fancy trunk and high-tech lock, and all that was inside was a broken crucifix necklace and a Halloween costume. A gray alien suit."

Zach stared out of his windshield and shook his head. Almost midnight. Four hours outside Raissa's shop and no sign of the voodoo princess. Oh, but he'd seen plenty of signs of Agent Fields. If the FBI's finest had been trained at the art of surveillance, it certainly didn't show. Agent Fields had parked his car directly in front of Raissa's shop hours ago, and every fifteen minutes or so, he got out of his car and banged on the shop door.

Stupid. Raissa knew Zach would run her print as soon as he could get it done, so he seriously doubted she was out on a hot date or tossing back beignets and coffee. No, if he had to guess, Raissa had flown the coop—whether permanently or temporarily remained to be seen—but he wasn't going to waste any more time watching Agent Fields doing nothing.

Zach tapped the keyboard on his laptop once more and got the name he was looking for—the owner of Raissa's building. He entered the name into the police database and finally came up with a phone number for the man. He was obviously asleep when Zach called but woke right up when Zach identified himself and asked about his building. It took him a couple of minutes to assure the man that the building was fine, and as far as he knew the tenant was fine, but she was a possible witness to a crime and he needed to speak with her as soon as possible.

The owner was only too happy to provide him with Raissa's emergency contact—Sabine LaVeche.

Zach hesitated for a moment, then told the owner

that there was a bum outside Raissa's shop banging on the door, and if he moved a bit to the left, the owner might end up replacing that plateglass window. He hung up before the owner could ask for details.

A few more minutes of laptop whirling and one more rather enjoyable round of watching Agent Fields make yet another pass on assaulting Raissa's door, and he had the information he was looking for. Sabine LaVeche, Mudbug, Louisiana. And unlike her friend, Sabine had pages and pages of information. He scanned the info for anything that might be able to help him find Raissa, even if it was only something he could threaten Sabine with.

Another psychic. Great.

And apparently a psychic with a death wish, he decided as he read the police report on what had to be one of the strangest and most convoluted cases he'd ever heard of. Faked deaths and war crimes and crazy aunts and people buried in the backyard of some of the wealthiest people in the parish. Zach would bet anything that Sabine regretted the day she'd decided to go on a manhunt for her family. He imagined that all the inheritance in the world wasn't going to erase that trauma from her mind.

He continued to scan the screen, hoping for a weak link, something he could use to his advantage. The last couple of sentences made him groan. Cancer. Jesus H. Christ! How was he supposed to strong-arm a dying woman who'd discovered dead bodies in her newly found family's backyard? That was a level of asshole even he wasn't going to be able to manage.

He shut the laptop and took one final look at Agent Fields pacing the sidewalk and yelling at someone on his cell phone. Enough of this. Cancer and dead-body-finding aside, he was going to locate Sabine LaVeche and tell her he had an emergency. It wasn't exactly a lie.

A little less than an hour later, he pulled into the town of Mudbug, what there was of it. It was tiny, just a single row of buildings and a neighborhood that stretched in front of the bayou, the houses there the sort that only old money could buy. He had no trouble locating Sabine's shop and parked in front. The building was dark, but then that hardly surprised him, as midnight had come and gone over an hour before.

He peeked in the store window, but all he saw was a replica of Raissa's store in New Orleans. This building had been listed as her home address, so he pressed the doorbell, hoping if she was asleep upstairs she'd hear it. He waited for a while, staring up at the second story to see if a light came on, but the building remained black and silent. He pulled his cell phone from his pocket and was just about to dial Sabine's home phone when a car turned onto Main Street, tires squealing as it rounded the corner.

The car slid to a stop in front of the hotel, and the driver jumped out, looking frightened and frustrated all at the same time. Zach felt his skin tingle and ducked behind his car, peering over the roof. The passenger finally stepped out, and he smiled. He knew it—Raissa Bordeaux. And whatever her middle-of-the-night adventure had been, it apparently required a laptop and an unhappy getaway driver.

He watched as the two women entered the hotel, then hurried across the street, careful to stay out of the glow of the streetlamps. The blinds were closed on the hotel windows, so he slipped by and stopped at the door. Locked. But then, that wasn't really unexpected. He bent down for a closer look at the handle and realized it was an old model and one easily opened with a credit card.

He pulled his driver's license out of his wallet and slipped it down the crack between the door and the doorframe. It hung in the frame for just a minute, and Zach mentally cursed himself for choosing his license instead of his grocery-store discount card. At least that didn't have his name printed on it. He wiggled the license a bit and pressed it down again. There was an audible click and he froze, listening for any noise inside the hotel. When several seconds passed with no reaction from inside, he eased open the door and slipped inside.

There was a dim glow in the room created by a lamp tucked behind a desk in the corner. Zach blinked twice and, after a scan of the room, decided he was in the lobby. The place looked more homey than corporate. With any luck, that desk in the corner would have a nice old-fashioned registration book. He eased over to the desk and pulled out the first drawer. Jackpot. He opened the book and flipped to the last page.

Eighteen fifty-six. What the hell?

He scanned the other entries on the page, then closed the book and shoved it back in the drawer. Obviously it was an old record used for display. He checked the remainder of the drawers but came up empty. Looking over at the computer tucked in the far corner of the desk, he sighed. Hacking wasn't exactly in his skill set, but it was either that or knock on every door in the building, which would only draw a bunch of attention he was trying to avoid.

He sat in the office chair and turned his attention to the computer. What was a good password? . . . *room service*, *mudbug*, *hotel*, *california*. Okay, so maybe he needed a better plan. He sat back in the chair and stared at the blinking password box.

"I never figured you for a breaking-and-entering kind of guy," a voice whispered in his ear.

Chapter Seven

Zach knew it was Raissa by the way his body responded. Her soft breath on his ear set his skin on fire, and he felt stirrings in places that had no business stirring over a suspect. He turned around in the chair and was certain his heart had stopped beating.

Raissa stood in front of him wearing a black silky tank with lace trim, black spiky shoes that had to be five inches tall, and from the looks of it, not much else. "I see you're not in uniform," Raissa said, her voice low and sexy. "Did you at least bring the handcuffs?"

Zach felt his blood rush to one part of his body, which didn't need the additional confusion, and down to another, which definitely didn't need the additional stimulation. His mind raced with all sorts of possibilities that had nothing to do with police work but everything to do with the discovery phase—starting with what she was wearing under that silk nightie. Agent Fields had said they couldn't question her, and by God, Zach couldn't think of a single question he needed answered at the moment.

Except maybe what she was wearing under that silk.

She smiled down at him, sexy, hot, and so clearly issuing a challenge. Zach rose from the chair and locked his lips on hers in a single fluid motion that made her gasp. He pushed her back against the wall, enjoying the momentary surprise that crossed her face before she grabbed his head and lowered his lips to hers once more. He brought his hands up to cup her face as their mouths parted and their tongues met each other in wild abandon.

Then something struck him on his neck and he dropped to the ground, certain he'd been hit by lightning.

"Got him!" he heard a woman shout. "Cover me, Mildred."

"Wait!" he heard Raissa yell in the frenzy.

His entire body screamed in pain, and when he turned to see what had happened, he got a blast of spray right in his face. "Shit!" His hands, still numb from the initial blast, covered his eyes, but it was too late. He felt the burning of Mace and hoped to God that the woman who had attacked him had a bigger weapon to use, because as soon as he could see again and move, he was going to shoot her.

"Are you all right, Raissa?" the woman asked. "We saw him strangling you."

Zach managed to get one eye partially open and saw Raissa staring down at him, her face a mixture of amazement and amusement. Two other women stood in front of her—an older woman with the Mace and a younger one with a stun gun. Jesus, what kind of hotel was this?

"Sabine had Beau hook up your security system to portable monitors and gave one to me and Mildred," the younger one explained. "We figured that way you'd have backup if anyone tried to sneak in here. And since Luc left this morning, I thought I'd stay here and help."

Raissa filled a plastic cup with water from a cooler next to the front desk and handed it to Zach with a smile. The other two women looked at each other, clearly confused, then at Zach, then back at Raissa. Then the younger one paled.

"Oh, shit," the young one said. "Here I was thinking

you dressed pretty damned hot to sleep alone, and oh, shit." She looked down at Zach and bit her lower lip. "He's Just One."

"The one and only," Raissa confirmed.

The young one looked down at him, a pained expression on her face. "I am so sorry. If I'd known you were him, I wouldn't have tased you, I swear." She tugged on the sleeve of the older woman's robe. "Let's get out of here."

The older woman put her hands on her hips and gave them all a stern look. "Not until someone explains to me what is going on in my hotel."

"He's not here to kill her," the young one said, then paused and gave him the once-over. "Well, on the other hand . . ." She grinned at Raissa and pulled the older woman out of the lobby. "You're in big trouble, Raissa," she called over her shoulder as she trekked up the stairs with the hotel owner. "Huge. Enormous." He could hear her laughing all the way up to the second floor.

Zach struggled up from the floor, trying to appear anything but mortally embarrassed. "Friends of yours?"

Raissa smiled. "Why, Detective, you don't think perfect strangers would attack a man over me, do you?"

Zach cast a glance at the staircase. "Maybe not. The young one was scary."

Raissa laughed. "Oh, you have no idea. Maryse is a scientist."

"Let me guess . . . a mad one?"

Raissa gave him a sexy smile and stepped so close to him that he could feel the heat coming off her body. "I assume you didn't spend time tracking me down just for some night action. Might as well come up to my room. You can use my bathroom to clean up and tell me why you broke into a hotel and risked assault by two crazy women."

Zach hesitated, knowing being alone with Raissa in a hotel room . . . with a bed . . . was about the worst idea ever. He's already completely lost control and paid for it with his eyesight and a burn mark on his neck, but as she walked past him and up the stairs, he realized he was walking slowly behind her.

Raissa's room was quaint and homey, as he'd expected it would be, but he was surprised with the size and the equipment. What was likely once a sitting area contained two folding tables lined with computer monitors. He took a step toward the tables and glanced down the row of monitors. Different views of the street and alley outside the hotel and the lobby inside the hotel displayed on the screens.

He looked over at Raissa, who was, unfortunately, slipping a silk robe over her skimpy negligee. It was just as well. Being electrocuted hadn't been on his list of things to do, but it was probably far less painful than the mistake he had been about to make.

Raissa reached for a bottle on the dresser and poured two glasses of scotch. "The bathroom's through the far door if you need to flush your eyes more."

Zach shook his head. "I think I'll see again. Hopefully not blurry." He pointed to the row of computers. "What the hell is going on here? You've got more security on this hotel than we have at the police department."

Raissa handed him a glass and motioned to two chairs pushed over to the side of the tables. She dropped into one and took a long drink of her scotch. Zach slid into the chair beside her, hoping he was finally going to get an answer to the question of the enigmatic Raissa Bordeaux.

"I'm expecting company," Raissa said. "And I'm not really interested in visitors at the moment."

"I can tell," Zach said, and rubbed his neck.

Raissa reached for a backpack next to her chair and rummaged through it for a minute. Finally, she pulled out a tube of aloe vera cream and handed it to Zach. "I'm sorry about the burn. I honestly didn't know that Maryse and Mildred had their own closed-circuit system hooked up. Heck, I didn't even know Maryse was here. I thought I was the only one who knew you were in the hotel."

Zach squeezed some of the cream onto his fingers and rubbed a bit onto his neck. "So why does a psychic need so much hardware? If you were for real, you should have known I was coming here before I did, right? So why the Fort Knox routine?"

"I don't mean to offend your manliness, but you're not the reason all this hardware is here. Right now, you are actually the least of my worries." Raissa tapped one finger on her glass and stared at the wall behind him. Finally, she looked directly at him. "You're not supposed to be talking to me, are you?"

"Well, no. Not exactly."

Raissa sighed. "Who did they send?"

Zach didn't bother to play dumb. Clearly, Raissa knew the drill. "Some prick named Fields."

Raissa laughed. "You gotta be kidding me. Hell, Fields couldn't find me if I was sitting on top of him."

Zach couldn't help feeling pleased that Raissa had the same opinion of Agent Fields. "Yeah, I liked him about that much myself. The idiot's parked in front of your shop, beating on the door every ten minutes. I told your landlord a bum was banging up his property. It should distract him for an hour or so."

Raissa smiled. "Fields is going to be royally pissed

that he's stuck at my house. He's sorta an early-to-bed guy."

Zach sobered and looked her directly in the eyes. "So are you going to tell me why you're wanted by the FBI and hiding out in a hotel room with Pentagon-level security? You wouldn't have given me that fingerprint if your secret still mattered. I knew that at the time. Something changed, but what?"

"What did Fields tell you?"

"Nothing, except that it was FBI business and the New Orleans PD was forbidden to contact you. Given the tip you provided on the Franco girl, my captain is about to have a coronary over that directive. I figured I'd just go ahead and ignore it and likely pay for it later."

"Unless you can find Melissa Franco."

"Yeah, there is that angle."

Raissa stared at him for a couple of seconds, then sighed. "The FBI wants me to testify against a mob boss, but they had some trouble keeping me safe. I left protective custody nine years ago and never looked back. Well, not for the FBI, anyway." She tapped one of the monitors. "I keep the mob boss in my sight on a regular basis, which is probably why I'm still alive."

Zach nodded. What Raissa said made complete sense, given her lack of background history. "Were you an informant?"

"I was an agent."

Zach straightened in his chair, unable to control his surprise. "Shit! I mean, I knew you could handle a weapon, but lots of criminals can, too. Not that I'm saying I thought you were a criminal . . . Oh crap, I'm messing everything up."

"It's okay. You'd have been stupid not to think I was a criminal. I would have." She smiled. "Although that does bring into question exactly why you were caught in a compromising position with a woman you thought was a crook."

"I didn't think that, exactly. Not really. Oh, hell, the reality is that all the evidence pointed to you being a criminal, but for some reason it never felt right. Intuition sounds stupid, but I guess that's all I've got."

"Intuition is far from stupid. It's kept me alive more times than I can count."

"Yeah, but still. An FBI agent? Wow. Sorry, but that's really not what I was expecting to hear—" He jumped up from his chair and stared down at her. "Holy shit. You investigated the other abductions. That's why you know so much."

"Actually, I fell into the investigation by accident when I was undercover on another case. In fact, investigating those abductions is what blew my cover. The bureau wasn't thrilled."

Zach sat back down. "What did you find?"

Raissa sighed. "You're going to think I'm crazy again."

"Maybe. But I'm not going to think you're lying. This case isn't exactly normal."

"I saw an alien suit in the closet of one of the people I was investigating. Not hanging, like you would a costume, but in a trunk by itself. A padlock was on the trunk but not fastened all the way, so I took a look inside. I had no idea what to think about something so weird and dismissed it, figuring I didn't want to know. Then a friend of mine told me about this abduction case he was working where the MO matched some previous cases. I asked about dates and times. Every time an abduction happened, this particular guy was 'unreachable.'"

"And the other girls had already been returned, so you knew about the alien part."

"That's the thing that really got me. I mean, why else would that suit be locked away like that unless it was something that could create a lot of trouble? It was too much of a coincidence to ignore."

"Why didn't you follow him?"

"He wasn't my primary, and he didn't live in New Orleans. So the next time he told my primary he was going to be off the grid for several hours, I went to Baton Rouge to follow him."

"And got caught," Zach finished.

"Yeah."

"And your primary . . . who was he?"

Raissa hesitated for a couple of seconds, then finally said, "Sonny Hebert."

Zach felt his heart pound in his chest. He stared at Raissa, at a complete loss for words the first time since he'd met her. "You were undercover in Sonny Hebert's organization?"

"Yeah, for almost two years."

"As what? I mean, what did you do that you got that close to him?"

Raissa gave him a small smile. "Can't you tell?" She pointed to the row of equipment. "I'm a computer whiz. I could move money in ways that even the banks holding it couldn't trace. And I dabble a bit with security systems. I'm probably indirectly responsible for the alarms being bypassed at the kidnapping scenes."

"Jesus. I can see where that might make you a valuable commodity in Sonny's world."

"Oh, you have no idea. Sonny paid me a quarter million a year. Not that I got to keep it."

"Holy crap! I think I'm playing for the wrong team. Damn my conscience."

Raissa nodded. "I damned mine a time or two when I was moving millions to tax-free shelters overseas. Or driving around in my 'company' car—a Bentley, by the way."

Zach whistled. "So Sonny caught you following up on his guy?"

"No, the guy did. Monk Marsella. He was Sonny's cousin and ran the Baton Rouge side of things."

"And you think this Monk is the guy who took Melissa Franco?"

Raissa frowned. "I did, but now I'm not so sure."

"Why not?"

"You remember that guy in the bar? You know, the one I was going to castrate with my nine-millimeter?"

Zach felt his heart beat stronger for a beat or two, but his mind had flashed firmly back to Raissa's lipstick-coated finger pressed against his cheek. "Yeah," he said, and cleared his throat, hoping it might clear up his mind. "Hard to forget."

"Spider hasn't likely forgotten, either. I picked Spider to question because he's a weak link, a real pansy compared to the others. He says no one's seen Monk in six months. I've asked around, and he's not lying, as far as I can find."

"So what happened to him? Somebody's got to know."

"I'm sure someone does, but I'm guessing he's not in rehab or taking a leave of absence in Bermuda. Even if someone suspected what happened, they're not going to say. It's not exactly safe to have an opinion on the boss's cousin coming up missing, especially if the boss is the only one with the rank to make that call."

"Yeah, I guess not." He tapped his fingers on the table for a minute, then asked, "So what do you think happened?"

"It doesn't matter what I think. I can't prove anything."

"It matters to me. I trust your instincts. You've been right about everything. In fact, you've been one step or ten ahead of me."

"Well, I did have the advantage of a historical point of reference, but you're right, I do have an idea. I think Monk is vacationing at the bottom of the Mississippi River."

"Then who kidnapped Melissa Franco?"

Raissa stared at him, her expression mixed with frustration and fear. "I have no idea."

She rose from her chair and put her glass on a tray on the dresser. "So, do you still want to pin me to a wall and frisk me?"

Her tone was light, but Zach could tell it was anything but sexual. He didn't blame her one bit. "Between being electrocuted, going partially blind, and finding out my main suspect is a damned FBI agent—who I've been forbidden to contact—and my new main suspect is likely dead, I think I'm too overwhelmed to perform."

"Isn't that the truth." Raissa sat down next to Zach with a sigh. "Besides, I figure I've got another hour or so before Agent Fields shows up here looking for me. It would be best if your car's not parked out front, I imagine."

"He's going to be a problem."

"Who, Fields? Hardly. Fields is lazy. He'll come here once, find out Sabine's out of town. Mildred will tell him no one's seen me and that will be the end of it.

Hell, he'll run from a town like Mudbug. The man thinks camping out means a four-star hotel instead of five."

Zach laughed. "Then you might have found a home base. I just hope you packed well. Your apartment is likely off-limits." He rose from his chair. "I guess I better get my car off the street, but I'm coming back tomorrow. I want to check a couple of things, and then I want to pick your brain."

"Next time, call first."

"Next time, I'll come in with police lights flashing and wearing a cowbell."

Raissa placed her hand on his arm. "That might be enough."

Chapter Eight

Hank Henry glanced up and down the street in front of the construction site and breathed a sigh of relief when he didn't see Rico Hebert's car anywhere. He was in the clear, at least for the moment. He had no doubt that Rico would turn up sometime that day. The man was a thug but completely reliable. If Rico said he was going to do something, you could bet on it.

Hank got out of his truck and saw Chuck waving at him from the doorway of the building. A young woman stood behind him. As Hank crossed the street and approached the building, his felt his pulse shoot up. He knew the woman, and that might not be a good thing at all.

"Hank Henry," Chuck said, "I want you to meet Lila Comeaux. Lila will be running this facility when it's open, and she's got some specific ideas about the look and feel of the place."

Lila smiled and extended her hand to Hank. "It's good to see you again, Hank. You look well."

Hank felt relief wash over him as he shook her hand. Apparently, she wasn't going to make an issue of his past. "It's good to see you, too."

"You two know each other?" Chuck asked.

Lila froze for a moment, and Hank knew she was struggling with exactly how to answer the question without betraying a confidence. He quickly decided to take the decision off her plate. "Yes, sir," Hank said.

"Lila worked at the rehab center I stayed at in Mississippi. She was a huge factor in me getting straight. I'm glad to know you're opening your own place. I know you wanted to move back home, and I think you'll be able to help a lot of people here."

Chuck looked over at Lila. "Are you okay with Hank working on this job? If there's any discomfort, I can make other arrangements."

"I'm thrilled Hank is going to work here," Lila reassured him. "Hank was a huge success for the clinic. He really has the determination to make his life something of merit." She smiled at Chuck. "And I'm very pleased to know that you're the kind of man that gives people an opportunity to do something worthwhile for themselves, despite their past. It makes me even more certain of my decision to hire you."

Chuck blushed a bit and looked down at the ground. "Well, hell, we all made mistakes. Youthful indiscretions and the like. Some of us were just lucky enough to pull our head out of our ass before getting caught. Don't mean you can't do things right going forward." He looked up at Lila and grimaced. "Oh, hell, now I've gone and said 'ass' in front of a lady. My wife will have my hide."

Lila laughed. "You said 'hell,' too, but I won't tell if you don't."

Chuck looked pained for a moment, then laughed along with Lila and Hank. "Guess I did at that. Well, if the two of you are finished with the reunion talk, I guess we best get to talking about cabinets." He pulled a notepad from his pocket. "Let's start with the reception area."

An hour later, Hank walked Lila to her car, unable to contain his excitement about the job before him. "Your ideas are fantastic, Lila. I think people will really feel comfortable with the environment you're creating."

"Thanks," Lila said and brightened. "You have some pretty good ideas yourself, and I was very impressed with the photos of your prior work. You have a rare gift." She placed one hand on his arm. "I'm so glad you're pursuing a great life for yourself, Hank. I look forward to working with you."

Hank's arm tingled at her touch and he felt a blush creep up his neck. Lila smiled at him, a warm, sweet smile that made him feel good all over. "I'll see you sometime tomorrow with those color swatches," she said, and slipped into her car.

Hank watched her car until it turned out of sight at the end of the street, and that's when he heard whistling behind him. He felt his spine stiffen and turned around, already dreading what he knew he would see behind him. Sure enough, Rico Hebert was half a block up, leaning against his car.

And he didn't look happy.

"Pretty piece of work," Rico said as Hank approached. "Girl like that might be worth making some time for."

"Don't even go there. She's my boss, nothing else."

Rico stared at him for a couple of seconds. "Looked awfully friendly for a boss, but hey, maybe you got one of them jobs with perks. Might be the reason you went straight."

Hank clenched his jaw and struggled against clenching his hand. Hitting Rico would be instant gratification and long-term suicide. "What do you want?"

"You know what I want."

"I already told you, I don't know anything about that psychic woman. And my ex won't talk to me since our divorce," Hank lied. "She's not going to give me information on her friends, especially given our past."

"That's a shame, because you see, we got sorta an issue on our hands now. And the boss would really like it solved, you know?"

"What kind of issue?"

"That woman took a powder. Ain't no one seen her since yesterday."

Hank put up his hands. "I don't know nothing about that."

Rico studied him for a couple of seconds. "Maybe not. Still, if someone told the woman that we was looking for her, that person might be in trouble, you know?"

"I haven't been anywhere but this job site and my house." He pulled his cell phone from his pocket and held it out. "Check my phone. You can see every call in and out the past week, and I don't have a home phone. I can't help you."

Rico looked down at the phone, then back up at Hank and nodded. "Maybe you should ask that ex of yours again. You know, as a special favor to Sonny." He walked back to his car and pulled away.

Hank watched until Rico's car rounded the corner; then he crossed the street back to the job site. "Hey, Chuck," he called to his boss when he walked in the clinic. "Can I borrow your cell phone for a minute? Mine's dead and I need to make a quick call to my ex-wife. There's some legal business I need to get settled up with her."

Chuck pulled his cell phone from his pocket and passed it to Hank. "No problem. Come see me in the back when you get done. I want to put together a plan for building the cabinets and need to talk to you about when to order the supplies."

"Sure," Hank said, and waited until Chuck was halfway down the hall before he punched Maryse's number into the cell phone.

Maryse looked away from her computer and down at her phone, frowning when she didn't recognize the number. She answered on the second ring.

"Hello?"

"It's Hank. Don't hang up."

"What do you want?" Maryse asked in the exasperated tone she reserved only for her ex-husband.

"Your friend, Raissa . . . she's got trouble."

"Tell me something I don't know."

"Okay, how's this? For two days now one of Sonny Hebert's guys has shown up at my job site wanting to know where Raissa is. He says that the reason she left is because I warned her about Sonny. He thinks I should find out where she is from you."

Maryse felt her pulse quicken. "What have you told him?"

"That you hate me and won't even talk to me."

Maryse blew out a breath. "I don't hate you, Hank. I honestly don't know how I feel, and I'm sure you understand that now is not exactly the time to explore that."

"I get that. I'm just afraid that when he doesn't get the answer he wants from me, he might decide to go straight to you. You need to watch your back, Maryse, and tell Raissa to do the same. These guys don't mess around."

Maryse swallowed and stared out the front window of her and Luc's new home. "I know. We're being careful. I mean, as careful as we can be."

"Damn it." Hank sighed. "It's times like these I'm almost grateful that Mom's not around to see just how big of a mess I made of my life. I know she was a hard woman to love, but she still deserved a better son than me, and you deserved a better husband."

"We all make mistakes. It's what we do afterward that defines us. Thanks for warning me. And Hank, you watch your back."

"Yeah."

Maryse disconnected the call and leaned back in her chair, a tinge of guilt running through her. She still hadn't told Helena that Hank couldn't be her biological son—hadn't told Hank, either. After everything she'd been through in the past couple of months, Maryse knew better than most that you never knew when your last conversation with someone might be. And where Helena was concerned, that was doubly true, as no one really had a clear grasp on why she was here to begin with.

She pressed in Mildred's number on her cell phone. It was time for them to come clean to Helena.

"Damn it, Blanchard!" the captain yelled, his face flushed red. "Can you explain to me why the FBI was in my office first thing this morning blaming this department for that woman disappearing?"

Zach put on his best blank look. "I have no idea what they're talking about, sir."

The captain stared at him, but he never averted his eyes. Finally, the captain sat back down and threw up his hands. "I've got the mayor's son calling me every hour on the hour about his daughter. I had to call the police to get the media off *my* front lawn. One of those reporters snapped a shot of me through my bathroom window. I was taking a pee, for Christ's sake. Can you just see the headline? MAYOR'S GRANDCHILD STILL MISSING WHILE POLICE CAPTAIN HOLDS HIS CRANK."

"Captain, I promise you I didn't warn the Bordeaux woman off. I had nothing to do with her leaving." Technically, it was all true, so Zach managed to deliver it with a straight face.

"That better be the case." The captain tapped a pen on the desk and stared out the window for a moment. Zach waited, then wondered if he'd been dismissed. He was just about to rise when the captain looked back at Zach. "That wasn't the only reason I called you in here," the captain said.

Zach remained seated, but sat up straight. Something in the captain's tone was off. "Sir?"

"I have a problem, Blanchard. I know you have zero propensity for bullshit and even less tolerance for political positioning, so I want to ask your opinion on this."

Zach stared at him. "You want *my* opinion? Uh, yeah, I mean, if I can help with anything, certainly I'll try."

"You said that Bordeaux woman is who gave you the tip on the other missing girls, right?"

"Yes, sir."

"And then the FBI comes storming in here to claim her, which tells me she's probably an informant who saw something she wasn't supposed to see."

"That would be a logical guess, sir," Zach hedged.

The captain pulled a folder from his desk drawer and slid it across the desk to Zach. "Then can you tell me why it took that Bordeaux woman to bring those other cases to our attention when the mayor took part in a kidnapping seminar two years ago that discussed those very abductions?"

Zach stared at the captain, certain he'd heard incorrectly. "You're kidding me. Then why isn't the FBI taking over the case? If they released the facts for a workshop, why wasn't a public plea ever made?"

"Because after the girls were returned unharmed, the cases went cold. No point in spending a lot of time on healthy girls when they get new cases every day. If I had to guess, the last thing the FBI wants the public to know is that they did little to nothing about this in the past, and now it's happened again." The captain pointed to the file and Zach opened it.

The first page was an itinerary with a list of workshop attendees. The mayor's name was third on the list. Zach flipped through the rest of the pages. Surely, there had to be a mistake. Maybe he'd been invited and hadn't been able to attend.

But the paperwork said differently.

Notes from the meeting clearly outlined the mayor's opinions on the subject of child abduction and the steps law enforcement should take when it occurs. There was even a picture of some of the attendees at the back of the file, and the mayor's smiling face was front and center. Zach slowly closed the file, his mind whirling with a million different thoughts, but not one of them any he felt like telling the captain.

There was no way the mayor had forgotten the information presented. It was too unique, too outlandish for one to forget. And there was the glaring fact that Melissa had been taken out of a home with a high-tech security system. A security system that someone obviously had known how to disarm. That either meant a pro or someone on the inside. But what in the world did the captain expect him to say?

"I'm sorry, sir," Zach said finally. "I can't even begin to imagine . . ."

"Yeah, you can. And so can I. The problem is that neither one of us can come up with a good, *moral* reason for a man who has information pertinent to the

kidnapping of his own grandchild to keep it quiet.
That's why I'm asking you what you think, before I
make a move that's career suicide."

Zach blew out a breath, the captain's position over-
loading his mind with dire consequences—for all of
them. "It could be he's hiding something else and
doesn't want us poking into his private life, particularly that seminar."

"But you don't think so."

"I don't think it's the best bet," Zach said.

"So what is?"

"Next year's an election year, and according to the
polls, the mayor's popularity is waning. Something
like this could create a huge sympathy vote."

"Motherfucking shit."

Zach nodded. "That pretty much sums it up."

"So, what do I do with this?"

Zach shook his head. "Either he knows something
about the kidnapping, or he's keeping his mouth shut
to hide something else. And I gotta say, captain, that if
it's option two and this isn't some political maneuver,
then you're not going to like whatever it is that's so
important he's willing to risk his grandchild."

Zach studied the captain as he pulled at his tie. His
face was an interesting mix of wanting to throttle
someone and the precursor to a heart attack. "We're
not going to get anything out of him," the captain said.

"No, sir."

"Then who might we get something out of? Someone's got to have suspicions."

"You want to know who would roll on the mayor?"

"Yeah. Blood isn't always thicker than water, and
he's got a shitload of relatives working for him. Which
one do you think will talk?"

Zach considered the long list of relatives that he was aware of. "I think my bet would be on the little girl's mother."

The captain sat stock-still, and Zach could tell he was rolling that idea over and over in his mind, playing out every possible outcome—good and bad—of pumping the mayor's daughter-in-law for family secrets. Finally, he gave Zach a single nod. "Do it."

Zach rose from his chair and headed to the door. Before he opened the door, the captain's voice sounded behind him. "And not a word to anyone."

That kinda went without saying.

Raissa, Maryse, and Mildred sat in Mildred's office, all looking at Helena, waiting for the bomb to drop. Helena stared back at them in disbelief, her mind not even capable of processing the information they'd dumped on her.

"But that's not possible," Helena said finally, looking far more pale than even a ghost should appear. "I gave birth to Hank. I know he's my son. Giving birth's not the sort of thing you forget all that easily."

"We're not doubting that part," Maryse said. "But your blood types are completely off. There's simply no way you and Harold could have produced Hank."

Helena's eyes widened. "I never cheated on Harold. It was Harold who made a habit of running around. Hell, I should have cheated on Harold, but I didn't, I swear. In fact, I hate to admit it now that I'm dead and don't even have a chance at another go, but Harold's the *only* man I've ever slept with."

Raissa glanced at Maryse and Mildred, who were both grimacing. It was pretty horrific, if one knew Harold Henry. And very, very sad. "There has to be an explanation," Raissa said.

Helena shook her head. "I can't imagine what. Are you sure, Maryse?"

Maryse nodded. "I double-checked with the doctors I'm working with in New Orleans, just to make sure I hadn't forgotten anything about blood types. They all said it's not possible for a combination of your and Harold's blood types to produce Hank."

Helena stared at her, a lost look on her face. "I don't understand. Hank was my miracle baby. I'd had problems, cysts removed, and Dr. Breaux said it was unlikely I'd be able to get pregnant. When I got pregnant with Hank, I was so surprised and excited. And now you tell me he's not even my son. I know he's done a lot of things wrong, but I still love him. What could have happened?"

"I'm so sorry, Helena," Maryse said. "The only thing we can think of is that someone mixed the babies up at the hospital."

"But then . . . oh God . . . that means my real baby is wandering around somewhere out there, and I never knew him." Helena looked ready to cry. Maryse looked over at Raissa, the plea for help written all over her face.

Raissa took the cue and stepped in. "Are you certain you gave birth to a boy?"

"Yes," Helena said. "I remember the doctor saying so as soon as he came out, and Harold grinning like an idiot. Probably the only damned time the man was happy."

"That helps," Raissa said. "I'm going to do a little computer work and see what other male births happened at the hospital at the same time. We'll get to the bottom of this."

Maryse bit her lip and nodded. "I'm really sorry we had to tell you. I guess we were hoping there was some logical explanation."

"Like my having an affair?" Helena asked. "That's a great thing to think about a person."

"It's not like anyone who's ever met Harold would blame you," Maryse pointed out.

"That's true," Helena allowed. "I don't know what to make of all of this. First, I wind up killed. Then I find myself wandering around the earth and causing trouble most everywhere I go, and now you tell me the baby I raised isn't even my biological child. I guess that should relieve me some, given how he turned out, but it's just sorta sad."

Maryse blew out a breath. "I know he's done some bad things in the past, but Hank is getting better and he's still your son, Helena, no matter what the tests say. No one can take that away from either of you."

Helena rose from her chair and nodded. "I guess not," she said, and walked through the exterior wall of the hotel.

"That went well," Maryse said. "This sucks."

Mildred nodded. "It's a very odd and hurtful situation, but you were right to tell her. She'll come around in a bit. I imagine this is a shocking blow, on top of everything else."

"What else is there?" Raissa asked. "I mean, besides being murdered and roaming the earth, then finding out your child isn't yours?"

"Helena was dying," Maryse said. "The autopsy showed cancer all over her lungs and a rare form of leukemia.

Raissa frowned. "Why didn't she tell anyone?"

"She didn't know. Apparently, her symptoms were very mild and confused with her asthma. No one thought anything of it, including Helena. It's weird, but not impossible, according to the scientists I talked to."

"That is a lot to absorb, especially on top of being dead and still here."

"I know you've probably got things to do today," Maryse said to Raissa, "but do you mind meeting me for breakfast tomorrow morning? I've asked Dr. Breaux for coffee. I thought maybe he'd be able to shed some light on some of this . . . or not. But he *was* Helena's doctor and he did deliver Hank. I figure if anyone's going to be perturbed enough by all this to dig into it, Dr. Breaux will."

Raissa nodded. Whatever happened to their normal lives?

"There's something else," Maryse said, and bit her bottom lip. "Hank called me yesterday and again this morning in a panic. I didn't get a chance to tell you this last night, because I didn't hear you come in, and afterward . . . well, I figured you had your hands full, or I hoped you did . . ."

"No such luck," Raissa said. "Electrocution tends to lower the libido."

Mildred started chuckling and Maryse flushed red. "Oh, shit. I'm so sorry. I didn't mean to ruin your night."

Raissa waved a hand in dismissal. "You didn't. It was going to be ruined anyway as soon as he found out the truth. That's not exactly an erotic teaser. So what did Hank have to say?"

"He said one of Sonny's guys was at the construction site hassling him. Sonny knows you're gone, and the guy was pushing Hank to see if he warned you off."

"Shit. I hope my leaving doesn't put Hank in a bad position."

"Hank said he can handle himself, but he wanted to

make sure you knew they were looking for you. I guess I'm hoping they'll think the FBI got to you, but that's probably too much to ask, right?"

Raissa sighed. "Since the FBI agent assigned to bring me in was parked outside my shop all last night and thinks banging on my door is the way to locate me, then yeah, it's too much to ask. Sonny's men only need a glance at Fields to know he's a fed. They probably already know Fields doesn't have me. I'm sure they were watching my shop if they know I didn't go home last night."

"Sonny knows you're friends with Sabine and me. They're going to look here next." Maryse looked over at Mildred, who nodded. "Mildred and I don't think you should open Sabine's store. You'll be on the other side of a plate-glass window. Might as well be a sitting duck. They'll know you're here, and it wouldn't take a genius to figure out where you're staying once they find Sabine's apartment empty."

Raissa nodded. "Or just sit at the end of the street and watch me walk to the hotel. I know they'll find me, but I can't back out on Sabine."

"Sabine wouldn't want you to do this," Mildred said. "I promise you that. If Sabine knew how this was going, she'd be on the first plane back."

Raissa shook her head. "It's really something, you know? Here I thought all these years I was hiding from life and people, trying to keep my distance, and I end up with the best friends a person could ever ask for. You guys are truly amazing."

A flush crept up Mildred's neck and onto her face. Maryse nodded. "I agree. We are amazing."

Mildred tapped Maryse's leg with her hand. "Stop bragging. I'm the only one who can brag about my girls." She looked over at Raissa. "Think about it, please.

Maryse can sit in that store, same as you, although I shudder to think what she'd make of reading tea leaves or whatever else you do. The appointments can wait. Sabine is only gone a few days and her regulars already know that."

"Okay," Raissa agreed. "Maryse can store-sit, but that doesn't mean I'm hiding out here like a thief."

"I was afraid you were going to say that," Maryse said. "I suppose you're going to do some snooping?"

"This may be my last chance to catch a kidnapper, and time is running out. In five days, Melissa Franco will likely be returned to her parents with no memory of what happened. I can't let him get away with it again."

"Have you heard anything from Sonny's house that can help?"

"I wish. He was only in his office for ten minutes or so this morning, and I could only hear typing. I'll keep checking, though. He's bound to talk to someone sooner or later."

"Do me a favor," Maryse said. "I know she's sorta a pain, but take Helena with you. There's a lot of advantage to having a lookout that no one else can see. And even though things don't always turn out so great when Helena's involved, they could have been worse if she hadn't been there." Maryse looked around and lowered her voice. "But don't you dare tell her I said that."

Raissa smiled. "My lips are sealed. But I need to find her first."

"She'll probably be sitting on the dock at her house," Maryse said. "She goes there when she needs to think."

"And we've given her plenty to think about this morning." Raissa frowned. "Speaking of which, if a stupid man in a well-pressed suit comes around here asking for me or Sabine, that's Agent Fields. I half expected him to turn up last night, but he probably thought Mudbug would have dirt roads and it would mar the paint of his pristine car. He'll be here today, though. He won't have a choice."

"He won't get anything out of us," Mildred said.

"Actually, I want you to tell him that Sabine is on her honeymoon. Likely he'll leave as soon as he hears Sabine's not home."

"Then we'll be sure he gets the message," Mildred said. "In the meantime, I took the liberty of parking your car in the garage behind the hotel, and pulled mine up front. I figured it wouldn't do for them to see your car parked here."

Raissa nodded. "I figured as much when we raced in here last night and I didn't see it out front. Thanks, Mildred. You're getting good at this cloak-and-dagger stuff."

Mildred sighed. "I'll just be happy when I can get back to running my hotel and pestering Sabine and Maryse for grandchildren. I'm too old for this crap."

Chapter Nine

Zach stood in the living room of a townhome that probably cost more than he made in ten years and looked from Susannah Franco to her husband, Peter. "So there were no issues with Melissa?"

"What kind of issues?" Peter Franco asked.

"The typical sort, like a fight, maybe?"

"Absolutely not," Peter said. "I hope you're not suggesting something foolish, like Melissa ran away. Nothing could be further from the truth, and the time you're wasting here is time you could spend looking for my daughter."

Susannah Franco placed her hand on her husband's arm. "He's just doing his job." She looked at Zach. "My husband's right. Melissa is a very happy child. I know all parents think their children are special, but Melissa truly is. She never has a harsh word to say and always finds the fun and joy in just about anything. She loves her life."

Zach nodded. "What about illness? Sometimes if a child is sick, they behave differently, or if they're running a fever, it can affect their memory."

Peter shook his head. "She wasn't sick. In fact, Melissa is never sick. She has allergies but a mild case at that. My wife is right. She is a very special child. Perfect, almost. Sometimes frighteningly so."

"Why do you say that?" Zach asked.

"I don't know," Peter replied. "It took us so long to conceive and we'd just about given up hope. I guess I just always had this feeling that I got something I didn't deserve with Melissa, and one day it would be taken from me." He gave Zach a bleak look. "I guess I was right."

"We're going to find her," Zach assured him. "When I called earlier I asked about the instructions for your security system. Were you able to locate those?"

"Oh, yes," Peter said. "They were filed in my office. I'll get them for you." He exited the living room and hurried up the stairway. Zach allowed himself one second of relief that he'd managed to get Peter out of the room, but then he turned his best investigative techniques on Susannah. The townhome wasn't that big, and Peter would be back any minute.

"Mrs. Franco," he said in a low voice, "before your husband returns, there's something I need to tell you."

Susannah's eyes widened. "Okay."

"Two years ago, your father-in-law was a member of a panel on child abductions. The cases covered were identical to Melissa's, but when questioned, he never volunteered that information. Can you think of any reason why your father-in-law would intentionally withhold information that could help find your daughter?"

Susannah gasped, the fear on her face plain as day. "No. I don't believe it."

"I saw transcripts of the panel and photos. If you know something about your father-in-law, you need to tell me."

"Is he a suspect?"

"At this point, he's a person of interest, but all of you are. That's the way this sort of thing works. Your father-in-law knew how to disarm the alarm. Melissa would have gone with him without a struggle."

"No," Susannah shook her head. "I won't believe it. I can't. He's overwrought and he forgot. There's no way Martin would hurt his granddaughter or Peter."

"Not even for a reelection win?"

Susannah's mouth snapped shut and she stared at Zach for a couple of seconds. "I don't know why he didn't give you the information, but there must be a good reason."

Zach looked her directly in the eyes. She met his gaze for one second, two, three—then she couldn't hold it any longer and looked away. "Are you sure about that?"

"I have to be," she said, her voice barely a whisper. "The alternative is not an option."

Helena sat in the passenger seat of Raissa's car, wearing a black leather outfit and dark sunglasses. Raissa wasn't sure whether she was going for Lara Croft or *The Matrix*, but she'd missed the mark on both counts. Raissa found herself longing for the days that she could only communicate with Helena through writing or holograms. Maryse may have been dead wrong about the MTV years being worse.

"I don't understand why you have to do this in New Orleans," Helena complained. "You're supposed to stay out of sight. And while I'll give you that the disguise is good, it's still not safe."

"It's not safe to do what I have to do in Mudbug, either."

"Why not? I thought you were some sort of computer whiz. They have the Internet in Mudbug."

"I am a whiz, but it would take time to create a diversion good enough to cloak the origin of the Internet signal. I simply don't have the time. So the safest way is to do my hacking at a public site and toss the computer when I leave. That way, no one can trace it to me."

Helena's expression cleared in understanding. "And no one will show up in Mudbug."

"Exactly. The last thing I want to do is put anyone in Mudbug in jeopardy, especially Mildred or Maryse."

"Well, I still think it's dangerous, but I guess that's what I'm here for, right? Lookout extraordinaire."

Raissa didn't miss the sarcasm in Helena's voice. "You're a great help. Maryse and Sabine wouldn't be around if not for your help. Your methods may be questionable, but your heart is usually in the right place."

"I suppose you're right." Her face brightened and she turned in her seat to face Raissa. "I don't suppose you'd stop at the grocery store on the way home and buy me a cheesecake?"

Raissa laughed. "What happened to the diet?"

"Hell, I didn't diet when I was alive. What's the point now?"

"Maybe the point is you're expensive to feed and don't need to eat, so it's a waste of money."

"Yeah, yeah." Helena waved a hand in dismissal. "So are wine, cigarettes, and gym memberships, and there's still plenty of those around."

Raissa glanced in her rearview mirror and frowned. There was a black car about a hundred yards behind them. It was tucked in behind a van, but Raissa caught a glimpse of it as the driver edged the car over, probably trying to see around the van. The thing that bothered Raissa was that the lane next to the van was completely clear. The car could easily pull around.

"What's wrong?" Helena asked. "You've got this weird look on your face, and you keep looking in the rearview mirror."

"I think someone is following us."

Helena spun around in her seat and peered out the back window of the car. "The van?"

"No. There's a black sedan behind the van, but it won't pass. It's been there for the last three miles."

"Do you recognize the car?"

"No, but I'm getting a bad feeling."

Helena turned around and fastened her seat belt. "That's not good."

"Why are you fastening your seat belt? You do know you're already dead, right?"

"God, everyone is always saying that. You're like a bunch of broken records. Of course, I know, but I'd still duck if someone was pointing a gun. It doesn't matter if it's irrational. Fear is fear."

Helena's logic never ceased to boggle Raissa's mind. So many variables with ghosts, and boy, did Hollywood have it all wrong. She glanced in her rearview mirror again and saw the blinker flashing on the van. She felt her stomach tighten. "The van is exiting." Raissa checked her mirrors and the highway in front of her, but there was no other car for miles.

Helena sat frozen in the passenger's seat. "Is the car following?" She clenched her eyes shut. "I can't look."

Raissa watched as the van eased off the highway at the last exit Raissa had passed. The black car slowed and Raissa felt her breath catch in her throat, but then the car sped back up and remained on the highway, now exposed. "Shit."

"They didn't exit?"

"No." Raissa pulled her pistol out of her purse, turned the safety off, then clutched the gun in her right hand. She checked her mirror again and realized the car was picking up speed. They were half the distance from her now that they had been just seconds ago. "This is bad."

Helena bit her bottom lip and Raissa could swear the ghost grew paler. "How far away is the next exit?" Helena asked.

"Five miles. We're sitting ducks. I should have taken the last exit and tried to shake them. Stupid! I'm losing my edge." She checked the mirror. Another thirty yards and the car would be on top of them, and it showed no signs of slowing.

"Hold on, Helena. This is about to get ugly."

She'd barely finished her statement when the other car struck them from behind, then dropped back. Helena curled up in a ball with her head between her legs and arms wrapped over her head. Raissa gripped the steering wheel with her free hand and just managed to keep the car on the road. "Damn it, Helena, I need help here."

Helena peeked out from under her arms. "What kind of help?"

"I have a plan. I need you to be ready to read the license plate off the other car."

Helena sat up and glanced in the passenger-side mirror. "There's no plate on the front."

"I know that. I'm hoping there's one in the back. Are you ready?"

Helena looked completely confused but nodded. "Go for it."

Raissa lowered the driver's side window and shifted her pistol to her left hand. She watched in the rearview mirror as the car built up speed behind her for another hit. Just before the car reached her, Raissa yanked the wheel to the left and slammed on the brakes. The other car shot by them on the right side. Raissa strained to see the driver, but the windows were tinted so dark, she could barely make out a silhouette inside.

Before the other driver got any bright ideas, like braking himself, Raissa held her gun out the window and fired a shot into the trunk of the other car. The driver swerved, but managed to maintain control. Raissa waited a couple of seconds to see what the driver would do. She prayed he'd take the warning and move on. The shot had been a warning. If she had to kill the man, things would get really sticky, and she couldn't afford to waste time sitting in a jail cell.

"Shoot him again!" Helena yelled. "Make it count this time."

The other driver, apparently realizing his mistake, leaped forward. Raissa pressed the accelerator as far down as it would go, but the other car kept inching away from them. Her finger twitched on her pistol, and she warred with herself over shooting out the tires. But then she'd be on the hook for whatever happened afterward. Damn it!

Raissa's chest and stomach hurt from the seat belt, and she brought her hand in the window, placed the gun in her lap, and loosened the belt. She took a deep breath, trying to control her racing heart.

"You're letting him get away," Helena complained.

"I'm not letting him. His car is a lot faster. There's a V-8 engine in that Cadillac."

"It's still not as fast as a bullet."

"I know. But I couldn't afford to waste a day or two in jail explaining myself to the police, and the FBI would be right there ready to expedite things as long as I agreed to be on the first bus out of here."

"Yeah, okay," Helena groused. "I guess I see your point, but I don't have to like it."

"I don't like it, either. I would much rather have put

a bullet through his head. Did you get a look at the back of the car?"

"There was no plate on the back, either," Helena said, huffing like a freight train.

Raissa looked over at Helena, who was struggling to loosen her seat belt. "Are things supposed to hurt ghosts?" Helena asked. "Because this seat belt is killing me. What the hell?"

Raissa watched as the black car disappeared over the next rise in the highway. *What the hell?* was a really good question.

Working on her best pout, Helena sat in a secluded corner of Starbucks across from Raissa. "I can't believe you're going to drink that caramel, whippy-doodle thingie in front of me."

"You can't exactly drink one in here," Raissa whispered. "I'll get you one when we leave."

"Promise?"

"God, you're worse than a three-year-old. Don't worry. You'll have your coffee in twenty minutes or less. That whole run-in on the way here has made me change my plans. I don't have time for the hacking I had planned, and it might not be the best idea, when I can convince someone else to do it for me."

Helena winked. "Must be nice having a cop on the side."

Raissa laughed and pressed in some numbers on her cell phone. "Zach, I need a favor."

"What kind of favor?"

"Can you track down the other missing girls? I thought that if we could find where they are now, we might be able to ask if they've remembered anything about their kidnapping, or if anything's happened to them since."

"Sounds reasonable," Zach said. "Just let me run it by the captain. He's been watching us like a hawk. We're not supposed to do anything unless it advances the investigation."

"Great. And, um, there's one other little thing."

"What kind of thing?" The suspicion was evident in his voice.

"Well, I got into a little trouble, and I was hoping you could—"

Zach didn't even let her finish. "What the hell happened now?"

"A car followed me from Mudbug and tried to run me off the road. I might have taken a shot at them in a *Top Gun* sort of maneuver."

"Damn it! I told you to stay put."

"Yes, but I had things to do."

"Like what?"

"Like get a coffee. So can you help me do a DMV search or not?"

He sighed.

"Now, see, this is exactly what the captain doesn't want us running off on," he said. Then after a pause, "Did you get the plate number?"

"No plates, but I have a make and model. Black Cadillac DTS—current year."

"You want me to do a search for every Black Cadillac DTS in New Orleans? Seriously?"

"It's a sixty-thousand-dollar car. There can't be that many."

"Fine, but if I lose my job over this, I'm sending you my mortgage bill."

Raissa smiled. "I'll make it up to you. Give me a call when you have the info."

"So why do you want to know about the other girls?" Helena asked as Raissa hung up.

"I don't know. It's just a feeling that they're all connected in some way other than appearance, but it's a strong feeling. Do you know what I mean?"

Helena nodded. "Yeah. Kinda how I felt right before I died. I knew it wasn't just another asthma attack or something simple. It was too late by then, but it's almost like carrying a wet blanket around on your shoulders. I've been carrying it ever since."

"Exactly. And it's the one thing that's nagged at me for years. There has to be some reason these girls were chosen. I simply can't believe it's random."

Helena nodded. "You think any of them remember something?"

"It's possible. Maybe nothing with extreme clarity, but they could be experiencing dreams or reactions to certain stimuli. Unless the brain cells containing information are completely removed or damaged beyond repair, there's always the chance that a memory can surface."

"But if that's the case, wouldn't they have said something?"

Raissa shook her head. "Not necessarily. I know it seems like they would want justice, but I found with victims that the more time had passed after the crime, the less interested they were in justice than in just trying to forget."

"Makes sense. So you think maybe they wouldn't have raised a flag, but if questioned directly they might fess up?"

"That's what I'm hoping."

"So do you think the guy in the Cadillac works for Sonny?"

"It's certainly possible. Sonny liked Cadillacs and he never had a shortage of automobiles. He had twelve when I worked for him."

"Jeez," Helena said, "what the heck does he need all those cars for? You can only drive one at a time. Does he have fifty kids or something?"

"No. he only had the one kid."

"The one that died?"

"Yeah. His wife had complications with the birth and had to have a full hysterectomy afterward. The one thing I can say for Sonny is that the whole time I was with him, I never saw him cheat on his wife. Most of the guys figured he'd cut her loose when she couldn't give him a son, but they're still married."

"A mobster with family ethics? Weird."

"His daughter's death really affected him. I've never known a man to grieve that way. Despite everything I knew he was into, I felt sorry for him. His daughter was his light. After she died, he never really seemed to snap out of it. I was afraid he was setting himself up for takeover, being weak and all, but I soon realized that I was the only one that noticed. I think the rest of them are missing the empathy gene."

"Probably a good thing for Sonny," Helena said.

"Definitely a good thing for Sonny. Well, since I'm deadlocked until I hear from Zach, what do you say we get you the biggest latte they make and get out of here?"

Helena frowned. "Um, I wasn't going to bring this up, but seeing as how you're probably light-years smarter than me, I'm going to go ahead and ask. How did they know it was you in the car? I mean, you're wearing an awesome disguise and your car's the same, but you switched plates with Maryse, and well . . ."

"They had to be watching. It wouldn't have taken a genius to see me having breakfast at the café with Maryse or walking back across the street to the hotel. All someone had to do was watch the back and they would have seen me leave and get the car out of the garage." She tapped one finger on the laptop and stared out the window. "Or maybe it was something else."

"I don't see what. Even if they were in Mudbug looking for you, no one would have recognized you in that getup."

"Even without this getup, I still don't look like I did when I was in the FBI. I've had facial reconstruction done."

"Shit," Helena said. "Maybe we should get that coffee now?"

"I think that's a great idea, and I'm going to call Maryse and ask her to pick you up, okay?" Raissa said, an idea already forming in the back of her mind. And if she was right, it wouldn't take long to prove it.

Ten minutes later, they were perched on the top level of a parking garage half a block down from the Starbucks. Helena was panting after walking up the stairwell. "You didn't tell me I had to hike for my coffee. What are you trying to do, kill me again? And what the hell are we doing here? This isn't where you parked."

"I know, but I wanted a good view of everything, and this is the best view around."

Helena pulled the lid off her coffee and continued panting in the cup. "No need letting good air go to waste. This is a little too hot."

Raissa shook her head and looked back at Starbucks.

"So why are we playing eagle eye up here?" Helena asked.

"Because I want to see who else shows up." Raissa pointed across the street at the parking garage where she'd left her car. "Look on the third level. You can see my car where I parked it on the end."

"Yeah, but there's no way that guy followed us after the exit. You would have seen him."

"I know. Just wait. If nothing else happens in the next ten minutes, we'll leave."

Raissa leaned back against a cement wall and watched Helena savor her coffee. Five minutes later, she pushed herself off the wall and pointed. "Look."

Helena looked down the street from the garage where a black car with dark-tinted windows had pulled to the side of the street. The car was parked with a clear view of the garage exit. Helena turned to Raissa, her eyes wide. "Is that the same car?"

"Same type, but it's not the car that hit us earlier. There's no bullet hole in the trunk of that Cadillac."

"So how did they find you so fast?"

"I think there's a GPS tracker on my car. See how they parked to have a clear view of the garage? They're not sure where I went, so they parked where they can see the garage, for when I return."

"I'll be damned. So that's how they found you."

"That's my bet."

"Then that means they put something on your car before you ever came to Mudbug."

"Yep."

Helena's eyes widened. "Which means that Sonny already knew how to find you, assuming it's him, of course."

"I think so. I've thought so since Hank paid me a visit."

"Then why wait all that time and try to kill you now, when it's harder? You got the FBI looking for you, a new buddy with the New Orleans Police Department shadowing you, and an assortment of crazy women in a hotel rigged with better security than the White House. Seems stupid to make a move now."

"It's very stupid. That's what makes it so interesting. Sonny Hebert may be a lot of things, but stupid isn't one of them. He's very deliberate, almost methodical, about everything. It's why he's made it this long without going to prison or being bumped off by another family member looking to take over."

Helena frowned and looked back down at the black Cadillac. "So what the hell?" Helena asked for the second time in less than an hour.

Raissa looked down at the black car and shook her head. The question was just as pertinent now as before. And just as unanswerable.

Chapter Ten

Zach stood on the top level of a parking garage, staring at Raissa over the top of his unmarked police car. "I don't like it." His captain had given him the go-ahead to pull information about the other missing girls, but hadn't thought there was anything there to warrant questioning them. Raissa, of course, thought different.

She shrugged. "There's a tracking system on my car and someone tried to kill me earlier. I don't like *that*.

"So are you going with me to this girl's house, or do I need to get a new car and do this with my fake police ID?"

Zach groaned, the ten million things that could go wrong with Raissa's plan racing through his mind. "I still think this is a horrible idea."

"No, you don't. You just don't want to get caught doing it." She gave him a critical look. "You know, with a laptop and a printer, I could make you a new police ID."

Zach placed his hands over his ears. "I'm not hearing this."

"C'mon. There's only one girl in New Orleans. She lives with her aunt. It's not like I'm asking you to round them all up for a lineup or the Spanish Inquisition."

"Yeah, that's what you say now." He opened his car door. "Get in before I change my mind."

Twenty minutes later, Zach pulled up in front of a

neat townhome in a quiet area of town. "I will introduce myself. Follow my lead, but don't say anything if it can be helped. Nice wig, by the way."

Raissa patted down her long brown curls. "Thanks. I have a blue silk nightie that goes perfect with this. If you're interested in seeing some of my other costumes."

Zach turned away, trying to block the mental picture of Raissa in blue silk and those sexy brown curls. He walked up to the front door of the townhome and could practically feel Raissa smiling behind him. He took a deep breath and rang the doorbell. He waited a couple of seconds and was just about to ring the bell again when he heard footsteps inside.

A second later, the door opened and a pretty young blonde woman peered out the door, safety latch firmly in place. "Can I help you?"

Zach opened his badge and held it up to the crack in the door. "I'm Detective Blanchard with the New Orleans Police Department. Are you Jennifer Warner?" he asked, giving the girl's new name.

The girl stared at him, a wary expression on her face. "Yes."

"I'm sorry to bother you, but I need to ask you a few questions. Do you mind? You can step outside if you're not comfortable with us being inside, or you can answer them through the door. You can have my badge if you want to call in my number." Zach held his breath that she wouldn't take that last option. He wouldn't even have time to clean out his desk, especially if Jennifer described the female partner that he didn't exactly have.

She looked at the badge again, then up at Zach. Finally, she closed the door and Zach heard the lock sliding back. The door opened a second later and she waved them inside. "I was just making some coffee," she said as she walked down a hallway into a kitchen. Zach and Raissa trailed behind.

Jennifer lifted the pot. "Would you like any?"

"No, thank you," Zach said. "We don't want to take much of your time."

Jennifer poured a cup of coffee and sat on a stool at the end of a bar, nervously fiddling with the handle on her mug. Raissa tugged on Zach's sleeve, and he took a seat along with Raissa across from the girl. As soon as he slid onto the stool, the girl relaxed. He glanced at Raissa. That woman could definitely read people.

"I guess I don't have to ask if you know who I really am," Jennifer said. "Is this about the kidnapping? It's been all over the news."

"Yes, but why do you assume that?" Zach asked.

Jennifer shrugged and stared into her coffee. "I don't know. I guess 'cause the missing girl sorta looked like me."

Zach studied her for a couple of seconds and decided that Jennifer was right. There was definitely a resemblance. "You do favor each other, but that's not the only reason. There are similarities regarding the disappearance that make us think it might be the same person or persons involved."

Jennifer looked up at him, her expression bleak. "What do you want from me? I told the police everything years ago."

"I know. I guess I was hoping that maybe after all this time you might have remembered something. Something you didn't mention before."

Jennifer stared at him for a moment, then shook her head. "I wish I could remember. I can't even walk down the sidewalk without wondering 'Is that the guy who took me—is that the guy?' Or maybe it was a woman.

I'm scared of them, too. I thought changing my name and moving in with my aunt would help, and it did, but only barely. I've been homeschooled since I was returned. I graduated high school last semester with top scores. I already have offers from Ivy League schools, but I'm afraid to go. I've been through seven counselors and no telling how many drugs, and I still won't leave this house without an escort. Trust me, Detective, I would love to remember." Her hands shook as she stirred her coffee.

Raissa reached across the bar and placed her hand on Jennifer's arm. "Your fear is real and valid. Counselors usually try to tell you otherwise, which is where they go wrong, in my opinion, anyway. What they don't tell you is that because of your experience, your senses are finely honed. You are far better suited to recognize danger than the average person."

Jennifer looked at Raissa, her expression wavering between wanting to believe and wanting to run for cover. "I'm a quivering mess. I'm not finely honed."

"Not yet. You've tucked yourself away for so long that when you go out now, you're on sensory overload. If you increase your public time slowly, even by five minutes a day, you'll find the anxiety will start to fade. Then you'll be left with an awareness, almost a sixth sense, about what's going on around you."

"Did someone attack you?" Jennifer asked.

"I was stalked and shot. And I learned to trust that feeling in my gut and when the hair raises on the back of my neck. Fear is a gift. A gift far too many of us have forgotten how to access."

"Wow." Jennifer's expression cleared in understanding. "That makes sense." She gave Raissa a shy smile. "You're the first person who's made me feel anything but neurotic. Thank you."

Raissa smiled. "You're welcome. So how does knowing you have an advantage make you feel? Strong?"

Jennifer thought for a couple of seconds, then nodded. "Yeah. It does. This is so cool. Now, I can go out in public a little at a time, and I'll remember that my being hyperaware is a good thing. I could get better, right?"

"Yep, maybe even in time for college registration next spring."

Jennifer's smile widened, and Zach could see how Raissa had opened a whole new world in the girl's mind with just a few sentences. He liked to consider himself tough and hard, but he couldn't help being moved.

After a couple of seconds, Jennifer's smiled faded and she looked over at Zach. "I don't know if this means anything, but I started having dreams right after I saw the kidnapping on the news."

"What kind of dreams?" Zach asked, feeling his pulse quicken. Buried memories often started surfacing in dreams or in states of semiconsciousness.

Jennifer frowned. "Weird. Like it's me in the dream, but I'm watching it from the outside, you know?"

Zach nodded, but didn't reply, not wanting to interrupt her thought process.

"I'm in this room, but all I can see is bright light. The first time I had it, I thought I was dreaming about dying, you know, with the white light and all. But the next time I heard voices . . . regular voices, not God or anything."

"Do you remember what the voices were saying?" Zach asked, pen and paper ready.

"A man says, 'We're running out of time.' Then another man says, 'I won't have what we need until Wednesday. The blood wouldn't do any good now. It's too thin.' Then the first guy says, 'I hope that's soon enough.' And the other guy says, 'Of course it will be. I can make anything happen.'"

Jennifer stared at the wall behind Zach for a moment, then shook her head. "And then I woke up." She looked directly at Zach. "I tried to remember more. I tried going back to sleep, hoping more would come, but finally I just decided it was my imagination working overtime after that news story." She bit her lip and looked at Raissa. "What do you think?"

"I think something in that news story triggered a memory that's been buried for a long time."

"So you think that really happened?"

"Maybe," Raissa said, "or it might be something similar, but your recall is fuzzy because you were drugged at the time."

Jennifer crossed her arms across her chest. "I wish I knew what they did to me. The doctors said there was no . . . you know." She blushed and looked down at her coffee. "But why would someone take me for no reason? And why would they need blood? And if my mind's confused and it wasn't blood, then what was it?"

"I can't imagine how hard it is for you," Raissa said. "At least I saw my attacker and can easily identify him. I know why he shot me. To have no answers has got to be hell."

"Do you think I'll remember more?"

"I don't know. It's impossible to know what triggers buried memories. You may have opened the door, and your memory will start unfolding. Or it may be another ten years before it happens again. Or . . ."

"Or it may never happen again," Jennifer finished. "And I'll never really know what happened to me."

"There is another way," Zach said, more determined than ever to make the kidnapping son of a bitch pay.

"If we catch the people who did this, I'll get everything out of them. I promise you."

Jennifer gave him a small smile. "You know, Detective, I believe you're telling the truth. I'm going to hold you to that promise."

When they climbed back in the car, Zach handed Raissa a stack of printouts with DMV information. "You were good in there," he said.

"Thanks," Raissa said. "It's hard not to feel for her. Knowing what you're hiding from is hard enough, even for an adult. I can't imagine living in constant fear of an enemy you don't know and whose purpose is a mystery." She flipped through the papers.

"Anything?"

"Yeah. There's a corporation listed on here that owns several of the same make and model—all black. It's one of Sonny's companies."

Zach blew out a breath, the desire to protect the woman beside him overriding all his other emotions. "If he tracked your car to Mudbug, he knows where you're staying. What's he waiting for?"

Raissa shook her head. "I don't know, but Sonny never does anything without a reason. How much trouble did you get in over pulling the information?"

"Let's just say that what the captain doesn't know won't hurt him."

"Oh, really? Mr. Anal-retentive Rule Follower was less than forthcoming with the big boss? Might cost you your job, you know?"

"Damn it, Raissa, there are things you don't know."

Raissa immediately lost her teasing tone.

"So tell me. We're in this together."

"It's a long story," Zach replied.

"Then give me the CliffsNotes version, and don't worry about the ending. I've probably heard a lot worse."

Zach took a breath, not sure how to condense what some considered the biggest screwup in his career. Not sure if he wanted to share something that personal with a woman he barely knew, regardless of how attracted to her he might be.

"Several years ago, I screwed up on a case. I'm still digging my way out."

"What kind of screwup?"

"There was a guy we had our sights on for killing an eight-year-old girl, and all indications were she was hardly the first. The lab screwed up the chain of evidence and he walked."

"Shit. That sucks, but a lab screwup is not your fault."

"No, but I leaked who the guy was to the victim's father."

Raissa frowned. "But the father still had the right to file a civil suit, even if you couldn't make a criminal one. I still don't see the problem."

"I didn't give him the information for a civil suit. I knew what he would do."

"How could you possibly know what someone would do?"

Zach looked over at her. "He was an ex-marine sniper. His wife died a couple of years ago in a car accident and that little girl was the last of any family he had. He had connections in all parts of the world and the training to disappear without a trace."

"So, what happened?"

"They both disappeared—the father and the perp. We never found bodies."

Raissa was silent for a couple of seconds. "And you

took the heat for telling him. He could have gotten the information anyway, and from the way you've described him, he definitely would have been the kind that went looking for it."

"Yeah, but that's not how Internal Affairs saw it, so they put me on notice. From that point forward, I was supposed to do everything by the book. No exceptions."

Raissa sighed. "And then you met me. Why are you risking everything, Zach? You barely know me."

"I know you're a tough, strong, intelligent woman who has sacrificed a third of her life to do the right thing. I know there's a little girl missing who might end up a recluse like the one we just left if I can't get some answers. I know this could happen again if we don't catch the guy now." He paused for a minute and took a breath. "I know I have to sleep at night, and sometimes things aren't black-and-white."

Raissa placed one hand on his thigh. "In our line of work, things are rarely black-and-white."

"So how do you keep from crossing the line?"

Raissa shook her head and stared out the window. "I don't think some of us can."

Maryse looked up from her laptop as the bells above Sabine's shop door jangled, then frowned when she saw the man standing there, stiff as a board, clad in a business suit, and still wearing his sunglasses inside. Definitely not a customer. She grabbed Helena's box of MoonPies and tossed them into the break room, then motioned for Helena to make herself scarce. "Welcome to Read 'Em and Reap," Maryse said as she walked over to the man. "Can I help you find something?"

The stiff pulled a pad of paper from his pocket and glanced at it for a second. "Are you Sabine LaVeche?"

"No. I'm Maryse, but I'll be happy to help you if you'd tell me what you're looking for."

The stiff frowned. "I'm looking for Sabine LaVeche."

"I'm sorry, Sabine isn't available."

"I need to speak with her—now. Tell me where she is."

Maryse bristled. "If you'd give me your name, I'm happy to tell her you stopped by, but there's no way in hell I'm giving out her personal information."

Maryse saw his jaw clench and his face flush a bit. She stared him directly in the eyes until he finally understood that she wasn't intimidated now and wasn't going to be later. Finally, he gave her a disgusted look and pulled his wallet from his pants pocket, then flipped it open to show her his FBI identification.

She barely managed to hide her utter relief that the stiff was merely a fed and not one of the Hebert clan. "Agent Fields?" Maryse gave him her best confused expression. "Why in the world would the FBI want to talk to Sabine?"

"That's confidential. Can you tell me where to find her?"

"She's in the Bahamas on her honeymoon. There's no way to get in touch with her."

Agent Fields blew out a breath of frustration. "When is she returning?"

"In three days."

"And when did she leave?"

"Yesterday."

"I'm looking for a friend of hers, a Raissa Bordeaux. Do you know Ms. Bordeaux?"

"Yes." It was all Maryse could do to hold in a smile. Agent Fields was so frustrated with her clipped answers, his expression looked pained.

"Do you know where I might find her?"

Maryse gave him her wide-eyed innocent look. "At her store in New Orleans?"

Agent Fields threw up his hands. "Obviously, if Ms. Bordeaux was at her store, I wouldn't be looking for her here."

Maryse shrugged. "Then I can't help you. I have no idea where she is." At that very moment, the statement was entirely true.

Agent Fields pulled a card from his pocket and shoved it at her. "If you see her, please give me a call. It's a matter of utmost urgency." Agent Fields spun around and exited the shop.

"What an ass," Helena said.

Maryse nodded. "A matter of utmost urgency? Is that even English?"

"Pompous, stick-up-your-ass English. I'm not clear on the grammar part, though."

Maryse walked to the front window and watched as Agent Fields got into a tan Honda Accord, adjusted his mirrors, checked his blind spot, then pulled onto Main Street and headed out of Mudbug. "That guy is wound way too tight." She was just about to turn from the window when a glint of sunlight flashed in her eyes. She looked farther down the street to see where the reflection had come from and saw a black sedan with dark tinted windows parked at the far end of Main Street.

"Helena," Maryse said and waved at the ghost. "Come look at this car. Is that the car that ran you and Raissa off the road this morning?"

Helena peered out the window. "It looks like it, but then all I know is it was a black Cadillac. Seems like the front would be damaged if it was the one that hit us, though."

"Yeah," Maryse said, "but when Raissa called earlier,

she said Sonny had several of that make and model, right?"

"Four is what you said, I think."

Maryse backed away from the window. "I need you to do something."

Helena gave her a wary look. "You? You hate it when I 'do something.'"

Maryse glanced back outside and walked to the cash register before she could change her mind. "I know, but this is different. We have to find out who the guy in the car is. If I walk down there, he'll leave. Well, best case, he'll leave."

"Worst case, he'll shoot you."

"There is also that." Maryse pulled a disposable camera from beneath the cash register and handed it to Helena. "Which is why I'm not the one who's going to walk down there."

Helena stared at her as if she'd lost her mind. "You want me to take a picture of him? Won't that be a little noticeable?"

"Yeah, for a minute, maybe. Hide the camera in your pocket until you get to the car. I'm still working on this ghost-logic stuff, but that should keep it fairly concealed. If you can't get a clear shot of them through the driver's window, then take a picture through the front windshield."

"Let me get this straight. You want me to stand in front of a killer's car and take a picture."

"All he'll see is the camera. You take the picture, and by the time he jumps out of the car, assuming he even does, it will be too late. You tuck the camera in your pocket and stroll back to the store."

Helena shrugged. "What the hell. Probably be more interesting than watching you type." She slipped the camera into her pocket and walked through the wall of the shop and onto the sidewalk.

Maryse moved behind a display of colored rocks so she had a clear view of the street without the driver seeing her in the storefront window. She peered over the top of the display and watched as Helena strolled down the sidewalk, then crossed the street to the black Cadillac. She bent over and peered into the driver's-side window, but apparently the tint was too dark for her to get a good picture, so she moved to the front of the car. Maryse sucked in a breath and clutched the top of the display.

This is for Raissa, God. If you could just help Helena get it right this one time.

Helena stood in front of the car, studying the windshield. She looked behind her, then moved one step to the right, apparently trying to cut out the glare. She glanced back at the store and gave Maryse a thumbs-up. Maryse tightened her grip on the display. *Please God. Please God. Please God.*

Helena pulled the camera out of her pocket, but it got stuck on the way out and flipped through the air, seemingly in slow motion, then landed directly in the middle of the hood of the car. Helena froze for a moment, then scrambled onto the hood and grabbed the camera. The car rocked with her weight, and Maryse could see frantic, shadowy movement inside. Helena kneeled on the hood and directed the camera at the driver's seat as the car roared to life and lurched in reverse.

"Oh, no!" Maryse gasped as Helena rolled off the hood of the car and into the street. She lay there for a second, completely still, and Maryse was certain she had somehow died again. Then she was up and running.

Clutching the camera in one hand held high above her head.

Maryse felt the blood drain from her face and she had to lean against the display for support. The display gave way, and Maryse and a million colored rocks spilled onto the floor of the store. She managed to pull herself up on her knees and peer outside, but the situation was dire. Helena was running as fast as she could, the camera still in plain sight. The car had stopped backing up and was now coming down the street after the floating camera.

Maryse managed to crawl to the front door of the shop and open the door a crack. Surely, the driver wouldn't hear her yell over the car engine. "Hide the camera," she yelled as loudly as she could, then slammed the door shut, rose from the floor, and peeked between the miniblinds on the door.

Helena stopped dead in her tracks, which wasn't exactly smart. The car came to a screeching halt, but not before it bumped Helena and sent her rolling down the street.

Dazed, Helena jumped up from the ground and tucked the camera in her pocket just as the car door opened. Maryse strained to see the driver, but he had his back to her as he scanned the street for the missing camera. Helena staggered down the street to the shop. The driver took one final look in the street, then jumped in his car and tore out of town.

Maryse waited until the car had turned at the far end of Main Street, then opened the door of the shop to allow Helena in. "Are you all right?"

Helena leaned against the wall and slumped to the floor, wheezing. "I guess so. I mean, what could happen to me, right? I'm glad you opened the door. I don't know if I could concentrate enough to walk through a wall right now." Helena reached into her pants and pulled the camera out. "I don't think it got damaged when I fell, or when the car hit me, or when I fell again."

Maryse took the camera and studied Helena. "You know, I hate to say this, but you're white as a ghost. I know it sounds stupid, but normally you have color."

"Of course I'm white. That scared the shit out of me."

"It doesn't seem fair, you still feeling fear when there's really nothing that can hurt you. Kinda a rip, if you ask me."

"Tell me about it." Helena looked behind Maryse at the mess on the floor. "What happened?"

"Scared the shit out of me, too." Maryse looked at the mess and sighed. "I guess I better call Raissa."

"Think this will scare her?"

"No. And that's what worries me the most."

Chapter Eleven

Raissa snapped her phone shut and stared out the windshield of Zach's car as they drove down the highway back to New Orleans. Zach looked over at her, and Raissa knew he was waiting to hear what was said in the phone call, but she wasn't sure how to relay the information without his going ballistic. And then there was the whole Helena angle. He definitely wasn't ready for Helena. No one was.

"Was that Maryse?" he asked finally.

"Yeah. Fields showed up at Sabine's shop earlier."

"Was there a problem?"

"Not really," Raissa said. "Maryse deflected him by saying Sabine was out of the country. He left his card. My guess is, Fields is done with Mudbug."

"So what's the problem? And don't even try to say there's not one. I saw the expression on your face, and that conversation was far too long to just be chatting about Fields."

Raissa rolled the story Maryse had told her around in her mind. How the hell was she supposed to explain it to Zach when a key component was a photo-snapping ghost? Finally, she blew out a breath and told him about the black car at the end of the street.

"Did Maryse get a look at the driver?" Zach asked.

"No, but she might have a photo."

Zach raised his eyebrows and Raissa shook her head. "It's a long, complicated story going back months, and I'd rather explain the details when I can show you myself. Maryse is on her way to a drugstore in New Orleans right now to get the film developed. One of those one-hour joints, so she can meet us somewhere in the city or back in Mudbug."

"What are you going to do about your car?"

"Nothing, right now. It's obviously not safe to drive." She waved her cell phone. "I'm glad I maintained an untraceable cell phone, or they'd likely be tracking me that way, too."

Zach shook his head. "This is all a bit much. I made detective five years ago, and I've never seen such cloak-and-dagger stuff in my life. I don't know how you've lived this way for so long. Hell, my captain's on the verge of a stroke and he's not even facing an opponent like Sonny Hebert." Zach sighed. "But in his defense, this case could cost him his job if it goes wrong."

Raissa looked over at Zach. "What do you mean? I know there's pressure on the department because it's the mayor's granddaughter, but that's status quo for this sort of situation."

"Not exactly." Zach hesitated for a moment, then decided that given Raissa's deductive skills, she might be able to help. He told her about his talk with the captain that morning and his subsequent visit with the Francos.

Raissa listened to the story, her eyes widening until he got to the part about talking to Peter Franco, and then she frowned and shook her head.

"Why are you shaking your head?" Zach asked.

"That's not right."

"What part?"

"That Melissa wasn't ever sick. Once a month, her mother took her to a specialist who has an office across from my shop. They usually stopped in my shop and bought Melissa candles."

"You're certain?"

"Of course, I'm certain. I've seen them once a month for probably six months or more. That's why I was so upset when I saw the details of the kidnapping on the news. This one was almost personal in a way, because I knew the victim."

"Why would the father lie?"

"I have no idea. Maybe we should ask?"

"If he's lying, he's not likely to tell the truth just because I ask him to."

Raissa shook her head. "Not him. The doctor."

Zach frowned and started to speak and she waved a hand to cut him off. "I know doctor privilege and all that, but this is the mayor's daughter who's been kidnapped. If the doctor knows something, he might tell us."

"No way. You're not going anywhere near your shop. One of Sonny's guys is probably watching it, not to mention the Agent Fields problem."

"I can handle Fields, and the FBI can't make me do anything. I'm not under arrest."

"Sonny's guys can probably make you do plenty, starting with giving up breathing."

Raissa turned in her seat to face him. "Who do you think stands a better chance against them—me or Melissa Franco?"

Zach rolled the options around in his mind for half a second. "Shit." He turned at the next red light and headed toward Raissa's shop. Raissa pulled off the wig and tried to fluff her hair into some semblance of normal.

A couple of cars were parked on the street outside of Raissa's shop, but none was a black Cadillac. She pointed across the street. "That's the office."

Zach pulled over close to the building and parked at

the curb. A man in his sixties with black and silver hair stepped outside the door and turned to lock it. "That's him," Raissa said, pointing at the man locking the door. She checked the street, then jumped out of the car.

"Dr. Spencer," Raissa called as the doctor slipped the keys in his pocket. He turned around and gave her a wave.

"Hello, Raissa. I haven't seen you in a while. Did you finally take a vacation?"

Raissa walked over to the doctor, Zach close behind. "Hardly," she replied. "But a friend did—her honeymoon, in fact—so I'm filling in at her shop."

The doctor smiled. "That's nice." He gave Zach a curious look, then looked back at Raissa. "Well, my wife has dinner on the table, so I better run."

"Actually," Raissa said and pointed to Zach, "this is Detective Blanchard with the New Orleans Police Department. He'd like to speak with you about Melissa Franco."

Dr. Spencer's eyes widened. "The kidnapped girl? Why would you want to speak to me?"

"Because," Zach said, "you treated her, but her father clearly stated to police that his daughter had never been sick. I want to know why he would think that."

Dr. Spencer shook his head. "You're mistaken. Melissa Franco was never a patient of mine."

"I saw her here," Raissa said. "Once a month. She and her mother always stopped in my shop after they left your office."

Dr. Spencer appeared flustered. "I'm sure if you check my records, you'll see I'm telling the truth. I've never treated Melissa Franco. I didn't even know the name until it was on the news."

Zach narrowed his eyes at the man. It was so clear he was lying, but about what part? "Dr. Spencer, there are other eyewitnesses who put Susannah Franco and her daughter in your office," he lied, "so you can either tell me what's going on now, or I can drag you down to the station, and we'll take all night to go over it." Zach pulled the handcuffs from his waist. "Your choice."

Dr. Spencer paled. "You don't understand."

"That's exactly my point," Zach said. "And I need to understand. Rest assured that I don't care what you were doing here as long as it had nothing to do with Melissa Franco's kidnapping, but I do have to know what you were doing. So what was it—were you having an affair with Susannah Franco?"

"Good Lord, no," Dr. Spencer said. "I'm a happily married man, and Susannah is young enough to be my daughter."

"That's never stopped 'em before," Raissa said dryly.

Zach shot her a warning look and turned back to the doctor. "Good. See, this isn't so hard, is it? So you weren't sleeping with Susannah Franco. Were you treating her?"

Dr. Spencer sighed. "No. I was treating Melissa, but I swear I didn't know that was the child's name until I saw her on the news. Her mother gave a fake last name. Paid cash."

"Isn't that unusual?"

"Yes and no. Susannah said their church took up a collection each week for Melissa's visits. It's not that uncommon among some of the churches here."

"And you never noticed that their clothes or jewelry didn't match the charity claims?" Zach asked.

"Well, no. They were always clean and tidy, but never overdressed or even dressed fancy. The mother always had on jeans and a top. The child had on the type of cotton clothes that children wear. I never saw any expensive rings or other jewelry."

Zach looked over at Raissa for confirmation and she nodded. The doctor was right. There was nothing about them that automatically made one think "wealthy." Even Raissa had never caught onto their status during the shop visits.

"I apologize, Detective," Dr. Spencer said, "but the reality is, if Ms. Franco was carrying an eight-hundred-dollar handbag or wearing a two-hundred-dollar polo shirt, I'd be the last to know. My wife does all the shopping for our household."

"So let's just say you didn't know," Zach said. "Melissa's picture has been plastered all over the news. Why didn't you come forward then?"

"What could I possibly know that could help the police?"

"I find all this secrecy disturbing. You've never met Peter Franco?"

"No. Ms. Franco claimed she was a single mother. She didn't wear a wedding ring, so I had no reason until recently to suspect otherwise."

Raissa stared at the doctor. "But, Doctor, this is the part that I don't understand. It's one thing for Susannah Franco to hide her identity, but Peter Franco told the police that his daughter has never been sick. Are you trying to tell us the man doesn't know his own daughter is ill? How can that be? Why wouldn't Melissa tell him about the treatment herself?"

A hint of red crept up Dr. Spencer's neck. "Because we didn't tell her what was really wrong with her."

Zach threw his hands in the air. "Well, why the hell not?"

Dr. Spencer took one step back, clearly unnerved by

Zach's obvious exasperation. "Her case was mild. Even the treatments weren't making her sick. Her mother said as long as the disease remained that way there was no use scaring her."

"So what, exactly," Zach asked, "did you claim you were treating her for?"

"Allergies. It's something that requires some blood drawn, regular care, and daily medication."

"And it doesn't bother you in the least that this woman obviously used you for her own purposes?"

Dr. Spencer gave Zach an apologetic look. "I wasn't trying to create a smoke screen for a crime spree, Detective. I only wanted to save a little girl a lot of worry, if it wasn't necessary. I know it's not the most ethical thing to do, but the mother really had the final word on the matter since Melissa is a minor. I was certainly unaware of all the other subterfuge."

"You said she takes medicine daily," Raissa said. "How much damage will be caused by her going without it?"

Dr. Spencer shook his head. "There's no way to know for sure, but the medication seemed to curb newly developing symptoms and relieve previously developed others. The longer she goes without the medication, the greater the chance she'll suffer a lot for it." Dr. Spencer pulled a card from his wallet and handed it to Zach, clearly worried. "If you need anything else, or when you find her, please call me. She'll need special care."

Raissa shot Zach a grim look. No further explanation was necessary.

Maryse flipped through the photos at the drugstore counter, then shoved them back into the envelope.

"They look great," she told the woman behind the counter, who scanned the envelope to ring her up. Maryse passed the woman some money, picked up the envelope, and headed to the back of the store for the restroom. Helena was already waiting inside.

"Well?" Maryse asked.

"There's a black sedan parked across the street. Dark tint on the windows, but no bullet holes."

"Shit." Maryse said. "I was hoping Raissa was being melodramatic worrying about me, but apparently she wasn't. And the film counter is in clear view of the street. I'll bet black-sedan guy knows exactly why I'm here, even if he can't figure out how I managed to take the pictures."

Helena nodded. "It would be too much of a coincidence for him to ignore."

"Okay, so he probably won't kill me right there in the street, right? I mean, it's the pictures he wants, and the negatives."

"I guess," Helena said, but didn't look completely convinced.

"We'll go with that for now." Maryse pulled the photos out of the envelope and pulled out the spare copies. "I had duplicates made. I guess I was expecting trouble of some sort."

"God knows why, since your life has been a cakewalk for over a month now."

"Oh, you mean since you showed up?"

"You can't blame all this on me. Hell, if I had that much power and control, I'd run the world."

"There's a frightening thought." Maryse handed Helena the duplicate photos. "Hold on to those and do not lose them. Regardless of how scary things might be, remember that the bad guy can't see you. Keep those photos under your clothes, and try not to crease the heck out of them."

Maryse stuck the other set of photos back into the envelope along with the negatives and closed the flap. She looked at Helena and blew out a breath. "Okay, I'm going to leave the store and get mugged or jacked or rolled—whatever the hip, trendy term is for getting your butt kicked by a picture-stealing thug. *You* are going to get in the car and wait for me."

Helena raised her eyebrows. "You sure about this?"

"No, which is why we have to leave now. Otherwise, I'll spend the night in this restroom." Maryse opened the door and stepped outside. "Get ahead of me and let me know if the car's still there. It might have been a fluke."

Helena hurried out the drugstore ahead of Maryse, then rushed back inside. "The car's still there, but it's pulled up right behind your car now. Are you sure you want to do this? We can call Raissa and Zach—have them pick us up."

"That just puts Raissa in his line of fire and Zach on his radar. I don't think he'll shoot me. The street's well lit and lots of people are there. Besides, if this goes as planned, he'll think he got what he wanted and go away, right?"

Helena gave her a skeptical look. "Okay, but just in case things don't go as planned—which always seems to happen, by the way—why don't you give me your cell phone? I can call Raissa if something goes wrong."

Maryse frowned. "Do you think she would be able to hear you through the phone?"

Helena shrugged. "She heard me when I was putting the bug in Sonny's house."

Maryse's expression brightened. "You're right. I'd forgotten about that." She pulled her cell phone from her pocket and handed it to Helena. "Raissa's number is the fourth one on the favorites list."

Helena slipped the phone in her pocket. "Are you ready to do this?"

Maryse took a deep breath and blew it out. "As ready as I'm getting." Helena walked out of the drugstore ahead of her. Maryse said a silent prayer and followed the ghost onto the sidewalk.

The black Cadillac was parked ten feet or so behind Maryse's car just as Helena had reported. It looked like the car that had been in Mudbug that morning, but Maryse had no way of knowing for sure. She tried to appear nonchalant as she walked to her car, clutching the photos in her hand. No use making them harder to steal, or she'd likely show more bruises for her effort than necessary.

She pulled her keys from her pocket and unlocked the car door, then stepped to the driver's side and reached for the door handle. So far, there was no movement from the black car, and Maryse was beginning to think they'd made a mistake. After all, Sonny and his men couldn't be the only drivers of black Cadillacs, or there wouldn't be a reason to manufacture them.

She peered into the car to make sure it was empty, but she only saw Helena inside, clutching the cell phone with one finger poised on top, ready to dial at any moment. Letting out a sigh of relief, she pulled up on the door handle, and that's when she felt a hand on her shoulder and something cold and hard press into her back. Serious miscalculation. The man must have been hiding in the alley next to the cars.

"Give me the photos," the man whispered, "and you can drive off with all your body parts intact."

Maryse felt a rush of fear like a tidal wave, and then

did what she always did at the wrong time—she got sarcastic. "Well, when you put it that way. I'm hungry and could really use my stomach." She lifted the envelope of photos above her shoulder. "I'll probably need my colon later."

The man removed his hand from her shoulder and grabbed the photos. "Smart-ass bitch," he said, and clocked her in the back of the head with his gun. Maryse remembered yelling once before she fell against the side of the car and slumped down on the sidewalk.

Maryse had no idea how long she'd been sitting on the sidewalk next to her car, but when she opened her eyes, she saw three people hovering above her.

An older lady bent over and peered down at her. "Are you all right, dear? Do you need us to call an ambulance?"

Maryse struggled to rise, feeling a bit dizzy. "No, I think I'm okay. Just a little woozy."

"Did that man steal your purse?"

"No. Just the things I bought at the drugstore. I wasn't even carrying a purse."

"A smart idea, with all the tomfoolery that's going on these days. Shall I call the police, then?"

"No, don't bother. They're busy with much worse things than this, and it seems there's never enough of them to go around."

"That is so true. You should still go downtown when you're feeling better and file a report. Likely they won't be able to do anything about your purchases, but they do keep a record of problem areas and try to patrol more often."

"I'll do that," Maryse said. "Thank you for stopping. I think I'll drive home now and soak in a hot bath."

The lady nodded. "Excellent plan. Lord only knows

what kind of grime is on that sidewalk. Are you okay to drive, dear? Can I call someone to come get you?"

"No. I think I'll be fine. I'll just sit here for a minute, then drive. If I have any problems, I'll call my friend to come get me."

"Well, okay. You be careful, now." The lady gave her a nod walked down the sidewalk, the other pedestrians trailing behind her now that the show was over.

Maryse slid into the car and clutched the steering wheel, trying to steady herself. The dizziness was mostly gone, but the fear still raged. "Holy shit!"

"Are you okay?" Helena leaned over, peering anxiously at her. "I didn't know what to do. It all happened so fast."

"I'll be fine as long as I don't have a heart attack." She ran her fingers lightly over the bump that was already forming on the back of her head. "Did you call Raissa?"

Helena nodded. "As soon as I saw him put a gun in your back. She could hear me fine. She and Zach are on the way, but we should get outta here, just in case that guy's still around."

"Good idea." Maryse started the car. "There's a restaurant a couple of blocks over, Wally's Seafood Place. It's well lit and probably crowded. Text Raissa to meet us there."

"I grew up with manual typewriters. What in the world makes you think I know how to send a text message? I was doing good to make the phone call."

"Never mind," Maryse said, and took her phone from Helena's hand. She sent the text, then pulled away from the curb.

"I wonder how Raissa's explaining my call to Zach," Helena mused.

"Probably the same way she explained my taking pictures of the man to begin with."

Helena's eyes widened. "I hadn't even thought about that. So what are you going to say if he asks?"

"Damned good question."

Chapter Twelve

Zach looked across the restaurant table at Maryse and wondered what she was hiding. Ever since Raissa told him there "might" be photos, he'd wondered how on earth someone had managed to take a picture of the guy without him noticing. Obviously, the answer was she hadn't gotten away with it, or she wouldn't have been attacked. But how she'd gotten all the way to New Orleans to have them developed was another mystery. It seemed to Zach that the guy could have run her over in the street right there in Mudbug and saved himself the trouble.

Which meant something wasn't exactly right about her story. The only thing Zach could come up with that made sense is that it wasn't Maryse who had taken the pictures. But whom was she protecting? Obviously someone close to her, or no one would have followed her to New Orleans to begin with. And someone with a death wish, assuming they'd walked up to the car of a potential killer and snapped a photo. Whoever it was, it appeared to him that Raissa was also in on the secret. She'd maintained a fairly straight face, but Zach got the feeling Raissa was reading information between the lines in Maryse's story.

"And then I came to on the sidewalk," Maryse finished up her story, "with some lady looking down at me. I couldn't have been out for long, but the guy was long gone."

"With the pictures," Zach finished.

Maryse nodded. "And the negatives, but I had a contingency plan." She pulled a set of photos out of the front of her shirt. "I had duplicate copies made and hid one on my body."

Zach narrowed his eyes at her. "Why would you even think to do that?"

Maryse took a sip of her beer. "I peeked outside and saw a black car at the corner. I was afraid they'd followed me."

"So you hid a set of photos in your bra and went strolling outside, knowing full well you were probably going to be mugged."

Maryse frowned. "When you put it that way, it doesn't sound so smart, does it?"

"Ignore him," Raissa said and took the photos from Maryse. "It was very smart and very brave. Besides, you called me and put the phone in your pocket on the way out of the store so I could hear what was going on, so you were sorta covered."

"Yeah . . . I guess that was pretty smart." Maryse took another drink of her beer.

"By the way, if you do something like that again, I'll kill you myself."

Maryse rubbed the back of her head. "Don't worry. From now on, I'm leaving all the Jane Bond stuff up to you."

Zach smiled. It was hard not to like a spunky woman, even if she had electrocuted him. And was lying.

"You did a great job," Raissa said as she flipped through the photos.

"Do you recognize him?" Zach asked, leaning over to view the photographs with Raissa.

"I think so, but I'm not certain. He looks sorta like the son of one of Sonny's guys. But the last time I saw him, he was a teenager, so I can't be sure."

Zach pulled out one of the photos that offered a clean view of the man's face. "I'll take this one and run it through the database."

"Don't you need a reason to do that?"

"I'll make something up." He tucked the photo in his shirt pocket. "I'm more concerned about getting you two back to Mudbug. There's a lot of long stretches of road between here and there." He nodded at Raissa. "If your car has a tracking bug on it, Maryse's may, too. Anything can happen on your way there."

"Don't worry," Maryse said. "I've got that part covered."

Zach looked at Maryse, trying to hide his amusement. "Do you, Ms. Bond? And just what do you have in mind?"

"I talked to Carolyn, the lady who owns the seafood restaurant in Mudbug, before you got here. She's expecting a delivery of seafood this evening. Fred, the seafood-truck driver, always makes Mudbug his last stop because he lives there. He's agreed to park behind this restaurant and give us a lift."

"You trust these people?" Zach asked.

"With my life," Maryse said, "or I would never have asked." She looked a bit guilty, then looked at Raissa. "There is one little catch, though."

"Uh-oh," Raissa said. "I don't like that look."

"The cab of the truck was modified for Fred's paperwork. There's only room for the driver, so we'll have to ride in the back."

Raissa's eyes widened. "With the fish?"

Zach chuckled, unable to hold it in. "Well, it's the safest form of sleeping with the fishes that you two could have. You probably shouldn't complain."

Raissa looked over at him and raised one eyebrow. "I'm so glad our predicament amuses you. Keep in mind, if you were planning any more midnight visits to the hotel, that the back of that truck is refrigerated. It could take days for *me* to thaw out."

Zach ceased chuckling, but Maryse took over for him.

"If you could see the look on your face," Maryse teased. "Don't worry. I'll put her in a hot shower as soon as we get to the hotel. Trust me, Mildred will insist on it, or the whole place will smell like the shrimp house."

A vision of Raissa in the shower flashed through Zach's mind, and suddenly the restaurant felt overwhelmingly hot. He was really going to have to do something about his feelings for Raissa, but the one thing that came to mind was probably the worst thing, given their situation. Then, on the other hand, he was already lying to his boss and harboring a fugitive. Having sex with her wasn't exactly a stretch.

Zach looked over at Maryse. "So, if I happen to show up for a midnight visit, you're not planning on electrocuting me again, are you?"

Maryse gave him a sly wink. "Not unless you want me to."

Zach laughed. "I have to ask, what does your husband do for a living?"

"He's an investigator with the DEQ."

"The Department of Environmental Quality, no shit? That's great. And an investigator. He must love your side activities. They're somewhat unusual for a scientist."

Maryse reached over and patted Zach on the arm. "When all this is over, I'll tell you the story of how Luc and I met. Or you could run me through the police system when you run that photo. A little light reading while you're waiting." She grinned at Raissa, who smiled.

Lord help him, now his curiosity was in overdrive. On the other hand, if Maryse had a police record, it might give him an idea of what she and Raissa were hiding. If not, he planned on getting it out of Raissa later that night. Through whatever means he deemed necessary.

It was close to midnight before Zach managed to get away from the police station. The captain had been understandably unhappy over his take on Susannah Franco, and Zach hadn't even told him about the conversation with Dr. Spencer. He couldn't figure out a way to get around to it without revealing his contact with Raissa.

The captain had considered everything Zach had given him, and they'd tossed around a couple of outlandish thoughts, but neither of them had been willing to commit to anything more than checking into the mayor's past and keeping a closer watch on the movements of all the immediate family members. Zach was tasked with doing the digging. The captain would tap some other discreet detectives for the closer-watch detail.

Zach turned onto the highway and headed toward Mudbug. He'd been relieved when he wasn't placed on watch detail. There was no way he could have continued his investigating with Raissa if he'd been parked in a fake cable installer's van outside the mayor's house. He also needed to be extraordinarily careful about being seen with Raissa from this point forward. Questioning Jennifer yesterday had been a big risk, and he wasn't certain what they'd gotten from the girl had been worth it, except for the help Raissa had managed to provide her.

The stark fear in Jennifer's expression when she had recalled her dream still bothered him. That someone's life could be so derailed by another was beyond unfair and made him even more determined to catch the kidnapper and see to it that he could never hurt another girl again. Always looking over your shoulder, not knowing when an enemy might strike, was enough to render even the strongest person immobile.

He shook his head, amazed that Raissa had not only managed to live that way for nine years but had done so right under the nose of the very men she was hiding from. Unfortunately, all indicators pointed to the end of her charade. There were far too many black Cadillacs around Raissa and her friends. He smiled for a moment, thinking about Maryse.

He'd called her bluff and pulled her file. He had to admit that it wasn't at all what he'd been expecting, and it made him rethink his position on her lying about how she took the photo. For all he knew, she may have strolled down the street and asked the guy to pose. Maryse's escape from death was a story that belonged in a Hollywood movie, if they could even get an audience to buy it, which he doubted. If there was one thing Zach had learned long ago, it was that truth is definitely stranger than fiction. Still, he couldn't help admiring the way Maryse had handled a seemingly impossible situation, and he said a silent prayer for the man brave enough to marry her. Her husband, Luc, must have nine lives.

It was almost one A.M. when he parked his car behind the hotel. Maryse had been kind enough to provide him with a key to the back door so he could slip in unnoticed. He unlocked the back door and slipped inside. Raissa's room was on the third floor, so he hurried up the stairs and down the hall, hoping she was still awake.

Light shone underneath her room door. A good sign. He lifted his hand to knock and stepped back in surprise when the door swung open before he had even touched it. It took him only a split second to remember the security cameras. Raissa had probably been tracking his movements since he'd first driven down Main Street.

She was wearing a black silk negligee with a plunging neckline and a sexy smile. "About time you got here." She reached out with one hand and pulled him inside.

As he followed her into the room, he checked out her backside and realized the nightie ended just below the curve of her rear. He felt his pulse quicken. *Get a grip. You can't jump the woman as soon as you walk in the room, regardless of how she's dressed.* He laid his keys on one of the tables and turned to face her.

She was standing close to him, and when he turned, she ran her hands up his backside and bit him playfully on his neck. "Fun business now. Boring business later."

Zach felt a rush of heat throughout his body and he grew hard immediately. "You get no argument from me." He lowered his lips to hers in a crushing kiss, their mouths mixed in a frenzy of pure animal attraction. He ran a hand across her breast, feeling the engorged nipple through the thin fabric, and she groaned.

"I know this is going to sound really bad," Raissa said, "but I'm not really interested in foreplay."

Zach hardened even more and was certain he'd split the zipper on his jeans. "My God, you're perfect."

He pushed the nightie's thin straps over her

shoulders and the silk slid to the floor. There was nothing else in the way. He ran his hands down her body and stopped at a scar in the center of her chest, just below her breasts. It was perfectly round, a shape he'd seen before. He looked up to ask, but she shook her head, unzipped his jeans, and pushed them down.

He almost lost control when she wrapped her hand around the hard length of him. Never had he wanted something so badly, knowing with every ounce of his being that it was a stupid thing to do. But damned if he was going to worry about that now. He slid his hand down and felt wet heat. He touched her with light, feathery strokes. She gasped and stroked him faster until he was on the edge.

"No foreplay," he reminded her. He pulled his jeans off his feet and retrieved a condom from his pocket. A couple of seconds later, he was ready for action. He pushed a pile of paper off the table with one arm and lifted Raissa onto it.

She pulled him to her and he entered her fast and hard. She ran her hands down his back, and he could feel her nails pressing into his skin. He lowered his lips to hers, kissing her deep and long while he thrust. She wrapped her legs around him and he felt himself being absorbed completely by this woman. Mind, body, and soul.

He felt the rise coming and he could tell she was on the verge, just like him. He thrust once, twice more, then one final thrust that sent them both over the edge.

He thought his mind would explode. Heat rushed over his body, but the last thing he wanted to do was cool off. He didn't want to let her go, but he wasn't sure how much longer he could stand without collapsing from sheer pleasure. The bed was at least ten steps away, so he yanked a spare blanket off the dresser with one hand, lifted Raissa off the table, and laid her down on the floor beside him, directly under the cool air of the ceiling fan. She leaned over to kiss him lightly on the lips, wearing a satisfied smile, then nestled her head in the crook of his arm.

Zach had been right earlier. Raissa was perfect.

When he'd gotten his breath back a bit, he rolled on his side and traced a finger down her chest and to the scar. "Nine-millimeter?"

"Yeah."

"Was it Sonny who shot you?"

"No. Spider."

"Spider? I thought you said he was a pansy."

"He is a pansy, which is why he shot me instead of bringing me in so Sonny could do it himself. Lucky for me he ran after the first shot."

"And you lured him into a booth in a seedy bar and shoved a gun in his crotch." Zach laughed. "You're my kind of woman."

"And you didn't arrest me for doing it." Raissa lifted one hand and placed it on the side of his face. "You're my kind of man."

Pounding on the room's door brought Raissa out of her satisfied haze. "Raissa," Maryse said in a loud whisper. "There's somebody out back. I'm opening the door." Raissa heard the key turning in the lock and looked at Zach, who was frozen, staring at the door as if he were headed for the chopping block. It was far too late to do anything about clothes, or blankets, since the only one within reach was the one they were laying on. So Raissa did what any other woman would do in that situation. She smiled.

Maryse opened the door and slipped inside. She looked toward the bed, but when she found it empty she looked the other direction and gasped. "Holy shit." She put her hands over her eyes. "I am sooooooo sorry. I had no idea you two were. . . . um. . . . working? On the floor? In the nude?"

She spread the fingers on one hand and took a peek. "Okay, well, maybe I'm not completely sorry."

Raissa laughed as she sat up and tossed Zach's clothes to him. "The bathroom's behind you. Put on some clothes before she gets any ideas."

Maryse lowered her hands as Zach slipped into the bathroom, and leaned slightly to the side so she could watch his backside. "You mean any more ideas." She grinned at Raissa. "Wow. Nice butt, but don't you dare tell Luc I said so."

All of a sudden, the grin dropped from Maryse's expression. "Holy crap—I completely forgot. The monitors. There's a guy out back." She grabbed a pair of jeans and a shirt from the dresser and tossed them at Raissa. "Would you mind?"

Raissa slipped into the jeans and shirt as she studied the monitors. "Where did you see him?"

Maryse pointed to a monitor showing the alley behind the hotel. "He was behind the hotel at the back door. He tried the door handle, and I figured he was going to try to break in, so I hauled butt down here."

Raissa studied the screen and frowned. "Then where is he now? The alarm never went off, so he's not in the hotel."

"Maybe we should have Helena look. She's in the room next to mine. I could send her outside."

Raissa nodded. "Do that, but get right back in here afterward. I don't want us separated if we don't have to be. Where's Mildred?"

"She had three glasses of wine at dinner tonight, so she's sleeping like the dead."

"Good, then tell Helena to keep this quiet so we don't panic her."

"Gotcha."

"Who's Helena?" Zach asked, and they both jumped. Maryse stared at him, her eyes wide, then rushed out of the room, shooting a fearful glance at Raissa on her way out.

"Who's Helena?" Zach repeated. "Another friend?"

"You could say that." Raissa frantically searched her mind for a rational way to explain Helena Henry. Finally, she decided to avoid the topic for the moment. "She has special abilities."

Zach raised one eyebrow. "Can she make herself invisible? Because I can't think of a good reason to send someone outside the hotel to look for this guy unless you want them dead." He stared at Raissa for a moment. "You don't want her dead, do you?"

"Of course not!" *Because she already is.* "I would never intentionally put another human being in danger." *Not a live one anyway.*

Thankfully, Maryse slipped into the room again and saved her from any more Helena questions. "Well?" Raissa asked.

Maryse shot a nervous look at Zach, then looked back at Raissa. "She was asleep, but she's headed downstairs now. If she sees anything, she'll come back up."

Raissa nodded and looked at the screen displaying the back of the hotel just in time to see Helena walk through the hotel wall and into the alley. She tapped the screen and Maryse stepped closer to look. Zach looked at the screen, then at Raissa and Maryse, wondering what the hell they found so interesting.

Raissa knew she was holding her breath as she watched Helena stroll across the alley to the garage. Neither Raissa's nor Maryse's car was in Mudbug, much less in the garage, but the intruder had no way of knowing they'd arrived by way of a fish truck. Helena walked through the wall of the garage, and Raissa looked over at Maryse.

Maryse's eyes were wide as saucers, and she inclined her head toward Zach. Raissa barely shook her head to let Maryse know that Zach was not in on the Helena connection. With any luck whatsoever, he'd never have to be. Raissa looked back at the monitor.

But her luck had run out.

A man burst out from the front door of the garage and right behind him came Helena. Raissa might still have been able to swing an explanation if it weren't for the trash-can lid and crowbar Helena was wielding like one of King Arthur's knights. The only blessing was that Zach couldn't see what she was wearing. Unfortunately for Maryse and Raissa, they could, and full body tights with a family crest on the front was not Helena's best look.

"What the hell!" Zach stepped in between Maryse and Raissa and leaned forward until his face was only inches from the monitor. "What is that?" He looked from Raissa to Maryse, neither of whom were speaking. "You both know something, and I want you to tell me what it is right now."

Raissa considered what it must look like from Zach's point of view and understood his disbelief. After all, floating garage articles chasing an intruder down an alleyway wasn't something you saw all that often.

Maryse gave the monitor one last panicked look. "I better head downstairs. I mean, there's no chance he's coming back to the hotel, right?"

"I seriously doubt it," Raissa said. "Go intercept."

Maryse nodded and hurried out of the room. Raissa watched the monitor until she saw Maryse open the back door and poke her head out. Helena appeared a couple of seconds later and slipped into the hotel with Maryse, dropping the crowbar and trashcan lid next to the back door. Raissa let out a sigh of relief that the excitement for the night hadn't involved injury or death.

"I want an answer," Zach demanded, "and I'm not leaving here until I get one."

"An answer to what?" Raissa tried on her best innocent look. "He was obviously looking for my car or maybe Maryse's and something spooked him, so he ran."

Zach's face flushed with anger. "You know damned good and well what spooked him. The man was being chased by a crowbar—a crowbar without a human being attached. Damn right he was spooked. I'm spooked, and I'm three stories up in a hotel room. It's like a B horror movie. What the hell is going on, Raissa? I know you and Maryse are keeping something from me. That whole picture-taking story never added up."

Raissa sighed and sank into one of the folding chairs in front of the monitors. "How open-minded are you?"

"In what way? Religion? Politics? Equal rights for cats?"

"To . . . um. . . . paranormal things."

"You're telling me your friend, this Helena, *can* make herself invisible? I'm not buying it."

"No, she doesn't make herself that way. Man, this is hard. The paranormal realm has so many avenues that we really don't know that much about. I'm learning every day, and it's been my business for over eight years."

Zach stared at her, clearly uncertain of what to say. "You told me you hacked information to convince your psychic reading clients you were the real thing."

Raissa nodded. "And that's true, but . . . uh . . . that part where I told you I talked to dead people . . . Well, it's actually only one dead person, and I didn't ask to talk to her, but she's there anyway."

There was complete silence in the room. Raissa was sure neither of them was breathing. Zach stared at her with a mixture of horror, confusion, and a touch of fear. His expression clearly said he'd not only bought into the ravings of a madwoman, he'd slept with her, too. He was probably mentally processing his severance pay as he stared.

"I know," Raissa said, "it's a lot to buy—"

"It's impossible to buy. I don't know what kind of game you're playing, but you're not going to play it with me." He shoved his wallet and keys into his pants pocket and turned to leave the room, but before he could walk out, Maryse stepped in.

"I thought there might be a problem with, well, you know," Maryse said, "so I came back to help."

"Oh, there's a problem all right," Zach said. "You two are crazy. And from now on, you're on your own."

Maryse shook her head. "We're probably crazy, but not in the way you think." Maryse looked to Zach's side and nodded. "Show him, Helena."

Zach looked to his right as Raissa's lipstick rose from the dresser.

Chapter Thirteen

Zach stared in amazement as the cap came off the lipstick and the dial on the bottom spun round, pushing a glossy burgundy color out the end of the container. The lipstick connected with the mirror and swirled out sprawling lettering.

Sorry I missed the show earlier when Maryse walked in on you two.

Zach was certain he hadn't blinked since the lipstick left the dresser, and he was pretty sure he wasn't breathing, either. "Who are you?" he asked.

Helena Henry.

Zach's mind raced. That name was familiar. He whirled to face Maryse. "Your mother-in-law?"

"Ex-mother-in-law, but yes."

Zach slumped into a chair, completely overwhelmed and exhausted from the day. Of all the things in the world he had seen, this was by far the most outlandish. Never in his life would he have believed it was possible. Hell, he still didn't believe it was possible, and he was looking straight at it. "I don't understand."

Maryse snorted. "You think *you* don't understand. I've been able to see Helena since the day of her funeral. The woman I hated the most in the world, and I was the only one who could see or hear her for a long time." Maryse sighed and looked over at the mirror. "Don't get your panties in a bunch, Helena. You know I don't hate you anymore. I'm just giving him the four-one-one."

I don't wear panties. The words appeared on the mirror.

Zach grimaced. He had, after all, seen a picture of Maryse's mother-in-law in her police file. "That was far more information than I ever needed to know."

"All right," Maryse said. "Show's over, Helena. It's time for you and me to go back to bed." Maryse mouthed *Sorry* to Zach and opened the door, then glared at the air, apparently willing the ghost to leave. "No, I don't think he's getting naked again," he heard her say as the door shut behind her.

Zach stared behind them, still unable to form words.

"Sorry to hit you with it like that," Raissa said, "but there's really no simple way to explain."

"Yeah. I guess not." He studied Raissa, who sat calm and collected on the edge of the dresser. "None of that bothers you?"

"No. I mean, not in the ways you might think it should. I learned a long time ago to never close my mind to possibilities. Every time I did it made a fool of me."

"But you and Maryse can actually see her?"

"And Mildred and our friend Sabine, although I wasn't able to until recently."

"So you did what, exactly, to make that happen? Dance naked with lit candles . . . ?"

"Well, Maryse has this theory that you develop the ability to see Helena when you've been targeted for murder. We've all come pretty close to biting it at some point fairly recently."

"Are you serious?"

"It hasn't failed as a theory for over a month now."

Zach ran one hand through his hair, trying to make sense of everything. Trying to make *normal* out of anything. "So when did you first see her?"

"The night I left the police station, after I told you about the other girls. Someone pushed me in front of a bus on the corner. Helena pulled me out of the street just in time."

"Jesus!" Zach rose and started pacing the small room. "That means someone was following you before you ever came to the station. Your cover was already blown."

Raissa nodded. "Yeah, I tried to dismiss it at the time, but Helena was sitting in my car across the street. I knew it wasn't a coincidence."

Zach stopped pacing and stared at her. "Do you realize what you're asking me to believe? In ghosts . . . curses . . . whatever you think is going on here? Damn it, Raissa, you'd already stretched my mind to the limits with your past as an agent and your undercover work, not to mention your theories on the abductions, but this . . . this is something I can't buy into."

"I'm not asking you to buy into anything," Raissa said gently. "You know what you saw. You're a sane, rational, intelligent man. There's no other explanation than the one I gave you."

Zach sat back down again with a sigh, unable to get control over his warring emotions. "I don't know whether to be amazed, or scared, or worried."

"I think all three is a safe bet." She sat down next to him and placed one hand on his leg. "I know how you feel—well, maybe not exactly, but sorta. It's going to be fine, Zach. Think of Helena as another form of weapon. She's a pain in the rear a lot of the time, but she has her usefulness."

"So the pictures Maryse had developed—provided by Helena, the ghost photographer?"

"I told you she had her usefulness. If she'd tucked the camera in her pocket and then managed not to get run over, the entire thing might have gone off without a hitch. You can't always depend on Helena for the best judgment or to keep her cool."

Zach shook his head, still trying to wrap his mind around everything. "Yeah, I guess I can see that, especially after that garage escapade. That guy probably won't sleep for a week. Which reminds me, did you recognize him?"

"No. It was too dark, and the feed wasn't clear enough for me to make out a face. I'll do some work on the footage and see if I can clean it up, but the most we're probably going to get off it is height, weight, and an estimate of age based on movement."

"I figured as much." Zach looked over at Raissa. "So is there anything else you're keeping from me—a husband, five kids, a cat? Because I don't think I can take any more surprises."

Raissa opened her mouth to answer, when one of the laptops at the end of the table started beeping. A loud, persistent, annoying beep. Raissa rushed over to the laptop and looked at the screen.

"What now?" Zach asked. "Don't tell me you've set a timer to brush your teeth or paint your toenails at two A.M."

Raissa motioned him over, so he rose from the chair and walked over to stand beside her. "There is *one* more little thing. This audio is from earlier tonight."

"Oh, no." Zach looked down at the laptop as Raissa clicked on a speaker icon. A man's voice, yelling and cursing at the top of his lungs, bellowed out of the laptop.

"I had Helena put a bug in Sonny Hebert's office."

Zach stared at the laptop, listening to the mob boss rant about his desire to kill his "demon" cat and bury it in the backyard. For the second time that night, Zach was totally speechless.

Raissa slid into the booth across from Dr. Breaux and signaled to the waitress for a cup of coffee. "Morning," she said, and nodded gratefully to the waitress when she slid a mug in front of her.

Dr. Breaux looked at her over the top of his newspaper, an amused expression on his face. "It's not even eight o'clock. It can't already be a bad morning."

Raissa poured a ton of sugar in her coffee, stirred, and took a long swallow. "Because it's not even eight o'clock is exactly the problem."

Dr. Breaux laughed. "So you're not a morning person."

"Not much. I'm more of a night owl, which tends to catch up with you when you agree to coffee with the chickens."

"If I'd known you weren't a morning person, I would have suggested seven just for a change of pace. It's good for the heart, you know?" He put down his paper and gave her his full attention. "So what was so interesting that it kept you up last night?"

Raissa felt the flush at the base of her neck and hoped like hell Dr. Breaux would think it was only the coffee heating her up. There wasn't anything interesting, really, unless you counted hot sex, an intruder, introducing a ghost, listening to an hour of Sonny Hebert cussing, more hot sex, and maybe thirty minutes of sleep. "Nothing much."

Dr. Breaux raised one eyebrow. "The young man would probably be crushed to hear that."

Raissa groaned. "It can't possibly be that obvious. It's because you're a doctor, right? I'm emitting some pheromone. Or I have a tic. Please tell me everyone else cannot just look at me and tell I spent last night with a man."

"Well, I don't know about all that pheromone stuff, but in all the years I've known you, I've never seen you flustered over anything. I realize that coffee you're drinking is hot, but it's probably eighty degrees in this café, and that coffee is not hot enough to make you blush."

"Maybe you could give me something to throw people off track. Poison ivy would be a good start. Then people wouldn't know."

Dr. Breaux laughed so hard he shook the booth. "Lord, Raissa," he said, wiping his eyes with his napkin. "I don't think you have to go to such extremes. Why, if I were you, I'd be happy to have spent a night worth blushing over. It's been a lot of years since my wife passed, but I'm not so old I can't remember one or two of them enough to wish she were still here, and that we were both a lot younger."

Raissa took another drink of coffee. "You're right. It's normal. It's natural. Everything in nature does it." She looked over at him. "Then why doesn't it feel natural to me?"

Dr. Breaux cleared his throat. "If you're having . . . female issues . . . I'd be happy to see you in a professional capacity."

"If only it were that simple. It's not the plumbing. That part is natural and exciting and everything it should be. It's the emotional side of things that's a problem."

Dr. Breaux shook his head. "Matters of the heart I cannot help with. Unless of course, you're having a heart attack."

Raissa laughed. "Not yet. But I'm not ruling it out."

Raissa looked up as the bells over the door jangled and Maryse rushed in.

"Sorry I'm late," Maryse said as she slid into the booth beside Raissa.

"No, you're not," Raissa joked.

Maryse blushed a bit. "I picked Luc up at the airport this morning. We had some catching up to do, so you're right, I'm not sorry I'm late."

Dr. Breaux gave them a wistful look. "Ah, to be young and in love again. I envy you girls."

"It's never too late," Maryse said. "There's a couple of eligible women in Mudbug I can think of."

"No, my time has passed. I'm married to my work right now, and in a year or so, I'll likely retire and spend the rest of my life sitting in a fishing boat off the Florida coast."

Maryse nodded. "Probably a lot more relaxing than a relationship. And definitely cheaper. Do you have any idea how much furniture costs? Luc and I looked at couches for the new house last week, and I swear I think I'm going to sit on the floor. Ridiculous."

Raissa laughed. "Says the woman who will pay thousands for a magnifying glass."

"That's a Meiji Epi-fluorescent microscope and is serious laboratory equipment. But I guess I see your point."

"Well, ladies," Dr. Breaux said, "I'm not senile enough to think two beautiful young women got out of bed early to have breakfast with an old codger like me just for fun. I have to assume something's on your mind, and I have to admit, I've been itching to find out what. I've simply drawn a blank trying to figure it out."

Raissa gave Maryse a nod. They'd already agreed that what they had to say would probably work better coming from Maryse, as she'd known Dr. Breaux her entire life. Raissa had suggested Maryse question him alone, but given her investigative background, Maryse wanted Raissa there to see if she caught things Maryse might miss. Raissa hoped he'd be forthcoming with his responses and there wouldn't be anything to miss.

Maryse laid a file on the table and pushed it over to Dr. Breaux. "You know after everything that went down last month with me, the police got permission to autopsy Helena Henry."

"Yes," Dr. Breaux said and picked up the file. "Is this it? They gave you a copy?"

"I have my ways," Maryse said, "and I'd really rather not explain them. The autopsy didn't prove anything as far as Helena's being murdered, but it clearly shows she had cancer. No one who knew Helena, including Hank or Harold, was aware of that. I was hoping you could explain."

Dr. Breaux frowned and opened the folder. He flipped the pages over one at a time, his brow scrunched in concentration. Finally, he placed the file on the table and shook his head. "I had no idea. The tests clearly show lung cancer and a rare form of leukemia, but Helena's complaints were the usual sort for someone with asthma. I never even thought. My God. So many people in this town lost to that disease. I guess it shouldn't surprise me so much, with her house sitting right on that polluted bayou."

"All we can figure," Maryse said, "is that she wasn't in a lot of pain and was dismissing it as age or whatever. You said she complained about something before she died?"

"Not just before she died—chronically. Her asthma always bothered her, and she aggravated the situation with her weight and constant exposure to plants and flowers with her gardening."

"So did she come to see you any time right before her death?"

Dr. Breaux frowned. "No, but she might have seen the nurse. I could check my records if you think it's important."

Maryse sighed. "It probably isn't." Maryse looked over at Raissa. Raissa gave her a nod to move on to the next topic. So far, Dr. Breaux had been forthcoming, not that it had gained them any ground. They might as well hit him with the doozy.

"There's more," Maryse said. "In looking over some of that information I got, I noticed something odd. When I looked into it, I got more confused."

"What's wrong, Maryse?" Dr. Breaux asked. "You sound so troubled by this."

"'There's no way Hank could have been Helena and Harold's son. The blood types rule it out."

Dr. Breaux stared at her, his mouth partially open. "I . . . well . . . that really doesn't have any bearing on anything, does it?"

"It might for Hank." Maryse narrowed her eyes at Dr. Breaux. "You already knew, didn't you?"

"I was the family doctor, so of course, I'd requested blood work on all of them at times, especially Hank, since he was prone to be anemic. The irregularities were hardly something a good doctor should miss."

"Stop hedging. His mother is dead, and his father is in prison. Hank might need to know his real medical history."

Dr. Breaux sighed. "I noticed the discrepancy, but I never asked about it. I always assumed that Helena had another man while Harold was in the service. I'm afraid many of the men I served with arrived home to children that weren't their own." He paused for a minute. "I have to say, I never saw signs of it, though. If the other man was still around when Harold came home, no one in Mudbug was aware. I figured as long as it was in the past, no good would come of letting anyone think any different than that Hank was Helena and Harold's son."

"So the babies couldn't have been switched at the hospital or anything like that?"

"Heavens, one wouldn't like to think so, although we hear about it in the news. I guess anything's possible, but that is far less of a possibility than a lonely woman seeking comfort."

Maryse looked over at Raissa, looking for advice on how to proceed. Raissa gave her a small shake of her head. There was nothing else to be done here. Helena had already been clear about her lack of outside relationships, and Raissa believed her. The ghost simply had no reason to lie and was obviously distraught over the entire mess.

"Dr. Breaux," Raissa began, shifting topics. "I wondered if you might know someone."

There were a couple of seconds' pause before he responded, but finally Dr. Breaux looked over at Raissa. "Who would that be?"

"A Dr. Spencer."

"I know two Dr. Spencers, as a matter of fact. Husband and wife pediatricians. Have a large practice in Miami."

"No, this Dr. Spencer is in New Orleans. He's a cancer specialist and works only with children."

Dr. Breaux frowned for a moment, then brightened. "Yes. Dr. Spencer was a guest speaker at a medical seminar I attended earlier this year. He did a very interesting panel on the increased rate of leukemia in children near manufacturing plants."

"But you don't know him personally?"

"No, can't say that I do. Why? Has he done something wrong?"

"Not that I know of. He was treating that little girl that was abducted on Monday."

"Really." They never said anything on the news about her being ill. Why, that's horrible. I hope she's found before her treatment is compromised." He shook his head, his expression sad. "I wonder what her prognosis is." He gave Raissa a curious look. "Did they say that on the news? I watched this morning, but I don't remember them covering anything like that."

"No. Dr. Spencer's office is across the street from my shop. The girl always came into my store with her mother after the appointments. She looked very healthy, if that makes you feel any better."

"Yes, that's good news. I guess we'll just have to pray that she's found before things worsen." Dr. Breaux looked over at Maryse and shook his head. "What interesting lives the two of you lead. You seem always to be right in the middle of the action." He gave them both a stern look. "Be certain you don't put yourself in a bad position with all this. There are lots of people who don't relish their secrets being exposed. You should both be well aware of that after the last couple of months."

"We'll be careful," Maryse said, and Raissa nodded.

Dr. Breaux stared into his coffee, his expression both confused and troubled. Maybe Maryse was right. Maybe he'd check into things. Things that happened twenty-nine years ago with the birth of Hank Henry.

Raissa still intended to do some checking on her own.

Chapter Fourteen

Zach sat across from Captain Saucier, trying to figure out the best way to lie to him and still not cause a heart attack. The man was clearly suffering from the strain. He kept running his fingers across the top of his bald head, probably wishing he still had some hair to pull out.

"Nothing," the captain complained, and banged one hand on his desk. "Four days and not a damned thing. Please tell me you've got something, Blanchard. Our futures here may depend on it."

"I might have something, but it's thin, and you're not going to like where I got it."

"I don't care if Satan himself showed up with a tip. I'll take anything at this point."

Zach took a breath and blew it out. "It wasn't Satan, but it could get us a one-way ticket to hell if anyone finds out."

The captain stared at him for a couple of seconds, then shook his head. "Shit. That Bordeaux woman."

"Yeah. She sorta called me. I gave her my card and—"

The captain waved a hand, cutting him off. "I know I'm likely to regret this, but I don't even care. Do you know where the woman is now?"

"No." At least that part was absolutely true.

"Could you track the call?"

"No." Since she'd told him the phone wasn't traceable, that part was technically true, also.

"Then fuck it," the captain said. "What did the woman have to say? Did she bother to explain why the FBI is after her? Or what she had to do with the kidnappings? Please tell me she knows something."

"She knows something, but I'm not sure what to make of it."

"I need to know that the information she provides is credible, so let's start at the beginning. What does the FBI want with her? Was she involved with the other kidnappings?"

"Sorta, but not in the way you're thinking. She claims she's former FBI."

The captain sat straight up in his chair. "Is she rogue?"

"No. She's the key witness in a huge case, but she fled protective custody when it was clear the bad guys could get to her anyway."

"And you believe this?"

Zach tried to appear nonchalant. "I can't see much reason not to. The FBI's looking for her, sure, but all they sent was that dick Fields. If she were wanted for criminal activity, especially kidnapping, wouldn't they have sent in a squad with guns blazing?"

"You have a point. Unless she voluntarily surrenders and puts on a set of handcuffs herself, Fields isn't likely to apprehend her. That guy must be related to somebody important to keep his position. He's useless. So was she on the kidnapping case?"

"No, but while she was undercover, she stumbled across something that made her think a member of her primary target's family was part of it."

"Undercover, huh? Please tell me she wasn't a secretary or something in the mayor's office. My ulcer is already killing me."

"No, it wasn't that kind of family, exactly."

The captain frowned. "Then what kind of family was it?"

"The Hebert kind of family."

Captain Saucier stared at him, a stunned expression on his face. "No shit. This broad claims she was undercover in the Hebert clan? No wonder she's been hiding. I'm surprised she's not hiding at the bottom of the Mississippi."

"Me, too, but apparently Ms. Bordeaux is much more resourceful than the FBI or the Heberts ever imagined."

"Unbelievable. Well, that's a twist I didn't see coming."

"Me, either, sir."

"So this Bordeaux woman thinks one of the Hebert family is involved? Did she say which one?"

"Yeah, but word is he hasn't been seen for some time now. She doesn't think he's vacationing. At least not alive."

"Shit." The captain picked up a pen and tapped it on the desk. "So what do you make of this? It could be a different Hebert now, but what the hell? There's never been a ransom request, so what's the angle? The Heberts aren't known to participate in not-for-profit activities."

"I was thinking the political angle," Zach suggested.

"With the mayor." The captain dropped the pen and sat back in his chair. "Okay. So the question is, did they take the girl to strong-arm some favor or did they take the girl per mayor's orders, to boost his reelection ratings for future favors?"

"I couldn't say."

"Did the Bordeaux woman give you anything else?"

"Yeah. A Dr. Spencer. Apparently Ms. Bordeaux knew the girl. Used to see her go to a doctor's appointment across the street from her shop. The mother and girl used to stop in her store afterward."

"And did you talk to Spencer?"

"He's a cancer Specialist and says the girl is sick, but apparently the mother lied about her identity, and even the girl doesn't know what she's being treated for."

"Does the father know?"

Zach shook his head. "I don't think so, and the mother's definitely hiding something. She looked scared to death when I mentioned the mayor's connection to the other kidnappings."

"Please don't tell me this kid's going to die."

"Dr. Spencer doesn't think so, but the longer she goes without her medication . . ."

"Shit. Can you find this Bordeaux woman?"

Zach shrugged. "I don't know. Are you telling me to go against FBI orders and look for her?"

The captain stared out the window for a while, then looked back at Zach. "Yeah, that's exactly what I'm telling you to do."

Zach rose from his chair, holding in a smile. He'd just been officially given permission to be in Raissa's company, and God help him, that was something he wanted badly. Plus, he tried to tell himself, it would make things much easier going forward . . . for the investigation.

"And Blanchard," the captain said as Zach stepped out of the office, "keep this between the two of us."

Zach nodded. It went without saying.

Maryse rang up a candle purchase in Sabine's store and handed the woman her change and a bag with the candle. "Thank you, and please come again. Sabine will be back this weekend. I'm sure she'd be happy to schedule a reading for you."

The woman smiled. "Thank you. I look forward to meeting her."

Maryse watched until the woman left the shop and crossed the street before hurrying from the counter to the break room. Raissa was perched on a chair at the break-room table with a laptop in front of her. Maryse pulled a chair next to her and took a seat. "Did you get in yet?"

Raissa nodded. "Piece of cake."

Maryse looked at the screen that prominently displayed the hospital's medical records and felt her pulse quicken. "You're sure no one will track it back to you?"

"Someone would have to know I've broken in to even begin a trace. Mudbug General has simply horrible security. A high-school student could hack their system and never leave a trace."

"That's great to know, considering all my medical records are stored there."

"Don't sweat it. No one bothers with hospitals unless they're looking for something to blackmail people over. And since most people go to clinics and pay cash for the blackmailable sorts of health issues, hospitals aren't exactly hopping with hackers."

"Okay," Maryse said, not completely convinced. "So did you find anything?"

"There were five babies born during the time Helena was in the hospital having Hank. Three were girls, so that leaves only baby Frederick Agostino."

"What a mouthful."

"Tell me. Take a look at that birth weight." Raissa pointed to a line on a birth record. "Surely if Hank had been an eleven-pound baby, Helena would have mentioned that."

"Are you kidding me? If Helena had given birth to an eleven-pound baby, we'd have heard about it every day of her life, and she'd still be complaining after death. No one does persecution drama like Helena."

Raissa closed the program with the hospital records and accessed a Web browser. She typed in a search for Frederick Agostino, and Maryse was surprised when a number of hits were returned. Raissa laughed and Maryse leaned in to read some of the results.

"A family-owned Italian restaurant. That explains the birth weight. Mama Agostino probably ate them out of restaurant and home while she was pregnant."

Raissa clicked on one of the links and a news article about the restaurant appeared, complete with a picture of the Agostino family. It was obviously taken with a wide-angle lens.

"Well, that blows another theory," Maryse said with a sigh. "Frederick is the spitting image of his mother."

Raissa shook her head. "That is truly frightening, but you're right. There's no way Frederick isn't Mrs. Agostino's son."

"Which means we still don't know what happened to Helena's baby," Maryse said.

"Or where Hank came from."

"Maybe when those aliens take one person, they leave another."

Raissa shrugged. "It's as good a theory as any other. You think Helena will buy that her son's from another planet?"

Maryse sighed. "I would."

Hank walked Lila to her car, anxious over what he was about to do. It was a risk. A huge risk, and Hank Henry was not the risk-taking kind of guy, not anymore. But

Lila was standing there in her yellow sundress, her long brown hair falling in gentle waves across her shoulder, and Hank was mesmerized.

He opened her car door for her and stood there with his hand still on top of the door. She placed her notebook inside and turned to smile at him. It was a smile that turned his insides into jelly and other places on him into something far less squishy. In all his years on earth, Hank had never met a woman who left him so unbalanced.

"Thanks," she said. "That first set of cabinets looks fabulous. I can't believe you got them built so quickly."

Hank blushed. "I might have worked a little overtime. I wanted to have something for you to look at when you came today."

"It's so exciting. Everything is going to look even better than I imagined, and the rooms are going to look like home and not a clinic." She placed one of her hands on top of his. "I'm so glad you're working here, Hank. You understand how important all this is. I'm very proud of you. And I have to say, I told you so."

Hank looked down at the ground. "Thanks, but I can't take all the credit." He looked back up at her. "You made a huge difference in my life, more so than anyone else ever has. You were a stranger, and you still believed in me. I didn't trust that at first. Didn't think it was possible for me to be anything other than what I'd always been. Probably still wouldn't if I hadn't met you."

Lila squeezed his hand and sniffed. "That's so nice, and it means a lot to me." She rubbed her nose with one finger and sniffed again. "My father was raised in harsh circumstances. He got into all sorts of trouble when he was a teenager, and people figured it was a given that he was going to spend most of his adult life in prison. But my mom saw something in him that no one else did, and she brought it out in him. He owns his own CPA firm and does really well."

"Wow. He must be really smart."

Lila grinned. "He was a bookie before that, so he said it just fit."

Hank laughed. "That's cool. Your mom must be a special woman. I guess that explains where you get it." He looked down at the ground again and fidgeted, trying to build up the courage for what he wanted to do. Finally, he took a deep breath and looked back up at her. "Would you like to have dinner with me sometime? I understand if you say no, since I was a patient, and now I'm an employee, and well, I know you have a reputation to protect—"

Lila placed a finger on his lips to stop his rambling. "I'd love to have dinner with you. I'm free on Friday." She leaned over and kissed him on the check. "I've got to run to my next appointment, but I'll see you tomorrow morning at eight for the walk-through with Chuck. We can make plans afterward."

Hank nodded, unable to speak, as Lila got in her car and pulled away from the curb with a wave. His cheek tingled where her lips had touched his skin, and he watched her car until it turned the corner at the end of the block and he could no longer see it.

"How touching." The voice sounded directly behind Hank and he spun around to face Rico Hebert.

"What do you want, Rico?" Hank asked.

"I want what Sonny wants."

"I've already told you I don't know anything. My ex-wife doesn't know anything, and her friend that might know something is out of the country getting married. I'm a dead end."

Rico nodded. "That's what you say, but that psychic

woman's still missing. Her shop's closed. She's not at home, and Sonny would really like to find her."

"Yeah, well, tell Sonny to get in line."

"Sonny doesn't wait in line. Why should he?"

"Because according to my ex-wife, the New Orleans Police Department and the FBI are looking for Raissa, too. My ex has already gotten the shakedown from all of them and told them the same thing she told me—no one knows where Raissa is."

Rico frowned. "That's very unfortunate."

"Look, unfortunate or not, apparently the woman's good at not being found. If the FBI can't find her, my guess is Sonny's not going to, either."

Rico studied Hank for a couple of seconds. "Maybe your ex-wife knows more than she's saying."

Hank shook his head. "No way. If my ex knew anything, she would have told the cops or that new husband of hers, and *he* would have told the cops. She's got some damned code of ethics that men like you and I simply wouldn't understand. Raissa's gone, Rico, and no one that cares about her knows where. My ex and her friends are frantic. They're not faking."

"Maybe not, but that would be unfortunate. You know, you not being able to find out and all." Rico inclined his head toward the clinic. "All kinds of accidents happen on construction sites. Bad electrical wiring and such. Some of these places are known to just go up in flames. Least that's what I hear."

Hank clenched his hand into a fist and gritted his teeth, trying to control himself. Hitting Rico was a surefire way to bring down the house of cards. "That's what insurance is for, I suppose," Hank said, trying to sound as if he didn't care.

"Yeah. Unless, of course, insurance thinks the guy

building the clinic did it himself. I hear insurance fraud is a real problem for business owners."

Hank felt his blood start to boil. He was going to blow it. He was going to throttle Rico Hebert to death right there in the street, and God help him, there wasn't a thing he could do to stop it.

"Hank." Chuck's voice sounded behind him.

Hank spun around and saw Chuck getting out of his truck just a few yards away from where he stood. It momentarily unnerved Hank that he'd been so focused on killing Rico that he hadn't even heard Chuck's truck pull up behind him. "Hi, Chuck."

Chuck glanced over at Rico, and Hank could tell he didn't like what he saw. "Is there a problem?" Chuck asked.

"No problem," Rico said. "I was just asking for directions." He nodded at Hank. "Thanks for the help."

Hank watched as Rico jumped in his car and drove away, then turned to face Chuck. "Sorry about that. Guy was a little weird. I think he was hopped up on something."

Chuck studied Hank's face for a couple of seconds, and Hank could tell he wasn't completely convinced. Finally, he nodded. "I just came by to drop off the rest of the front-office designs." He handed a tube to Hank. "Might as well give them to you. It's the front-desk layout and the ideas you came up with for furniture in the lobby. Great stuff, by the way."

"Thanks. It's hard to believe I actually get paid for this. This is fun."

Chuck nodded. "Shows in your work, too. I tell you, it's a rare person that finds they can make a living at something they love. You and me are lucky men,

Hank." He looked over at the clinic. "You done for the day?"

"Not quite yet. I have one more cabinet to stain. I wanted to get one coat on all of them today, so I can finish them tomorrow."

Chuck clasped one hand on Hank's shoulder. "Sounds good. I'll see you tomorrow morning for the walk-through with Lila."

"Yes, sir," Hank said as Chuck walked to his truck and hopped inside.

Hank waved as Chuck pulled away from the curb, then crossed the street to the clinic. Maybe another hour and he'd be done for the evening. Then he could go home and figure out what the hell had motivated him to ask Lila on a date. If he couldn't come up with any reasonable explanation for canceling besides being scared, which wasn't exactly something a man liked to admit, then he was going to have to call Maryse and ask for a restaurant recommendation. And what to wear. Jesus, dating was filled with difficulty.

He closed the front door to the clinic behind him and locked it just in case Rico was lurking anywhere nearby. He didn't doubt the thug would plow right through a locked door if he really wanted what was on the other side, but at least Hank would hear him coming. He headed down the hall to the last room in the clinic. He'd been using that room to assemble and finish the cabinets, and his first masterpiece was resting in the center of the room, all stained except for the corner unit. He grabbed his can of stain and paintbrush and got to work on the cabinet facing.

Hank heard the intruder as soon as he entered the building. He probably thought he was being quiet, but the click of the front door lock releasing echoed straight through the silence of the clinic. Hank grabbed a screwdriver from his toolbox and slipped behind the row of cabinets he was working on. He paused one second, two seconds, trying to figure out where the person was, but there was only silence.

He edged away from the cabinets and pressed himself flat against the wall, then crept down the hall until he reached the doorway. He peered around, but the hallway was empty, and he couldn't detect the sound of another person moving around inside the building at all. But he knew what he'd heard, and the hair standing up on the back of his neck told him he hadn't been wrong. He was a lot of things, but fanciful wasn't one of them.

For the first time in a long time, he wished he'd broken the law and bought a handgun. He'd hoped it wouldn't be necessary, but that had been a foolish thought. Battling whoever was out there with a screwdriver didn't seem like the best option, but he couldn't think of another one.

He waited a couple of seconds but didn't see or hear a thing. Finally, he slipped out of the room and down the hall, careful to avoid stepping on anything that would give away his position. He peeked into each room as he passed, but they were empty. When he reached the lobby, he peered around the corner from the hallway and scanned the room. The door was shut, but he could see it was unlocked.

Had the intruder been a common thief, looking for construction-site tools? Maybe he'd left after hearing Hank in the back. That must be it. Hank crossed the lobby and opened the front door. The lawn and street in front of the clinic was empty, and the only cars on the street were those he'd seen earlier in the day. Absolutely nothing seemed out of place. Letting out a sigh of relief, he closed the door and locked it.

When he felt the sting of the needle, he immediately knew he'd grossly miscalculated.

The intruder must have been hiding behind the frame for the front desk, and whatever he'd been stuck with was making him woozy. Hank turned, trying to get a good look at his attacker, but the last thing he saw before crashing to the floor was two huge eyes and a bug-shaped face staring back at him.

Chapter Fifteen

Raissa closed the folder she'd been studying and tossed it onto her hotel-room bed. Maryse looked up from a set of paperwork. "Frustrated?"

"To say the least. Six hours of combing these files, and nothing. There has to be something those girls have in common besides looks. Why would anyone go to such lengths to abduct them and return them for no good reason?"

Maryse nodded. "There's a reason. We're just not seeing it. I keep waiting to hear about a ransom note, given the last girl was the mayor's granddaughter, but if there's been one, it's being kept really secret."

"Zach would have told me if there had been a ransom request. It would change everything."

Maryse cocked her head to the side and studied Raissa for a couple of seconds. "So, you want to talk about your relationship with Just One, or do I have to leave it all to my very vivid and creative imagination?"

"It's not a relationship, so there's really nothing to talk about."

Maryse raised her eyebrows. "Looked relationshippy to me when I walked in on you two naked. I couldn't help but notice the cleared area on one of the folding tables *and* that the bed wasn't rumpled in the least. That says something."

"*That* says hot, wild sex, and that's all there is to it."

"You sure?"

Raissa sighed. "How can I not be? Even if this all

turns out for the best, and Melissa is safely back with her parents—even if the kidnapper is caught and jailed—that doesn't remove my biggest threat. As soon as this is over, I'll have to leave, whether the FBI takes part in it or not. I'm not safe in New Orleans any longer, and if I stay, I put everyone I care about at risk."

Maryse frowned. "So can you just not testify?"

Raissa shrugged. "They can subpoena me anyway. Then the price of freedom would be lying under oath, and that's *if* I manage to make it to court alive, which is questionable, given the FBI's inability to protect me in the past."

"That sucks, but it's only for another six months, right? I mean you could hide out until the statute of limitations has passed, and then you're in the clear."

"If Sonny lets it go. Remember, I was his confidante for two years. He chose me. He trusted me. This isn't just business for him—it's personal."

"But wouldn't your death just bring the heat on him all over again? I mean, if you've passed the time limit on what you could testify to, doesn't it make more sense to just leave you alone?"

"Mob business isn't always about common sense, although I have to admit that Sonny's more controlled than most. But six months is still a long time. Long enough for people to realize what they had was a flash in the pan due to a highly emotional situation. Six months after the fact, all that emotion and stress is gone. Things are normal."

"So what makes you think you and Zach can't do normal?"

Raissa laughed. "I don't know the first thing about normal, and I get the impression that Zach is trying to manage it but failing dreadfully. My less-than-conventional ways of handling things would only make things tougher for him, especially given his job. His captain is already watching him closely and if he knew half of the things Zach's already done for me against orders, he'd be fired in a heartbeat. I'm a huge liability, no matter what."

"Do you think you'll ever go back to law enforcement?"

"I will never go back to the FBI, and based on Zach's description, the police department appears a bit too stringent for my methods, too. But I have to admit that even though this entire situation with the abductions is very serious, I find myself enjoying it on some level."

Maryse nodded. "It's like my research. Even though I've lost people I love to cancer, I can't help getting excited when I'm working. The disease is still out there, and it's still killing people, but I get a personal thrill from things that would appear very minor to anyone else. A guilty pleasure, almost."

"Exactly. And don't get me wrong, between my business and the security gigs, I still got to use some of those skills—the hacking, surveillance. It was all part of the game, but it's not the same as doing it full-time and in the open."

"Maybe you should go solo, like Beau. Heck, he may even consider a partnership of some sort. You two would be a deadly combination."

Raissa momentarily considered Sabine's husband, Beau, and his private-investigation service. It wasn't the worst idea she'd ever heard, even if she did it alone in another state with another name. Despite what was logical, Raissa still doubted her ability to remain in New Orleans much longer or to ever return. It was simply too dangerous for everyone around her, but the last thing she wanted to do was press Maryse to accept that when they were up to their neck in things. "It's a thought."

"Did you ever have anyone to rely on, or who was dependent on you before? I mean, I figured if you did, they'd either have to go into protective custody with you or you'd have to leave them, right?"

Raissa nodded. "Those are the choices, but fortunately for me, my parents were already gone before I went undercover. I was so focused through high school and college, I didn't give men a second thought." She stared past Maryse and looked out the hotel-room window. "There was a guy once. We met at the FBI Academy."

"What happened?"

"He died."

Maryse's eyes widened. "Oh, wow. I'm sorry. I didn't mean to bring up anything bad."

"You didn't. My relationship with him was all good. He was a great guy—dedicated to his job and an assortment of nieces and nephews. Sturdy, but not in a boring way, you know?"

Maryse nodded.

"He was interesting and funny and I really enjoyed spending time with him. He always made me laugh, even when the academy training was getting the best of me."

"What happened?"

"He was on a special task force for missing kids."

Maryse gasped. "The missing girls . . . that's how you knew about the cases. He was the agent on them."

Raissa nodded, her mind flashing back to the night Ben had told her about his case. "We met at an all-night diner, in a part of town that Sonny's men wouldn't be likely to enter. Ben had flown in from D.C. for the day—that's all the time he could afford to take off. The latest kidnapping had happened two days before, and he wanted my advice."

"And he wanted to see you."

"Probably. I'd been under over a year and a half by then. We'd only seen each other four times since I'd gone undercover, but I still wanted to jump him right there on that table in the diner."

Maryse smiled. "You two were good together."

"I'd like to think so."

"So did he get killed investigating the kidnappings?"

"No. That's the worst part of the whole thing. A drunk driver hit his taxi on the way home from the airport. That cheap, greasy dinner in a rundown café was the last time I got to spend with him."

Maryse placed her hand on Raissa's arm. "I am so sorry."

"One of life's ironies, right? He spent every day of his life putting himself at risk, and everything was cut short by a drunk. What a waste."

Maryse nodded.

"It just makes you think twice, you know? About how no matter what, you're never really safe. And then with our job, we were at risk even more than regular people. Makes you think hard about getting involved again."

"If Sabine could take that risk, then you can, too."

Raissa sighed. "Fortunately, I don't have to think about it. I can't say for certain how Zach feels, but I seriously doubt he's mentally picking out matching luggage. I'm a temporary distraction during a temporary situation, and soon I'll be gone. No risk at all." She picked up another folder and started to read.

"Your parents . . . were they still alive when you went into the FBI?"

"No. My dad died when I was eight. He was a fighter pilot and died in a training accident testing new aircraft. My mother passed my last year of college. Congestive heart failure. It ran in her family, and after my dad died, she never really took care of herself. She just sorta faded away."

"That sucks, but at least you have some good memories." Maryse stared down at the folder in her hands.

"I do," Raissa said, her heart going out to her friend. Maryse had never known her mother. She'd died when Maryse was too young to remember her. So, despite all the regrets and blame Raissa might fling at her mother, Maryse was right—there were still years of good memories she could draw on.

Maryse looked up at Raissa, her brow scrunched in thought. "What about the parents?"

"I just told you about my parents."

"No, sorry. Not your parents, the girls'. Maybe it's the parents who have something in common."

Raissa thought about all the families. "Well, they all live in different states. Until now, there were no political affiliations."

"Professions?"

Raissa slowly shook her head. "All your basic blue-collar type work. A mechanic, a fireman, a fisherman . . . I can't see how that has anything to do with—"

Maryse waved a hand. "Before. What about before they were firemen and fishermen and all that?"

Raissa picked up a file and scanned the history. "All I've got here is a couple of years before the kidnappings. I don't know that anyone went back further, as kidnappers rarely need that long to plan. Why? What are you thinking?"

"I don't know. I mean, it's not likely they met in college, given the professions, but what about the military? Did anyone ever ask them if they knew the other families?"

Raissa stared at Maryse. "I don't think so. There's no record of it, anyway."

Maryse frowned. "I suppose we'd go directly to jail if you hacked the military, right?

Raissa smiled. "Oh, yeah, but don't worry, I've got a better idea."

"What's that?"

"The Social Security Administration." Raissa reached for a spare laptop and Mildred's car keys.

Maryse sighed. "Yeah, much safer."

"Actually, it is. They have simply horrible security."

"There's a pleasant thought." Maryse placed a hand on Raissa's arm. "Let's try it my way first."

"Your way? Maryse, you've been holding out on me?"

Maryse grabbed one of the spare laptops and plopped back on the bed. "Hardly," she said, and started typing. "Give me the father of the first girl."

Raissa picked up the file and read the name.

Maryse tapped on the keyboard, hit enter, scrolled a bit, and clicked the mouse. She looked up at Raissa with a triumphant smile and turned the laptop toward her.

Raissa leaned over and stared in amazement. "Facebook? Your big investigative trick is Facebook?"

Maryse nodded and tapped the screen. "Look at the history. He's listed everyplace he ever worked, including his military service. When his wife got pregnant, they were stationed in North Carolina." Maryse turned the laptop around and waved a hand at Raissa. "Give me another name."

Raissa grinned and picked up the file. The young

dog had just taught the old dog a new trick. She'd opened the file to read off the name when the computer next to her started beeping.

Maryse looked up in alarm. "What is it?"

"It's the bug in Sonny's house." Raissa tapped some keys on the keyboard and Sonny's voice boomed out of the laptop.

"Damn it!" he yelled. "Why haven't you brought me anything? What the hell are you waiting for?"

"Taylor or Raissa, whatever she calls herself now," another guy said.

"Forget her," Sonny said. "Have any of you found out anything at all about that kidnapping?"

There was silence for a couple of seconds, then finally another guy said, "There's no word on the street, Sonny. That kid wasn't taken by anyone we know or have business ties with. Maybe it's just some perv, you know?"

"Get out," Sonny said. "Except you, Rico."

They heard the door click shut and then someone sighed.

"I don't like this," Sonny said.

"Neither do I, but the guys are right. This wasn't any of our associates or competitors. They're baffled we're even asking."

"I want to know what Monk Marsella involved this family in."

"Does it really matter, now? I mean, Monk's been gone for months now."

"Yeah, it matters," Sonny said, "because I want to know what was so important that it got him killed, and why it's happening again. Don't tell me the cases aren't related."

"I'm not saying that. Our sources indicate the police are looking into the old cases as well. They've made the connection. Probably from Taylor. She's a problem, you know. I think you ought to let me take care of her."

"No. If anyone can figure out what's going on, it's her. She's brilliant, or she'd never have fooled me. Leave her to work with the police. They'll never figure this out without help, and time's running out."

"You going soft, Sonny? This really ain't none of our business."

"Watch what you're saying, Rico. I ain't soft, but this is a kid we're talking about. We don't deal in wives, and we damned sure don't deal in kids. You know the rules. You want this family associated with whatever perverted shit is probably being done to those girls?"

"No, I suppose not."

"What about Hank Henry?"

"Ain't nothing going on there that I can see," Rico said. "I've been watching him close like, but he only goes to work and home. Ain't nobody else hassling him or anything."

"Keep watching. I'm sure that's the name Monk said before he died. If Hank isn't doing anything, then he must know something."

"Maybe, or maybe Monk just thought he did. The guy wasn't all that bright, you know?"

"Yeah, but it doesn't take smarts to run up on something bad," Sonny said. "Keep checking on Taylor, too, but you do not have authority to move on her, got it?"

"I got it, for now. But afterward . . . when this circus is over?"

"I'll deal with it then."

There was some shuffling and the door opening and closing, then silence. Marysc looked over at Raissa, her eyes wide.

"What in the world is Hank involved in now?" Maryse asked.

"I don't know, and I'm willing to bet Hank doesn't know, either. Apparently he's mixed up in something to do with Monk, but even Hank doesn't know what."

"Are you sure?" Maryse asked, drily.

Raissa nodded. "Yeah, I'm pretty sure. He was spooked that night we talked. I can usually tell when someone's holding back, but Hank just looked clueless. Whatever he knows, he doesn't realize how important it is. Or maybe he doesn't know or remember at all. Either way, he's not safe. I need to call and warn him."

Maryse nodded. "So if the Heberts didn't take that girl, who did?" Maryse asked.

Raissa looked at Maryse, a million thoughts—mostly bad—rolling around in her head. "I have no idea, but apparently Sonny thinks I can find out."

"I don't understand. If Sonny told his guys to leave you alone, then who's been trying to kill you?"

"That's a really good question."

It was close to midnight when Zach let himself into the Mudbug Hotel. He half-expected to find Raissa already in bed—or at least he hoped—but when he pushed the door open, it wasn't exactly the scene he'd envisioned on the forty-five-minute drive to Mudbug. Raissa was in bed, but she was wearing more clothes than he'd imagined, and he hadn't counted on her being surrounded by paper, either.

"Am I interrupting?" he asked, realizing she was so engrossed in whatever she was doing that she hadn't even heard him open the door.

"Crap!" Raissa jumped up from the bed at the sound of his voice. "Why are you sneaking up on me?"

Zach laughed. "Are you kidding me?" He waved one

hand at the rows of computer equipment. "You could have seen what I was wearing as soon as I drove into town if you were watching your security. Unlike your ghostly friend, I cannot walk through walls, nor am I invisible."

"That's a good thing, or you'd be dead."

"True. Speaking of dead people, she's not in here, right?"

"Helena? No, why?"

"Well, I was sorta hoping you'd have on fewer clothes, so I thought maybe she was here."

Raissa laughed and jumped up from the bed. "I promise to have on fewer clothes later, but first I have to show you what Maryse and I found."

Zach's mind immediately shifted from carnal thoughts to the case. No way Raissa was this excited over nothing. "What did you find?"

Raissa grabbed a bunch of papers off the bed and sat at the table, spreading them out in front of her. Zach pulled up a chair next to her, ready for the show. "Maryse and I spent the afternoon going through the FBI files, trying to make a connection among the girls."

Zach placed his hands over his ears. "I'm not hearing anything about hacking."

"Wimp." Raissa said and pulled his hands down. "I wanted to find the common denominator in the abductions. I've never believed it was on looks alone. It just doesn't feel right, you know?"

Zach nodded. He thought there was far more to it than they had been able to discern. "So you found something about the girls?"

"No, their parents."

"Like what? They lived in different places, had different jobs . . . No reason their paths would cross."

Raissa smiled and handed him a stack of papers.

"Unless they were all in the military. Check those papers. Three of them were stationed at Myrtle Beach."

Zach looked down at the first sheet. "Facebook? You're hinging a kidnapping investigation on Facebook."

Raissa shrugged. "I wanted to hack the Social Security Administration. Maryse's way was safer."

Zach gave a silent prayer of thanks. "And legal. Remember legal?"

Raissa waved a hand in dismissal. "Forget that. Don't you see—they were all at the same base. The last guy doesn't have a Facebook account, but what do you want to bet he was stationed there, too?"

"Were they all there at the same time?"

"No, but within the same year, seventeen years ago."

"And the FBI never caught that before?"

Raissa shook her head. "They wouldn't have looked that far back initially, and when the lead investigator died, it got shuffled around a bit. There was a lot of terrorist activity going on then and most of the agents were redirected."

"Then it went cold."

"Yeah. They probably figured whoever did it was dead or in prison, and the reality is, the predators who don't return kids alive are a higher priority than the one guy who returns them all seemingly unscathed."

"So he got conveniently off radar and no one noticed a connection."

"Until now. And guess who else just happened to be present on the base during that time?"

"Please don't tell me it was the mayor."

"Okay, I won't tell you, but you need to check this bio we pulled off the City of New Orleans Web site. The mayor spent his last year of service as an instructor . . ."

". . . in Myrtle Beach. Shit."

"Guess who else was there?"

"I'm afraid to ask?"

"Our friend Dr. Spencer."

Zach ran one hand through his hair. "Did he have that listed on his Facebook page, too?"

Raissa grinned. "No. We called and asked."

Chapter Sixteen

Zach stared at Raissa, unable to wrap his mind around everything she'd just told him, much less what any of it meant. "You're sure?"

"Yep. Dr. Spencer is ex-military and did a part-time stint on the base when they were short on medical personnel. A lot of the boys had returned from the Gulf War and needed care. He flew up there two weeks a month for over a year."

"And the military just gave you this information because you asked?"

"Not me, Maryse. She explained who she was and the project she's working on—she has government funding, you know—and besides, the officer who worked in records is from New Orleans."

"So he gave out information over the phone to a stranger because she has government funding and he used to live in New Orleans."

Raissa nodded. "I was impressed with Maryse, too. She explained that she was considering him for work on her project, as he's a cancer specialist, but wanted to make sure he was telling the truth about his work with the military, since she has the utmost respect for military personnel and didn't want him sneaking in the door with a lie. She didn't ask for details, more like job-reference sort of stuff—what he was there for and when."

"You think Spencer knew the victims' parents?"

"I can't prove anything, but I think it's far too big a thing to be a coincidence."

Zach shook his head. "I agree, but what does it tell us?"

Raissa sighed. "I have absolutely no idea. That's why you found me sitting in bed with stacks of paper—my back hurt from the chair. But I still haven't made sense of it. It's all fascinating and can't possibly be irrelevant, but for the life of me, I can't come up with anything that fits."

"This case just keeps getting stranger."

"And that's not all." Raissa told him about the conversation between Sonny and Rico.

"Do you know this Hank?"

"A little. More secondhand than anything else. Apparently he owed the Heberts money and did a few jobs to pay off his debt."

"But you don't think he's involved with the kidnapping?"

"I don't see how. He's not the kind of guy you'd trust with delicate work."

Zach nodded. "I don't like the Hebert angle of this one bit. I don't care what Sonny said tonight. He could just as easily change his mind about you tomorrow morning and alert his guys by cell phone. You won't have any idea he's coming."

Raissa waved a hand at the computers. "That's why I'm always prepared."

Zach ran one hand through his hair, his emotions warring inside of him. Finally, he said, "Maybe you should talk to Agent Fields. See what the FBI is offering."

"No way."

"But—"

"I'm not cutting out of here until this is over."

Zach could have sworn his heart stopped beating for just a moment. *Moron. You always knew she'd have to leave.* But had he? Had he really given any thought to what would happen to Raissa when the case was over? And when had it become important? He was attracted to her, and he admired her, and worried about her, but that was all. Right?

"Zach?" Raissa's voice broke him away from his thoughts.

"Huh." He looked at Raissa. "Sorry, I was thinking."

"Obviously. You didn't hear the last two things I said. Well, did you figure anything out during all that thinking?"

"No," Zach said, "not really." Except that he'd complicated his personal life right along with his career, all with the same woman. It had to be some kind of record.

"Well, I say we call it a night and start on this again tomorrow when our brains aren't fried."

"Sounds good to me."

Raissa gave him a sexy smile and started unbuttoning her shirt. "So let's see what I can do about that 'fewer clothes' thing you mentioned earlier."

"Raissa, what exactly are we doing here?"

Raissa stopped unbuttoning her blouse and looked directly at him. "I thought it was obvious."

He stared at her—the black lace of her bra peeking out the top of her partially unbuttoned blouse—and his mind warred with other parts of his body that were far more powerful. "You're right," he said, and took over on the buttons where she'd left off. Raissa knew exactly what he was asking, but she'd intentionally avoided the question. For that matter, he'd allowed it. He opened her shirt and pushed it over her shoulders.

But they were going to have to talk about it sometime. Sooner would probably be better than later.

Bright and early Friday morning, Chuck and Lila stood in front of the clinic. Chuck punched in Hank's cell-phone number for the fourth time in the last ten minutes, but Lila could hear the call go straight to voice mail.

"I'm sorry," Chuck apologized. "I just don't know what's keeping Hank. He's usually so punctual, and he always calls if anything comes up."

Lila frowned, trying not to think of all the wrong reasons for Hank to be late for their meeting. She didn't want to believe his change was temporary. Surely, something had delayed him, and he'd be there soon. "That's okay. Maybe we should just start the walk-through without him. I'm sure he'll be here soon."

Chuck nodded and reached for the door. He stopped short when he realized it was already unlocked. "What the heck?" He turned the knob and pushed the door open. "Hank? You in here?" He looked back at Lila. "Let's go check."

They stepped inside and Chuck called out again, "Hank? Where are you?" Nothing. Chuck walked down the hallway of the clinic, checking in the rooms as he went. Lila followed behind.

"Chuck?" A voice yelled from the front doorway.

Chuck turned around and saw his assistant foreman, Jimmy, standing in the doorway. "Yeah, Jimmy, we're back here. Looking for Hank. You seen him?"

Jimmy walked down the hallway to join them. "Nah, but I just got here. Had a flat on the truck this morning. Musta picked up a nail." Jimmy pointed to the back of the clinic. "Hank was working on a set of cabinets in the last office when I left yesterday. He's probably got his iPod playing and can't hear you."

"Maybe so," Chuck agreed, and headed for the back office.

Lila hurried after him, hoping the explanation was that simple and that benign. Chuck stopped short in the doorway. Lila inched to the side of him and peered into the room. It was empty, but something was wrong. She took it all in—the tools left out on the floor, the table saw that was still plugged in. She started to take a step into the room and her foot brushed against something on the floor. She looked down and realized it was an open can of stain.

"This isn't right," Lila said.

"No. It feels all wrong," Chuck agreed. He nudged the can of stain with his boot. "That stain has been open for a long time." He pointed to the top of the ladder in the corner. Hank's wallet and keys were perched on top where he always placed them. "Jimmy," Chuck called out. "You see Hank's truck out there?"

Jimmy opened the back door and looked outside. "Yeah, it's here. Same exact place it was yesterday. Weird."

Chuck backed out of the office and motioned for Lila to follow him. "We're going outside, and I'm going to call the police. Don't touch anything, okay?"

"Chuck, what in the world is going on?" Lila felt the blood drain from her face and she stumbled in the hallway. Chuck grabbed her arm and steadied her, guiding her out of the clinic and onto the front lawn. Lila took a deep breath, then looked at Chuck. "What is it? You know something."

Chuck pulled his cell phone from his pocket and

dialed 911. He told the dispatcher he wanted to report a break-in and possible missing person. "They said someone will be here shortly," he said and closed the phone. "There was a guy parked across the street yesterday talking to Hank. It didn't look like a friendly sort of conversation."

"What did he want?"

"I don't know. Hank tried to play it off that the guy wanted directions, but I didn't buy it. And I didn't like the look of the guy. Now this. There's no way in hell Hank Henry left this clinic with power tools plugged in, stain uncovered, and his wallet and keys still on that ladder—not voluntarily, anyway."

Lila covered her mouth with her hand, worry and fear washing over every square inch of her body. "Oh, no."

Chuck looked Lila in the eye. "I know about all that doctor-patient-privilege stuff, but if you know what Hank was involved in before he went into rehab, I think I need to know. I think the police are gonna need to know."

Lila nodded, not concerned in the least about the ethics of the situation. All she wanted was Hank, safe and sound and staining cabinets at her clinic. "He got into trouble gambling. Owed the wrong people money. He worked it off, but never gave me details as to how, exactly. He only said that work is what sent him to rehab."

"What people?" Chuck asked, the fear in his eyes clear as day.

"The Hebert family."

Chuck closed his eyes and blew out a breath. "Dear Lord," he whispered.

Even though it was every bit of eighty degrees outside, Lila shivered.

* * *

Zach was still sound asleep when his cell phone started ringing. He reached for the nightstand, but all he found was air. Confused, he opened one eye, and that's when he remembered that he wasn't home—he was in a hotel with the hottest and most dangerous woman he'd ever met.

He hopped out of bed and dug through a pile of hastily discarded clothes scattered across the hotel-room floor. Finally, he located his pants and pulled the phone from the pocket, managing to answer the call just before it went to voice mail.

"Damn it, Blanchard!" the captain yelled. "What the hell took you so long to answer? It's eight thirty, and your ass was supposed to be at the station at eight. You got ten minutes to get here before I demote you to dogcatcher."

Shit! "Uh, that's not going to be possible . . ."

"It's possible from anywhere in New Orleans."

"I'm not exactly in New Orleans."

"Well, where the hell are you?"

Zach paused. "Uh . . . following up on a lead?"

He heard Raissa laugh and covered the speaker part of his phone.

"Did that lead require you to spend the night? Oh, no, do not tell me that your 'lead' involves crystal balls."

"Of course not, sir." His balls were absolutely not made of crystal. "I'll be there in forty minutes. I promise."

He snapped his phone shut and shoved it in his pocket along with his wallet. Then he grabbed his keys off the dresser. "I can't believe you let me sleep this late."

"Late? Good Lord, please don't tell me you're a morning person."

He looked over at her lying back in the bed, all

rumpled and sexy. "I could probably be persuaded in that direction, but not today. The captain's in one of his yelling moods. I need to go take some abuse." He gave Raissa a quick kiss. "I'll call you as soon as I run Spencer through the database."

It was forty-two minutes later when Zach pulled up in front of the police station and hurried inside. He'd deal with parking in a tow zone as soon as the captain got done yelling.

"Blanchard!" the captain sounded off before he'd even gotten completely through the doorway. "My office—now!"

Zach saw Detective Morrow smirk as he rushed past his desk, but for once, he didn't even care. He had far bigger fish to fry. Hell, he had the whole Atlantic Ocean of fish to fry. He hurried into the captain's office and closed the door behind him.

The captain was pacing the length of his office and Zach almost ran into the man when he entered the office. "We've got trouble."

Zach felt his pulse rise. The captain's voice was different from when he'd talked to him at the hotel. Something was up. "What kind of trouble?"

"Another missing person."

Zach felt a rush of blood to his head. "You're kidding me. That's not the MO."

"It's not another girl. This is an adult male."

Relief washed over Zach. "Then it's probably not related."

"I know. Likely this has nothing to do with the Franco case, but it's the second goddamned missing person in a week. I'm catching hell all the way around here, Blanchard. I hope that psychic woman was able to give you a lead."

"Nothing solid yet, but there's a couple of things I want to look into."

The captain nodded. "You tell me as soon as you have something. First, I need you to check out this other case. Make sure it has nothing to do with the Francos."

"I don't think that's a good idea. I'd be wasting time when I could be looking into those leads."

"I know that, but you're also the only one in contact with the Bordeaux woman. I want you to see the crime scene so you can relay the details to her. Make sure there's not something in the FBI files that was missed or that we weren't given. I don't want that information second- and thirdhand."

"No problem, sir. I'll get on it right away."

He took the sheet of paper with the crime-scene address on it from the captain and hurried through the station and back to his car. At least he hadn't been there long enough to get towed. He pulled away from the curb, his tires squealing. This was a colossal waste of time. If the captain hadn't been insistent, he'd have found some way to get out of it. He glanced down at the address and turned right at the red light.

Ten minutes later, he pulled up in front of a construction site. An older man and a woman stood out front with a patrolman. They both looked worried. Zach crossed the lawn, displaying his badge as he approached. "I'm Detective Blanchard. What's going on here, B and E?"

The patrolman shook his head. "No sign of forced entry, and nothing missing but the cabinetmaker."

"Maybe he's sick or didn't want to do the job any longer."

"No way," the older man said. He extended his hand. "I'm Chuck Daigle. I own the construction company building this clinic." He waved a hand at the worried woman. "This is Lila Comeaux. She's the owner of the clinic. We both know the man who's missing, and neither of us thinks this is in character. In fact, we'd swear to it."

Zach held in a sigh. He'd heard that all too often. "Any signs of a struggle?"

"No," the patrolman answered, "but there are some irregularities that make me think these two might be right. Let me show you."

Zach followed the patrolman into the clinic and down the hall, Chuck and Lila trailing behind. They stepped into the last room, and the patrolman pointed to a ladder in the corner of the room. "The guy's wallet and keys are on top of that ladder. His truck's out back and hasn't moved from where it was parked yesterday."

"There's more," Chuck said. "The table saw was still plugged in. There was an open can of stain right there in the middle of the floor with the brush right beside it, and from the way the stain was set on top, it had been open for a while. There's no way he just left things like that."

Zach walked around the room, studying the area. Considering it was a construction site, the room was pristine, but then, since he was staining cabinets in this area, it needed to be. He took a look at the cabinets and decided it was probably some of the best workmanship he'd ever seen. Everything about this guy said orderly and dedicated. As much as he hated to admit it, something was wrong with this picture.

"Anyone check where he lives?"

The patrolman nodded. "I sent a guy by there as soon as I saw the scene here. Apartment manager let him in, but the place looks fine. No sign of forced entry and no sign of the guy."

Zach blew out a breath and lifted the wallet from the ladder. "I'll take his wallet and keys, run him through the system . . . see if we can come up with anything. So who is this cabinetmaker?"

"His name is Hank Henry," Chuck said. "He's really been doing a fine job here. Something must be wrong."

Zach froze. Surely, it wasn't the same Hank that Raissa had mentioned last night. The one that Sonny Hebert's men were "watching." He flipped the wallet open and pulled out the driver's license. It was a lousy picture, like most licenses. He needed to run the guy as soon as possible.

The patrolman nodded his head toward Chuck. "Chuck tells me Hank's had some trouble in the past but nothing to speak of since being on-site, until yesterday."

"What happened yesterday?"

"There was a guy," Chuck said. "Looked like he was hassling Hank."

"Did you ask about it?" Zach asked.

"Yeah, but the guy said he was asking for directions, then took off. I don't think it was the truth. The guy . . . well, I don't know how to say this without incriminating myself, but he reminded me of some of the ilk I had to deal with when I first got started in construction. You know the type."

"The type that shake you down for money if you want to stay in business?" Yeah, Zach knew the type, and it was hitting far too close to home.

"Yeah," Chuck said. "I'm not saying that's what was going on, but I don't believe the guy was asking for directions, either."

"Would you recognize the guy if you saw him again?"

Chuck nodded. "I'm pretty sure I would."

"Good. I'll send someone over with some pictures . . . see if you can help us with another angle to investigate. Will you be here all day?"

"Until five or so." He reached into his pocket and handed Zach a card. "Give me a call. If I'm not here, I can meet anywhere to look at the pictures. Doesn't matter what time."

"Great," Zach said, and slipped the card into his pocket. "If there's nothing else I need to see here, I'm going to head back to the station and get working on this." He pulled his cards from his pocket and handed Chuck and Lila each one. "If there's anything you can think of that you forgot to tell me, please call me anytime."

As soon as Zach got into his car, he reached for his laptop and connected with the police database. He typed in Hank's information and waited while the system searched. A couple of seconds later, a clear picture of Hank Henry appeared on the screen. Shit.

He stared at the screen, hoping his initial reaction had been incorrect, but even with a closer look, he knew he wasn't. This was the guy he'd seen going into Raissa's apartment that night. The one she'd met in the alley. He'd completely forgotten about it, with everything else going on. And then it hit him where he'd seen the name before—in the police records on Maryse's many adventures.

Hank Henry was Maryse's ex-husband, son of a murdered ghost.

Knew him secondhand, my ass. Raissa Bordeaux had a lot of explaining to do.

Chapter Seventeen

Raissa walked into the coffee shop in downtown New Orleans wearing blue jeans, a polo shirt, and a black bob. She ordered her usual latte and took a seat in a far corner nearest the exit, where she had a clear view down the street of her shop, and more importantly, Dr. Spencer's office. She saw Helena huff down the sidewalk, then look back and glare. Because Raissa had refused to drop an invisible passenger off in front of the building and wouldn't buy Helena a latte until they left, Helena was pouting.

Raissa grinned at the agitated ghost and wondered if Helen would find anything of interest in Dr. Spencer's office. She rather doubted it. Surely he wasn't stupid enough to keep information on whatever he was mixed up in right there, where a search warrant could find it. But criminals weren't always smart, and Helena was invisible.

Despite Zach's assurances that he'd do a thorough check on their friend Dr. Spencer, Raissa was pretty sure he didn't have clearance for military records. Having Helena check out his office was a long shot, but you never knew what a long shot might turn up.

She opened her laptop, intending to make a list of all the items they'd discovered that didn't add up. Sometimes seeing the facts in print made her mind turn in a different direction, find a connection she hadn't seen before. Instead, she stared at the blank document, her thoughts drifting off to the night before, and Zach.

She'd been stunned when he asked what they were doing. She knew exactly what he wanted to know, but the reality was, she didn't have an answer. At least not one that made it seem anything but cheap and tawdry, and that's not at all how she felt. Zach brought out feelings in her that she'd never felt before. She'd never met anyone else who agonized with what was right and what was policy the way she did. He struggled with everything, as she had before her stint with Sonny.

That stint had changed everything. That and the kidnappings. The bad guys weren't all bad. The good guys and the rules weren't all good. And for the first time in her life, Raissa had had to learn how to live in shades of gray. Some people managed it easily, but Raissa felt it said a lot about a person if they struggled with creating a balance.

She let out a sigh. Not that any of it mattered. The reality was, Raissa's time in New Orleans was fast drawing to an end. One way or another, time was up in two days, assuming the kidnapper stuck to his MO.

Melissa Franco would be back at home with no memory of what had happened and unable to provide them a single lead. And Raissa would quietly disappear.

Again.

Raissa blew out a breath and stared out the plate-glass window across from her table. She'd run before, many times. There had been six other towns, six other identities, and countless other jobs before she'd landed back in New Orleans as Raissa Bordeaux. But this was the first time she'd felt she belonged. She had a job she enjoyed, that challenged her on some level even if it wasn't the thrill ride she was used to. She had all the money she needed from the security gigs, a comfortable apartment, and some of the best friends anyone could ever ask for.

And she had Zach.

Well, *had* was too strong a word, but Raissa liked to believe that if things were different, they might have made a go of it. It had been a long time since Raissa had allowed anyone that close to her. It scared her and excited her and depressed her all at the same time. It was going to be hard to let go . . . of everything.

Her cell phone's ringing yanked her out of her thoughts and she glanced at the display. Zach. That was fast. She opened the phone. "You got information on Spencer already?"

"No," Zach replied, his voice tight and hard. "I have another problem. One I'm hoping you can help me with."

Raissa felt her heart rate speed up. "What's wrong?"

"I was watching your apartment one night, and I saw you with a guy. He was hiding in the alley, but you brought him up to your apartment. I need to know what your relationship is with him."

Raissa frowned, completely confused. "You're in the middle of a kidnapping investigation and you're calling me about some jealous, macho stuff?"

"Give me a break. I'm calling because there was another kidnapping last night, and that guy I saw go into your apartment is the one missing. The same guy you claimed to only know secondhand, remember?"

Raissa clenched her phone. "What happened?"

"Looks like someone snagged him from his work site yesterday evening or last night. He came to see you damned near in the middle of the night, Raissa, and I already ran a check on him. I know all about Hank Henry's past. The construction company owner said some guy was at the site yesterday. He thought the guy was hassling Hank. Who's tailing him?"

"Rico Hebert."

"Damn it! You told me he wasn't involved in the kidnappings."

"I don't think he was."

"Then what did they want from him? The fool didn't learn the first time?"

"It wasn't Hank they wanted. Rico was shaking down Hank for information on me. He told me about it immediately after it happened."

"So that night he came to your place . . ."

"Was the first time I'd ever met him."

"And he thought it would be smart to accost you in an alley? What in the world did he tell you that couldn't wait until the next day?"

Raissa took a deep breath, knowing Zach wasn't going to like that she'd kept this from him. "He told me that one of the Heberts asked him to kill me."

There was dead silence on the other end of the line, and Raissa could practically feel Zach's anger over the phone. "Why didn't you tell me?"

"Because if they'd wanted me dead, I already would be. I think they were sending a warning, hoping I'd pack and leave. They knew Hank was no killer and probably figured he'd tell Maryse, who'd tell me."

"And that's why this Rico kept hassling him? You *did* leave. Why stay on the guy?"

"I don't know for sure. All I can figure is that since Monk mentioned Hank's name before he died, Sonny thinks he knows something about the kidnappings. I think he's got a tail on him to see if it leads anywhere."

"Like figuring out what Monk was into?"

"Exactly."

"And what do you think?"

"I think Hank is clueless. If he saw or heard something he wasn't supposed to, he has no idea what it is. I covered that ground with him already. He's not faking, or I would know."

"So maybe he just owed this Monk money, like he did everyone else in the state."

"Maybe, but then why was he kidnapped? Easier to just put a bullet through his head to leave a message for others who are thinking about banking with the Heberts."

"Shit. This situation is getting out of hand. A missing girl, a missing gambler, a lying doctor, a mayor with a shaky background, and far too many black Cadillacs for my taste."

"I know, I know. I'm trying to make sense of it, but then something else happens and I get even more confused than before. There has to be something we're missing. Did you get the check on Spencer yet?"

"No. I'll run it as soon as I get to the station and tell my captain about Hank. Not that I have any idea what I'm going to say."

"Just tell him what you got from the crime scene and witnesses. We'll figure it out, Zach, I promise. I need to call Maryse. I need to warn her and Mildred to be extra careful."

"Good idea. I'll call as soon as I can. Worry about keeping *yourself* safe, while you're at it."

Raissa disconnected with Zach and dialed Maryse's number. No answer. Damn. She didn't want to panic Mildred or Maryse. This might all amount to a bunch of nothing, even though she had a very bad feeling. Finally, she sent Maryse a text message asking her to call as soon as she got a chance.

She'd use the time in between to get everything down in writing, including this latest bit of trouble. And she'd figure out how to tell Maryse that her ex-husband was missing . . . again.

Ten minutes later, she shut her laptop and looked up to see Helena exiting Spencer's office. She glanced down at her watch. That was fast. She shoved the laptop in her bag and bought a coffee for Helena before leaving the shop to meet her on the street. How in the world was she supposed to tell the ghost that her son was missing? Raissa quickly ran through all the facts she had on Hank and potential scenarios, and finally decided to hold off for now.

They could be wrong. Hank could have fallen off the wagon and gone on a gambling bender and would show up in a day or two. Then she would have worried Helena for nothing.

And if the Heberts have him . . .

Her gut clenched. But it didn't change her decision. If the Heberts had gotten to Hank, then telling Helena now or later wasn't going to change the outcome. She tried to look normal as she hopped into the car. Helena was already sitting in the passenger's seat, gazing longingly at the latte. Raissa passed the cup over and pulled away from the curb.

"You weren't there very long," Raissa said. "Did Spencer show up or something?"

"No. There wasn't a lot to look at."

"What do you mean?"

"The place is almost bare. There's still a receptionist area with all the décor and computers, and the exam room looks like an exam room, but his office is almost wiped clean. No files, no books, no pictures. Did he say anything to you about moving?"

"No. In fact, he told me a couple of months ago that he'd renewed his lease for another three years."

Helena took a huge gulp of coffee and sighed with contentment. "You think he's making a run for it."

"It certainly looks that way."

"But what's he running from?"

Raissa shook her head. "If we had the answer to that, I think we'd blow this whole case wide open."

Maryse looked up as the bells over Sabine's shop door jangled, hoping it was Mildred or Raissa, but instead a petite, pretty blonde woman stepped hesitantly inside. The store had been swamped with business that morning, and the last customer had left only seconds before. Maryse had been hoping to return a call to Raissa, who'd sent her a text message earlier, but so far, there was no sign of a break in store traffic.

Maryse plastered on a smile and walked over to the woman. "Good morning. Can I help you find anything?"

The woman clutched her purse. "I hope so. Are you Maryse Robicheaux?"

Maryse studied the woman's face, trying to figure out if she was supposed to know her, but absolutely nothing came to mind. "Yes, I'm Maryse."

"My name is Lila." She extended her hand. "We've never met, so don't worry about offending me."

Maryse shook her hand. "Was it that obvious?"

"You're Southern. It's sorta a given."

"What can I help you with, Lila? If you're interested in a reading, Sabine will be back next week."

Lila's expression grew serious. "I wanted to talk to you about Hank."

"You know Hank?" Of all the things in the world Maryse figured the woman may want, information on Hank was the last thing that she would have thought of. "You don't look like a bookie, loan shark, or cop."

Lila blushed. "I'm not any of those things. I'm his boss."

"I thought his boss was some guy named Chuck?"

"Chuck is the owner of the construction company, but I'm the owner of the clinic that's being built. Hank's building the cabinets." Lila tucked a strand of hair behind her ear, her hand shaking.

Maryse placed her hand on Lila's arm. The woman was clearly distressed, and if it had anything to do with Hank Henry, she probably had good reason to be. "Let me put out the CLOSED sign and we can talk in the break room. I have tea and coffee and might even be able to stir up something stronger."

Lila gave her a grateful nod. "That would be great."

Maryse flipped the sign in the front window and locked the door. She motioned to Lila and headed to the back of the store to the break room. "Have a seat," Maryse said, and waved a hand at the tiny table and chairs squeezed into one corner of the room. "I'll get us something to drink."

"Oh, I don't want to trouble you." Lila said, and slipped onto a chair in the corner. She sat completely upright, and Maryse could see the stress on her face.

"It's no trouble," Maryse said. "I'd just put on a pot of coffee before you came in. Would you like some? If not, there's soda, water, and tea. Anything stronger and I'd have to make a trip upstairs to Sabine's apartment."

"Coffee would be great."

Maryse poured two cups of coffee and sat them on the table along with a caddy of creamer, artificial sweetener, and sugar. Lila opened a packet of artificial sweetener and added it to her coffee, then began to stir the life out of it.

"You said you wanted to talk about Hank," Maryse prompted.

"Yes, but I really shouldn't bother you. This was a mistake. I just thought . . . But now that I've met you, there's no way . . ."

Maryse placed her hand on Lila's arm. "No way, what? Is something wrong with Hank? Is he in some kind of trouble?"

"He's missing," Lila said, her voice barely a whisper.

"Oh, well," Maryse struggled for the right words since it was clear that the woman was distraught. "Hank's not exactly proven to be reliable in the showing-up-for-things category. In fact, you might say he made a professional career of coming up missing for a couple of years."

Lila nodded. "I know about your relationship—how he ran off and left you to deal with everything alone."

"Really? I didn't know you could get that kind of information in a job interview."

Lila blushed. "I shouldn't tell you this, but I was Hank's counselor when he was in rehab. Please don't let anyone else know. It's not ethical for me to talk about things he said to me at the center."

Maryse leaned back in her chair, her mind trying to process what Lila had said. "Rehab? While I was hunting for him under every cypress tree on the bayou, he was in rehab?"

"Part of the time, yes, and I can tell you that he has a lot of guilt over what he put you through. He stated clearly from the first day of therapy that he was wrong, and you were a wonderful person who didn't deserve to be saddled with someone like him. I know it's hard to believe, given the way he treated you, but Hank has great respect for you. I think that's part of the reason he couldn't bring himself to contact you."

"So it had nothing to do with all his gambling debts I got stuck with, huh? I find that hard to believe."

Lila nodded. "I understand. When Hank first left you, he had gotten in with a rough crowd. Some of them you met when they were trying to collect, but that wasn't the worst of them. He finally realized that his life was headed to an early end, and he checked himself into rehab in Mississippi. It's probably what saved his life."

Maryse sighed. "I guess I don't really have any room to complain anymore, as he sorta took a bullet that was meant for me a month ago."

Lila shook her head. "You have every right to complain. The Hank Henry that you knew wasn't a worthy enough person to have a relationship with anyone, but you have to believe me when I tell you he's changed. He's really trying to do the right thing, and this job is the start of a real future for Hank."

Maryse turned up her hands. "Then if he's really changed and the job is great, why did he take off again? And how do you think I can help you?"

"Chuck and I think Hank was kidnapped."

"What?" Maryse sat straight up in her chair.

"We called the police. They looked things over and agree that it looks suspicious."

"Holy crap. Are there any suspects?" Maryse shook her head. "What am I saying? This is Hank. The list of suspects is the same as his list of creditors."

"There was a guy at the site one day that Chuck didn't like the look of. Hank was talking to him, and Chuck said Hank looked aggravated, but when Chuck asked about it, the guy said he was just asking for directions. Chuck didn't really buy it. He said Hank looked nervous after talking with him, but Chuck didn't press him. He wishes he had pushed, now. He's blaming himself, which is wrong."

"What did the guy look like?"

"Chuck said he had dark hair, dark sunglasses, and drove a black Cadillac."

Maryse felt the color wash from her face. "A black Cadillac? Chuck is sure?"

"Yes. He said he remembers specifically because he
· looked at the car to buy one, but ultimately he didn't
want to pay for it. Why? Is that important?"

"It may be." Maryse studied Lila for a second. The
woman was clearly worried. She'd stirred her coffee
during the entire conversation but had yet to take a
single sip. "I'm just wondering why you're here telling
me all of this."

Lila blushed. "Um, well, one of the days before that,
when Chuck thought he saw the Cadillac, Hank came
in and asked to use his cell phone. He claimed his was
dead, and he needed to call his ex-wife. I guess maybe
we just thought he might have told you something."

"Did you tell the police about that call?"

"No." Lila frowned. "What's going on, Maryse? Do
you know something about Hank that you're not telling me? I saw your face when I mentioned the black
Cadillac. Is Hank in trouble? Is there anything I can
do?"

Maryse stared at her, finally understanding why
Lila was talking to her. "You care about him."

Lila looked down at her coffee. "Well, of course I'm
worried when anyone I know comes up missing."

"That's not what I meant, but I won't push you."
Maryse sighed. "Hank *did* call me that day, but it's not
him that's in trouble, or at least we didn't think it
was. He was stuck in the middle of a situation involving a friend of mine, and he called to warn me so I
would warn her."

"What kind of situation?"

"I can't really tell you much without breaking a confidence, but suffice it to say that some very bad people
are looking for her. I promise you, *she's* above reproach,
but the people who are looking for her are some of the
same people that Hank was involved with before.

They know he was married to me and that she's my friend, so they've been trying to shake him down for information."

"But Hank wouldn't give them what they wanted."

"No, and in all fairness he doesn't know the answers to their questions. We all thought it better if he didn't."

Lila nodded. "That makes sense. You're certain your friend is telling you everything?"

"I'm positive. I can tell you that the local police and the FBI are trying to protect her. This is huge, Lila. She's in a life-threatening situation, and the fallout reaches far beyond her. She's just as unhappy about that and feels guilty as hell, but I promise you, there's nothing she can do about it that is not already being done." Maryse sighed. "I'm sorry I have to be so cryptic, but the police have really forbidden me to talk about anything."

"Please, don't apologize. I understand completely. Well, not really, but I understand why you can't provide me with details. The FBI? Wow. I shudder to think what your friend's gotten in the middle of that rates that kind of attention."

"It's been kinda hairy. That's for sure."

"And the New Orleans police are also aware of this situation?"

"Yes." One of them, anyway.

"Then they'll be able to connect the dots to Hank's disappearance?"

"I will call my contact and make sure that they do, if they haven't already."

"Thank you." Lila opened her purse and pulled out a business card. She wrote a phone number on the back of the card and handed it to Maryse. "The woman that's in danger—if there's anything I can do, please let me know. I have connections with several safe houses."

"Thank you. That's really kind, but you don't know my friend. She doesn't exactly duck things well."

Lila nodded. "If you hear anything that you can share, I'd really appreciate a call. That's my cell number on the back of the card. Call anytime."

"Of course," Maryse said.

Lila rose and Maryse followed her to the front door of the shop and drew back the dead bolt. "It was nice to meet you," Lila said. "I only wish it were under different circumstances."

"Me, too," Maryse said as Lila slipped out the door. At the last minute, Maryse tugged on her sleeve. "He's doing a good thing for my friend. Hank, that is. I want you to know that. You're not wrong in believing he's changed. I believe it, too, and I'm definitely the last person to say something good about him unless it's warranted."

Lila smiled. "Thank you. I'm glad I haven't been wrong."

Maryse closed the door behind her and turned the lock in place. She was officially closed for the day. She pulled the pay-as-you-go cell phone Raissa had gotten her from her pocket and punched in Raissa's number. Things were getting much, much worse.

Chapter Eighteen

It was noon before Raissa and Zach met up at a café in downtown New Orleans. Zach looked stressed, and Raissa couldn't blame him. Ever since he'd told her Hank Henry was missing, she'd only thought the worst. She'd managed to reassure Maryse when she called hours before that Zach was in charge of the investigation and knew everything they did about Hank and the Heberts. Which was practically nothing. Both of them had already agreed to delay telling Helena until they knew something more concrete.

Raissa took a bite of her chicken sandwich, even though food was the last thing on her mind. "So did you get anything on Spencer?"

"Nothing good. Guy's clean as a whistle when it comes to the police database. I figured as much."

"I may have something."

"Oh, yeah? What?"

"I had Helena do a search of Spencer's office. She didn't come back with much."

"How does that help?"

"I mean she *really* didn't come back with much. The place is almost empty."

Zach's eyes widened. "You think he's getting ready to cut out?"

"If he hasn't already. He knows you're looking at him, since you questioned him the other day. He might figure it's only a matter of time before someone connects the dots between him and the parents of the other kidnap victims."

"Damn it. What good does the information do us if we can't use it? I can hardly get a warrant from his home based on military personnel giving Maryse confidential information, and I have zero way of explaining how I know his office is cleared out."

"Maybe we should question Dr. Spencer again. The police could have gotten a subpoena for information, for all he knows, and if he's guilty of something—and it sure as hell looks like he is—the last thing he'd do is go running to the police to tell them about his suspicions that we broke into his office."

"Maybe, but it's a huge risk. If this whole case shakes loose over that information, how am I supposed to justify knowing what to ask him?"

Raissa frowned. He was right, and that frustrated her. Mainly because she hadn't thought that far herself. She was so focused on finding Melissa that she'd forgotten anything that might happen afterward. And while she could probably get away with taking a hit for it, she didn't want to ruin Zach's career.

"I did find something I wanted to run by you," Zach said.

"What's that?"

"You know how the captain has me checking into the mayor's family's background? Well, an interesting thing happened when I tried to get information on Susannah Franco."

"What?"

"She didn't exist until she was eighteen. I find that a little strange, and way too familiar."

Raissa's mind raced with possibilities. "Could have been in witness protection with her parents and taken on another identity when she turned eighteen. Or she could have changed her name for any number of reasons."

"Changing your name doesn't get you a new Social Security number."

"No. So what does her Social Security card say?"

"Susannah Forrester."

"She never changed it after she married. I wonder why."

"I think I can guess," Zach said. "Because Susannah Forrester died thirty years ago."

"Then who is Peter Franco married to?"

Zach shook his head. "I have no idea, and I wonder if Peter Franco does, either. They met in college, and all I can get from teachers and other acquaintances is that she was an only child and the rest of her family is deceased."

"So what are you going to do?"

"The real Susannah Forrester lived in a bayou town on the outskirts of New Orleans. I figure Mrs. Franco had to know her to assume her identity. I'm going there as soon as we finish lunch to poke around. Do you want to ride along?"

Raissa bit her lip, trying to decide. Heck, yeah, she wanted to go, but she'd promised Maryse she'd head back to Mudbug after lunch to check for any Sonny recordings and fill Helena and Mildred in on the situation with Hank. Maryse had sounded panicked when Raissa talked with her earlier, so she knew her friend was hanging on by a thread. "I can't. I've got to get back to Mudbug and handle the Hank issue with Maryse. And Mildred needs her car."

Zach narrowed his eyes at her. "You aren't thinking about questioning Spencer yourself, are you? Because that would be the dumbest thing in the world to do."

Raissa blushed, as it had crossed her mind that

Spencer's office was only a couple of blocks from the café. "No, I'm not thinking about doing that."

Zach stared at her.

"Okay, so I thought about it, but I can't come up with a good enough excuse to do it. I promise I'll go straight to Mudbug."

"And call me when you get there."

"I promise."

"I mean it, Raissa." Zach rose from the booth and leaned over to kiss her hard on the mouth. "You're already taking enough risks. I want you around to see the end."

"The end is what I'm afraid of. We're running out of time."

"We know more now than the FBI ever did. I know it's a jumbled mess, but I'm just as certain that it's all relevant. We'll make sense of it in time to catch them."

Raissa watched him through the plate-glass window of the café until he drove away, then reached for her wallet, tossed some bills on the table, and left. The only good thing so far was that between the stress and giving all her sweets to Helena, she'd lost a couple of pounds.

She'd just gotten in Mildred's car when her cell phone began ringing. She looked at the display. Zach? She flipped open the phone and answered.

"Are you still at the café?"

"No. I just got in my car, why?"

"We have a huge problem."

"What happened?"

"I just got a call—homicide."

Raissa felt the blood rush from her face. "Oh, no. Not Hank."

"No. Dr. Spencer."

Shit. Raissa banged one hand on the steering wheel. "There goes our best lead."

"That's not the half of it. His body's in your store. I'm headed over there now. I know you don't want to run into Fields, and I can't promise you they won't ask me to hold you in custody until they figure this out, but I think you should get over there."

"I'll be there in a minute." She started the car and pulled onto the street, tires squealing. What the hell was Spencer doing in her shop? Who had killed him? And how? The questions outweighed the answers by a mile. It seemed that the closer they got to the truth, the more convoluted everything became.

The usually calm street was filled with vehicles, most of them with flashing lights. Raissa parked a block away and started up the sidewalk to her shop. A patrolman stopped her at the end of the block. "This is a crime scene, ma'am. No one's allowed past at this time."

Raissa pulled out her license to show the patrolman. "Your crime scene is in my shop. I got a call from a Detective Blanchard."

The patrolman checked her license and nodded. "Right this way, Ms. Bordeaux. I'll take you to the detective."

The patrolman waved at another officer to take his position and escorted her to her shop. There was a crowd of people outside, and as they stepped to the door, the paramedics came out, pulling the gurney. The body was completely covered.

"Wait," she said and stopped the paramedics. "May I?" She motioned to the body.

The patrolman nodded, and the paramedic pulled back the sheet to expose Dr. Spencer, with a clean bullet hole in the middle of his forehead.

The paramedic pulled the sheet back over Spencer's body and wheeled it onto the ambulance. The ambulance driver turned off the lights and they pulled away. No sense in hurrying on this one. Raissa turned and followed the patrolman into her store.

Zach stood next to the counter, talking to a member of the forensics team. He saw her come in and broke off his conversation to walk over. He thanked the patrolman, then pulled her to the back of the store to a section with the shape of a body taped on the floor. "He had a screwdriver, so we figure he was trying to open this door. That's the stairs to your apartment, right?"

"Yeah." Raissa shook her head. "But what was the point? Why come after me? You're the police. I'm just the nut who owns the psychic shop."

"Yeah, but you were with me when I questioned him, so he knows you're involved, and that's not all. We found his car in the parking garage behind his office. A black Cadillac."

Raissa stared at him. "No way. It's Sonny's guys following me. We know that. And besides, Spencer's name wasn't on the DMV list."

"It's registered to his wife." Zach glanced around and leaned his head toward her. "It has a bullet hole in the trunk," he whispered.

Raissa didn't know what to think. "Dr. Spencer tried to run me off the road? How did he even know to find me in Mudbug? He doesn't know any of my friends. He'd never know to look for me there."

"That is a damned good question, unless it was Spencer who put the tracking device on your car."

"But why? We questioned him after he tried to run me off the road. After I'd already figured out the trace was installed."

Zach shook his head. "I don't know what's going on

here, but I don't like it. It smacks of a professional hit, which smacks of your friends the Heberts. Maybe you're wrong about Sonny being involved. Or maybe some of Sonny's family is into business he doesn't know about. All I know is that witnesses said the shot was fired from the driver's side of a black Cadillac driving down the street. Now, how many people do you know who can land a bullet right between a guy's eyes while driving?"

"Not many. What are we going to do? Spencer was the best lead we had."

"Which is probably the main reason he's dead. I'm going to call the captain about getting a search warrant for Spencer's office and home, but it won't happen immediately. Meantime, I'm calling in Morrow to cover this."

Raissa frowned.

"I know, he's a dickhead, but he's also an idiot. With any luck, he won't find any evidence that incriminates you in all this."

"So what are you going to do?"

"I'm going to continue with my original plan to check up on Susannah Franco. Someone close to the Francos bypassed that alarm system. I originally thought it was the mayor, but now I wonder. Anyway, get the hell out of here before someone else decides to question you."

"Okay, wait," Raissa said, confused. "Won't your captain have a stroke if you let me get away?"

"He sorta sanctioned contact with you in order to get leads on the kidnapping case."

"Sorta?"

"Yeah, as in, I'm allowed to contact you as long as I don't get caught. Then, my guess is, he wouldn't know anything about it."

"Then I guess I'll sorta get the hell out of here before I make things even messier."

"Get back to Mudbug and close yourself in somewhere safe. I'll call you as soon as I have some information on Susannah Franco."

Raissa hurried back down the block, her head low so maybe no one would remember what she looked like and associate her with Zach, at least not right away. None of this made sense. Why had Spencer tried to kill her? Was he tied to the Heberts? And who had taken Hank Henry and for what reason? Even more important, where was he now?

The first thing she needed to do was check the feed from Sonny's. If Sonny's men had anything to do with Spencer's murder, she'd be able to hear all about it, provided they were in Sonny's office. She got into her car and headed back to Mudbug as fast as Mildred's ancient sedan would allow.

Zach's phone rang the instant he climbed into his car. He knew it was the captain without even looking at the display. He could swear that even the ring had a desperate, angry sound to it. He pressed the button to answer and the captain's voice boomed out, making him wince.

"Damn it, Blanchard! What the hell is going on? You tell me this morning that you don't have any leads to speak of, then the doctor you questioned about Melissa Franco turns up dead in the psychic woman's shop. I guess you've got plenty of leads now. What I want from you are some answers."

"I wish I had them, Captain. All I can tell you is that it looks like Spencer's been stalking Ms. Bordeaux, but neither of us know why."

"How do you know that the Bordeaux woman didn't kill him herself? Maybe they were having an affair.

Maybe she thought he'd kidnapped the kid, and she's lost it from so many years of hiding out."

"I'm sure that's not the case, sir."

"How can you be sure?"

"Because when Spencer was shot, I was sitting in a café with Ms. Bordeaux having lunch. And witnesses saw a black Cadillac, not an old tan sedan. It wasn't her, but it has all the signs of a hired hit."

"Which puts us right back to the fucking Heberts."

"It looks that way."

"So would you like to tell me why you called Morrow to take over for you on the hottest piece of evidence that we've got so far?"

"I'm tracking down some background information on Susannah Franco."

"Please don't tell me the mother has anything to do with the disappearance of her own child."

"Okay, I won't tell you that, but I have to wonder."

"Wonder about what?"

"Why the Social Security number Susannah Franco's been using belongs to a woman that died over thirty years ago."

There was dead silence on the other end of the phone, and for a moment, Zach wondered if the captain had finally had that heart attack he kept threatening the department with. "Sir, are you still there?"

"Yeah, but I'm starting to wonder for how much longer. Jesus H. Christ, Blanchard. You call me as soon as you have any information on the Franco woman. I'll make sure the detail watching her doesn't let her out of their sight. Is there anything else that can pile onto this case?"

"As a matter of fact, remember that kidnapping you sent me on this morning?"

"Yeah, the adult male. So? Probably out on a bender."

"I don't think so."

"Do I even want to know?"

"The guy was a friend of a friend of Ms. Bordeaux's and an ex-associate of the Heberts. He warned Ms. Bordeaux earlier this week that one of the Heberts asked him to kill her."

"Blanchard. I've changed my mind."

"About what, sir?"

"Don't call me again. When I can handle it, I'll call you."

Forty minutes later, Zach was perched on a hard chair covered in hideous fabric and sipping tea from china cups with Magdalena LeBlanc, Susannah Forrester's old friend and neighbor. Zach took a sip of the tea and tried not to grimace. Why in the world did people actually like that crap? "So, Ms. LeBlanc, did Susannah have any children?"

"Oh, heavens, no. Susannah was an old maid, like me. That's why we were such fabulous friends. Neither of us had others to answer to once our parents passed away. Why, we were fancy-free and living the life."

Zach smiled. "Sounds like a good life."

"Oh, it was the best, up until Susannah got sick. Breast cancer. Wasn't testing then like there is today. Why, she just wasted away. It's such a shame."

"I'm very sorry to hear that. I'm sure you miss her."

"Every single day. So tell me, what's a New Orleans detective doing all the way out in the boonies asking about Susannah?"

"Her name came up in a case I'm working on as a possible relative to a suspect. I thought maybe if she had kids . . . But looks like I'm out of luck."

"She never had her own kids, but she had a niece she

was very fond of. Used to send her money from time to time."

"Do you remember the niece's name?"

"Annabelle was her name. Annabelle Forrester. Her father was Susannah's brother, who died in the war."

"Did Annabelle have any children?"

"Oh, I don't know. After Susannah passed away, I never saw her again. She'd just recently married before Susannah's death, but I don't recall anyone telling me the young man's name. I'm really sorry I can't be more help."

Zach rose from his chair and took her hands in his. "You've been a great help, Ms. LeBlanc. Thank you for your time and the tea."

Zach left the house and hopped into his car. If Annabelle Forrester had married and had a child, she might have named that child after her favorite aunt. He'd passed the courthouse on the way into town. He'd try to find a marriage license and birth record there.

Chapter Nineteen

Raissa burst into her hotel room and ran straight to the laptop linked to Sonny's house. She sat down at the table and clicked to start the audio file. Sonny's voice was the first thing she heard.

"How the hell could you let this happen, Rico?" Sonny yelled. "You were supposed to stay on Hank Henry until I said otherwise."

"I *was* on Hank. He went back inside the work site. I had the GPS on his truck, so I drove around the block and picked up something to eat. I wasn't even gone ten minutes."

"Apparently, ten minutes is all it took for him to disappear. You are going to make this right, Rico."

"How am I supposed to do that?"

"You're going to put out word to every family member, bookie, prostitute, and bum in New Orleans that we're looking for Hank. Someone had to see something. If anyone gives you information that leads us to Henry, I'll pay ten g's."

"Ten grand for Hank Henry? You gotta be kidding me."

"Just do it, Rico."

The sound of the door shutting echoed over the computer; then Raissa heard Sonny slam his hands down on his desk, as she'd seen him do so many times. And that was all of the recording.

She checked the time—four hours before. Sonny's guys had a four-hour jump on trying to locate Hank.

Not that it mattered. Raissa didn't have the network that Sonny had. But why did Sonny want him so badly? There had to be a reason, but damned if Raissa could come up with anything that made sense.

She needed her files, and they were in the trunk of Mildred's car. Surely there was something in those files that would connect the dots. They were so close. Raissa could feel it. She checked the monitors, but all she saw in the alley was the city garbage truck, making its weekly pickup. She grabbed Mildred's car keys and headed out the back of the hotel, pulling the door shut behind her. The sun was already setting behind the row of cypress trees on the west side of town, reducing the sunlight to a dim glow on the alley between the hotel and the garage.

She hurried across the alley in front of the garbage truck and slipped the garage key into the lock. The garbage truck passed and she heard the footsteps behind her, but before she could reach for her weapon, a hand grabbed her shoulder and spun her around. Looking directly at Sonny Hebert, Raissa realized she'd made the miscalculation that might cost her her life.

"Don't yell," he said in a low voice. "I can't afford for anyone else to notice me. I'm sure the garbageman already thinks I'm crazy for following that stinking truck down the alley, but I knew if you were staying here you'd have cameras."

Raissa nodded, her heart pounding as if it would beat out of her chest. She wondered if this was how it was all going to end—in an alley behind the Mudbug Hotel.

"I hear a friend of yours is missing," Sonny said. "He's in a warehouse on Canal Street. A brown building with blue stripes. You've got about two hours before he's removed."

"Removed?"

Sonny glanced nervously over his shoulder. "Yeah, and I'm afraid this time might be permanent."

"This time?"

"Shhhh. I can't tell you everything, because I don't know all of it. What I do know is if you want to see him again, you better get over there now." He whirled around, hurried down the alley. A couple of seconds later a nondescript late-model sedan passed the end of the alley, with Sonny at the wheel. He barely slowed and cast one glance at her, then drove away.

Raissa dug into her pocket for her cell phone. She didn't realize her hands were shaking until she pressed in Zach's name. "I'm going to a warehouse building on Canal Street. One with blue stripes. I just got a tip that Hank Henry is being held there, but we have to move fast to get him." Raissa jumped into her car and fired up the engine.

"What the hell?" Zach said. "Where did you get this tip?"

"Sonny Hebert," Raissa said as she hopped into her car and pulled away from the curb, her tires screeching. "And since I'm still alive I can only assume he's not interested in killing me. At least not right now."

"How do you know the whole thing isn't a setup to get you somewhere that he can kill you?"

"I don't, which is why I need you to meet me there. I'll be there in forty-five minutes."

"No fucking way! I'm more than forty-five minutes away. Don't go there, Raissa."

"Too late, I'm already on my way. Your choice, Detective." She disconnected the call and pressed the accelerator. Her cell phone buzzed at her from the passenger's seat, but she let it ring, choosing to concentrate on driving well beyond the speed limit without killing herself.

Zach would be there. He wouldn't let her walk into something she might not walk out of.

She hoped.

Zach cursed when Raissa disconnected, and it was all he could do not to fling the phone against a wall. Not that he could afford to do that at the moment. Likely he was going to need it soon to call for backup, an ambulance, or the coroner. He was about an hour outside of Baton Rouge, which put him at almost the same distance from the warehouse as Raissa, but already behind her in travel time.

The county clerk who'd been helping him locate documents slid a couple of sheets of paper across the counter toward him. "These are the records you were looking for, Detective Blanchard. Do you want to pay the fifty cents or would you like me to bill the New Orleans police department?"

Zach punched in Raissa's number and waited until it went to voice mail. "Damn it!"

The clerk stared at him in surprise.

"I'm sorry," he apologized, "but I have an emergency." He tossed a five-dollar bill on the counter for the copies, grabbed the papers, and ran out the door, yanking his keys from his pocket as he crossed the street. He tore out of the parking lot and was doing eighty miles per hour by the time he hit the interstate.

He dialed the station. "Captain, I need backup to a warehouse with blue stripes on Canal Street. I got a tip that Hank Henry is being held there."

"Where on Canal Street?"

"I don't know."

"Damn it. That street's miles long."

"Tell them to start on the north side. I'll start on the south." He dropped the cell phone into the passenger's seat, and only then did he remember the copies. He grabbed them from the passenger's seat and looked at them. The first was a marriage license for Annabelle Forrester and Franklin Marsella. The second was a birth certificate for Susannah Forrester Marsella. Too much of a coincidence not to somehow be related to the missing Monk.

Zach felt his blood run cold. The mayor's daughter-in-law was the Hebert connection, not the mayor. He reached for his cell phone, ready to call the captain back with this bit of information, but stopped. The captain had already made it clear he didn't want more clues with no connecting dots, and right now, keeping Raissa safe was his priority. He'd tell the captain about his suspicions concerning the mayor's daughter-in-law once he'd made sure Raissa was okay and they'd found Hank Henry. He pressed the accelerator down even farther and prayed that he got to the warehouse in time.

Thirty-five minutes later, he turned the corner on the south end of Canal Street, frantically scanning the street for any sign of Raissa. He felt a wave of relief when he saw Mildred's car parked in front of a ware-house building just like the one she'd described, but Raissa was nowhere in sight. He jumped out of his car, pulled out his weapon, and hurried toward the ware-house entrance, scanning the street as he went. There were no other cars in sight and the entire area seemed completely abandoned.

The perfect place to commit a crime.

He slipped through the open door and looked down at the dusty floor. Prints led in different directions, but the majority broke off to the right. He crept down a long hallway, following the footprints, checking each room as he passed an open doorway. At the end of the warehouse, he looked into the last room and felt relief wash over him when he saw a very alive Raissa. Then a closer look revealed her hovering over a not-so-alive-looking Hank Henry, and his pulse began to race again.

Raissa looked up as he entered the room. "I've already called an ambulance. They should be here any minute."

Zach looked down at the pale man laid out on what appeared to be a hospital gurney. "He's alive?"

"Yeah, but I think he's drugged or something, and he looks really weak. Give me your handcuff key."

Zach looked confused for a moment until Raissa lifted Hank's right hand. He was handcuffed to the bed. Zach passed his key ring to Raissa and began to walk the room. "Did you see anyone when you got here?"

"No one. The street was as empty as the warehouse. But he didn't get here, chained to a hospital bed, by himself."

"No. Definitely not." Zach ran one hand across a window seal, then looked down at the floor and frowned. "This room has been cleaned. Spotless, as a matter of fact."

Raissa nodded. "Yeah, I noticed that. They're careful."

Zach shook his head. "You don't have to disinfect a room to remove prints, and I doubt even the best forensics team would find much, given the dust in the rest of the building."

"I don't think it was to erase evidence."

Zach looked over at her. "Why else then?"

Raissa looked down at Hank and bit her lip. "I think he's in a hospital bed for a reason. I think maybe they were going to do something to him. Medically."

Zach stared. "You think someone sterilized this room to perform a medical procedure? Jesus, does he have any incisions?" Theft of body organs was fairly rare, but it still happened.

"No incisions. It's the first thing I checked. It looks like everything is intact." Raissa looked up at Zach, a grim look on her face. "Maybe they hadn't gotten to the surgery part yet. Maybe that's what Sonny meant when he told me Hank would be removed."

Zach felt his face flush with anger. "Sonny Hebert has some explaining to do. I ought to go arrest him, now."

"Don't."

"Give me one good reason why not."

"I overheard a conversation between Sonny and Rico. Sonny's men put word out on the street this morning that Sonny would pay ten grand if anyone could tell him where Hank was."

"Why would he offer the money, then tell you?"

"I don't know. But I get the impression that Sonny knows or at least suspects something about what's going on here, though he isn't involved. Not directly, anyway. Even if that's the case, he took a big risk telling me where to find Hank, which tells me that whatever is going on is too reprehensible for even Sonny to let pass. He may be the only person who can lead us to the answer. If you lock him up, he won't be able to instruct his men."

"I can damn well demand the answer."

Raissa shook her head. "Strong-arming Sonny is the fastest way to get him to dig in his heels. He has to think he's running the show. It's the only way he operates. If you put the pressure on him, he'll back out of this whole mess, and I don't know what might happen then. To Melissa."

"Yeah, that's the part that worries me the most." Zach told Raissa about the marriage license and birth certificate.

Raissa stared at him, stunned. "Susannah Franco is related to Monk Marsella? So Monk was kidnapping the girls, and Susannah is related to Monk. But now Monk's gone and so is Susannah's daughter. What are we missing here?"

"I don't know. Damn it!" Zach paced back and forth across the room. "Do you think Sonny knows what happened to Melissa?"

"I think he has suspicions, but I don't think he knows where to find her. Sonny would never tolerate someone hurting a child."

"Great. A mobster with morals."

"I know how much you hate it, Zach, but you have to trust me on this one. I *know* Sonny Hebert, better than most people. You can't force him into anything or you'll lose. For whatever reason, he's looking into this kidnapping, and I have to tell you, he's likely to get results faster than we can."

Sirens sounded outside the warehouse and Zach glanced outside to see the paramedics hurrying into the building. "Back here!" he shouted, and waved them to the back room.

He looked over at Raissa, who stood to the side while the paramedics loaded Hank onto the gurney. Her expression was filled with fear and worry. Not that he blamed her. This case had thrown him more curveballs than opening day at Yankee Stadium.

Alien kidnappings, fugitive FBI agents, unauthorized medical procedures, and Sonny Hebert being helpful.

What the hell had they gotten involved in?

* * *

Dr. Breaux was leaving Hank's room as Raissa and Zach made their way down the hall. Raissa closed her cell phone, having just finished telling Maryse to spread the word that Hank had been found and was safe, and that she'd call back as soon as she'd spoken with Dr. Breaux. Zach flashed his badge and Dr. Breaux nodded and motioned them over to the side.

"I'm Dr. Breaux," he said, and extended his hand to Zach. He nodded at Raissa. "Good to see you again, Raissa. I hear Sabine returns tomorrow."

"I'm looking forward to it. How's Hank?"

"Fine. In fact, he's in excellent condition. I can't find any indication of trauma—his vital signs are perfect. I don't understand what's going on here. Can you tell me anything?"

Raissa hesitated. She looked over at Zach, who took over. "All we really know, sir, is that Hank was reported missing from his job this morning but was likely taken sometime yesterday evening. As for what happened after that, we were hoping you might give us a clue."

"His medical condition doesn't tell me anything at all. There's a small puncture mark on his left arm, but that could be anything. Where did you find him?" Dr. Breaux asked. "All the paramedics could tell me is that he was unconscious when they picked him up. Was he on another job?"

"No," Zach replied. "He was found in an abandoned warehouse. The room Hank was kept in was totally sterilized, and I found him handcuffed to a hospital bed. He wasn't conscious."

Dr. Breaux stared at him, then glanced at Raissa. "But that's just crazy. You're serious about this?"

"Yes, sir. I would never joke about a kidnapping."

"Well . . . I guess I just don't know what to say. I mean, I've heard of organ harvesting, of course, but it's one of those things you never think you're going to actually come in contact with. Especially among your living patients."

"So you think that's what was going on?" Zach asked.

Dr. Breaux frowned, obviously confused. "What else could it be? Why sterilize an area? Why chain a healthy man to a hospital bed? That puncture mark on his arm makes a lot more sense now if you assume someone kept him drugged or on an IV."

"You've got a point," Zach agreed. "Someone went to Hank's job site prepared to abduct him without a fight, which means it was all planned. The question is, who planned it and why Hank Henry?"

"How did you happen to find him?" Dr. Breaux asked.

"An anonymous tip," Zach said. "One of those things that rarely works out but this time turned out to be true."

"But you have no way of tracing the source?" Dr. Breaux questioned. "Surely, the police have methods of identifying that sort of thing."

"If it's a phone call or e-mail, sometimes, although technology still allows for the high-tech person to work around the system. But this was a note delivered by a kid on the street. He couldn't identify the man who gave it to him."

Raissa's eyes widened at Zach's story, but she had to admire his ability to make up something believable on the fly. The less anyone knew about Sonny Hebert and Raissa, the better.

Dr. Breaux shook his head. "Well, I wish I could help more, but there's simply nothing about Hank that can tell me what might have happened to him."

"Is he conscious?"

"Yes, but he says he doesn't remember anything."

"Damn," Zach said.

"You've got your work cut out. I understand."

Zach nodded. "Can we talk to him?"

"Sure. I'm keeping him overnight for observation just because of the circumstances, but there's not really anything wrong with him that I can find, except he's a little woozy from whatever they gave him. Should have the tox screen back in a couple of hours."

Zach pulled one of his business cards from his pocket and gave it to Dr. Breaux. "When you get the tox screen back, please give me a call."

"Of course," Dr. Breaux said, and slipped the card in the pocket of his hospital coat. "If that's all you need, I have a couple more patients to check on."

"Yes, thank you," Zach said, and motioned Raissa toward Hank's room.

Hank was propped up in bed when Zach and Raissa entered the room. Raissa was relieved to see the color was back in his face, and Hank looked equally relieved to see her.

Raissa walked over to the bed and sat on the side. "I'm glad to see you in one piece."

Hank nodded. "Same goes for you." Hank looked as if he wanted to say more, but he cast a nervous glance at Zach, then back at Raissa.

"Oh, sorry," Raissa said and point to Zach. "This is Detective Blanchard. He's a friend of mine. You can trust him."

"Then I guess he'll do." Hank gave her a small smile. "Would you mind passing me a bit of water? I wasn't in the mood to be waited on when the nurse was in earlier, but she says I need to take these." He lifted a disposable cup with two pills in it.

"Sure," Raissa said, and poured water from a pitcher

into a paper cup. "Pain meds?" she asked as she passed the cup to Hank.

Hank tossed the pills in his mouth and drank the cup of water. "No. I don't have any pain to speak of. Just kinda weak. They gave me a vitamin B shot and some iron pills. Said it should perk me back up in a bit."

"That's great news. I was really worried when I saw you unconscious. I had no way of knowing what they'd done to you."

Hank nodded. "That makes two of us. When I came to, here in the hospital, I was afraid that the men who were looking for you had gotten to you. I haven't told Sonny's men anything, but they haven't let up with the questions."

"I know you haven't said anything," Raissa said, "and I honestly think Sonny has those men asking questions just to keep me on edge. They've known where to find me all along."

"How do you know?"

"Because Sonny and I had a little chat in the alley behind the Mudbug Hotel."

Hank's eyes widened. "Holy shit! How are you still breathing?"

Raissa shook her head. "I think Sonny has a bigger problem than me, but for the life of me, I can't figure out how it all ties together. He's the one who told me where to find you."

Hank sat up straight in bed. "No way!"

"Yeah, I thought it was crazy, too." Raissa thought about the scene with Sonny outside of the shop and shook her head. "It was weird, Hank. He was alone, I'm sure of it, but he was jumpy, like he was afraid somebody was watching. I've never seen Sonny jumpy. Not even the possibility of the feds watching him made him flinch in the past."

Hank nodded. "That's true. The man has balls of steel."

"Until now. We need to figure out what's going on. Dr. Breaux said you couldn't remember anything. Did you even see your attacker?"

Hank looked down at his lap, a blush creeping up his neck. "I remember one thing, but I didn't want the doc to think I was crazy."

Raissa felt her pulse quicken and would have bet money that she knew exactly what Hank was about to say. "Who was it, Hank?"

Hank looked up at her, his expression completely bewildered. "I was abducted by an alien."

Chapter Twenty

Mildred, Maryse, Luc, and Helena were waiting for Raissa and Zach at the Mudbug Hotel. Zach was introduced to Luc, and with the pleasantries out of the way, they all crowded into the kitchen in the back. Mildred passed around coffee, water, and anything stronger if someone wanted it. Zach chose stronger. It wasn't as if he was driving afterward, and the things he'd seen that day warranted a stiff drink.

"Somebody say something," Helena complained. "I want to know what happened to my son."

"Helena's getting restless," Maryse said. "Can someone please give her the four-one-one on Hank?"

Zach started for a moment before he realized Maryse was talking about the ghost. He looked around at the group of people, but no one else seemed fazed. "Can all of you see her?" he asked, unable to help himself.

"Everyone but me," Luc said. "At least, not anymore. I was able to see her for a week. That was enough."

"I don't understand a bit of this," Zach said, "but my mind's too full to absorb it all. Raissa, why don't you fill them in."

"For starters, as I said to Maryse when I called, Hank is fine. He's a little weak, but he wasn't hurt. The New Orleans police are grilling him now, but you should be able to see him in an hour or so." Then Raissa went on to tell the crowd about Sonny's tip and how she found Hank, the conversation with Dr. Breaux, and lastly, their conversation with Hank.

"Aliens?" Luc stared at Raissa. "What the hell have you and my wife been up to? I swear I can't leave for a couple of days."

Everyone laughed except Zach, who sorta knew how he felt. He couldn't even leave Raissa alone for a couple of *hours* or things went sideways.

Raissa and Maryse took turns filling everyone in on the investigation and the alien connection. There were many gasps and dropped jaws, and a fair amount of cussing.

"It's so outrageous," Mildred finally said. "I just hope it all ends soon. I pray for normal every night when I go to bed."

Maryse tugged at Luc's sleeve and said, "Helena wants to go to the hospital and see Hank. Let's take her now, then go home. I'm exhausted."

Zach and Raissa made their way upstairs to Raissa's room. "I was thinking of picking up a couple of shrimp sandwiches from the restaurant, okay?" Raissa asked as they walked into the room.

"That's great. I'm starving." Zach pulled his cell phone from his pocket. "I need to call the captain and tell him about Susannah Franco."

"You're doing that tonight?"

"Yeah. He'll send someone into the office tonight to make the family tree add up first, but he'll want to put the screws to her in the morning. He'll just have to figure out an angle to use, as no one but you ever suspected Monk Marsella as the original kidnapper."

"All he really has to say is that there were discrepancies in her background and they want answers."

"True. I'll suggest that. I told her they were all 'persons of interest' as far as the investigation went, and that it was standard protocol. She shouldn't be surprised."

"Probably not. I'm going to hop in the shower, then go get the sandwiches. I want to go over the girls' files again after that. There's something at the back of my mind, but it's not clear."

"Did Hank's situation make you remember something?"

Raissa frowned. "No, but I just have this feeling that there's something I should know, and it hasn't clicked."

Zach nodded. "Then we'll go over the files until it does."

"Two more days," Raissa said, and sighed before heading into the bathroom.

Two more days to find Melissa Franco or the kidnapper would get away with it again.

Lila knocked softly on Hank's hospital-room door, not wanting to disturb him if he was sleeping. There was no answer, but the door was ajar, so she pushed it open and peeked inside. The room was dim, with only a night-light shining at the side of the bed. She started to walk inside, then realized there was an older woman sitting at the side of the bed, her hand over Hank's. Lila heard faint singing that sounded like a lullaby.

She stepped back, not wanting to interrupt, and almost collided with Maryse. "Oh, I'm so sorry," she said.

"No problem. Are you here to see Hank?"

"Yes, but I didn't want to disturb him. I peeked in, but he's sleeping, and there's another woman in there."

Maryse frowned. "There's no one else here that I know of." Maryse stepped by her and pushed open the door. She looked back at Lila. "There's no one here."

Lila stepped into the room and looked around.

Maryse was right—it was empty except for Hank. Lila sighed. "I must be losing it."

"Trust me, I know the feeling. The lighting in here's not all that great, either."

"Is it all right to see him? I mean, I'm not interrupting anything . . ."

Maryse waved a hand in dismissal. "Not at all. My husband's waiting for me in the car outside. I just checked in with the nurse and everything's fine." She smiled at Lila. "I'm sure he'll be happy to see you. I've got to run." She walked down the hall with a wave over her shoulder.

Lila took a deep breath and stepped into the room. As she approached the bed, Hank stirred and opened his eyes. "I thought I heard something. Were you singing?"

Lila shook her head. "I just got here, but I heard singing, too." She looked around the room but didn't see anything that could have created the noise.

"Probably in another room or something," Hank said.

"You're probably right." Lila stood at the side of his bed, fiddling with the bottom button on her blouse. "You don't know how happy I am to see you."

Hank reached up and took her hand in his and pulled her toward the bed. "Have a seat and relax." He smiled at her. "It's hard to see you so far away. Everything's still a little fuzzy."

She sat on the side of his bed and studied him as he pushed himself up to a sitting position. "How do you feel? Did they catch the guy who did this? Maryse called, but she didn't have any details, other than that you were fine."

Hank felt his heart leap into his throat at the concern in Lila's face. He swallowed once and tried to keep his emotions from his voice. Lila was his client and used to be his therapist. Even though she'd agreed to go to dinner with him the last time he'd seen her, the fact that she was visiting him in a hospital after his kidnapping was a clear indication that he had no business involving someone like Lila in his sordid life. At least, not on a personal level.

Keep things professional. "I feel fine, just a little tired. I don't think they've caught the guy. I don't know how they could, as I have no earthly idea who did it."

Lila gave him a worried look. "Chuck said a guy had been hanging around the site. He thought he saw him hassling you the night you disappeared, but said you passed it off as nothing. Based on his description, it sounded like someone from your past."

Hank sighed. "It *was* someone from my past, but I don't think that's who took me. The guy who took me bypassed a locked door and managed to creep up behind me without me hearing. He stuck me with a needle. I got the impression that he was taller than me. The other guy is shorter and not sneaky at all."

Lila bit her lip. "But he was hassling you? And he has friends, right?"

"Yeah, I guess he could have gotten someone else, but I'm not involved in anything. I swear."

"I went to Mudbug and talked to Maryse. Chuck said you called her one day with his phone, and I guess we hoped she might know something that could help. I hope you don't mind."

"I don't mind at all. It's nice that you and Chuck were trying to help. So what did you think about my ex?"

Lila laughed. "I think you were right saying you were crazy to let her get away. I think she's great."

Hank nodded. "She is, just not great for me. I see it

now, but at the time, I guess I thought she could save me. I was wrong for using her that way. I'm still hoping she forgives me someday."

"I think she already has. So do you think this was about her friend?"

"I don't know. The guy Chuck saw had been trying to get information on Maryse's friend, especially after she turned up missing from her apartment and business."

"Why does he want her?"

"I honestly have no idea," Hank said. "I warned her after the first visit, and she disappeared afterward. I called Maryse when Rico started coming around the job site. I borrowed Chuck's phone for the call in case they were tracing mine. I never asked why they were after her, and I don't want to know. It's safer that way."

Lila nodded but still looked worried. "That's what Maryse said. But even though you didn't know anything, the guy kept coming back. Why didn't he just look somewhere else?"

"That's not the way these guys work. They think if they put pressure on you, you'll figure out a way to get them what they want, even if you don't have it. They like shortcuts."

"This woman is still in danger then. Is there any way I can help?"

Hank looked at Lila, unable to keep the smile from his face. "You're really something, you know. You know the kind of guys I'm talking about, and here I was kidnapped right after a run-in with them, and you're worried about the woman they're after. You're a wonderful person, Lila. Probably the most wonderful person I've ever known."

Lila blushed and stared down at the floor. "I'm just

trying to do the right thing. It's no more than anyone else would do."

Hank used one finger to lift her chin until he was looking her eye to eye. "It's more than most people would do, especially for a stranger, and you know it." He looked at her a moment longer and tried to command his racing heart to still. He knew what he was about to do was a horrible idea, but for whatever reason, his mind simply couldn't convince his body to agree.

He leaned forward and pressed his lips to hers, fully expecting her to pull away. Instead she lifted one hand to his cheek and kissed him back, a soft lingering kiss that made him warm all over. He pulled back a bit and looked at her.

She sighed and smiled. "I thought you'd never kiss me."

Hank stared at her. "You wanted me to kiss you?"

"Of course. I would have liked to have dinner with you, too, but it looks like you're going to have to take a rain check, as I'm not really fond of hospital food."

Hank stared at her in disbelief. "I just never figured . . . I'm sorry, but I don't think you should be involved with me. Look at all the shit—stuff—that just happened, and I don't even know why." He shook his head. "No, that's wrong. I know why. It's because of who I was. If I'd never been that person, these things wouldn't be happening to me now. It still all comes back to my bad choices. I'm not an innocent."

"You can try to run me off, Hank Henry, but you'll find I'm tougher than you think. What about the woman in danger? Does Maryse know if she's safe?"

"She's not only safe, she's the one who rescued me."

Lila gasped. "Then it did have something to do with her."

Hank shook his head. "We don't know. That's the really weird part. This guy who's been looking for her is the one who told her where to find me, but he was all secretive, like he didn't want anyone to know."

"So his men took you, then he changed his mind?"

"I don't think so. I mean, I could be totally wrong, but I think there's something major going on here. Like I said, I don't ask questions, and I'm guessing I wouldn't get many answers even if I did."

"I asked Maryse about her. All Maryse would say is the woman was above reproach and that the right people were trying to protect her."

Hank nodded. "Yeah, she came to the hospital courtesy of a New Orleans detective who was looking at her like anything but a suspect. I think she's in good hands."

"Maryse said the feds were looking into things, too." She sat up straight and stared at Hank. "Do you think she's a fed?"

Hank stared at Lila in surprise. "You know, she's tough and smart and clearly not under arrest. And she knows how to handle a weapon. I've seen that firsthand." He shook his head. "Damn if you're not onto something. Her being a fed would explain everything."

"Well, maybe not everything, but probably a whole lot."

"A fed. I bet that's it. No wonder everyone's tiptoeing around her. That cop with her looked like he was guarding the Hope Diamond."

Lila smiled. "Maybe he thinks he is."

Raissa closed her cell phone and tossed it on the dresser.

"Maryse?" Zach asked.

"Yeah."

"How's Hank?"

"Good. Helena got to see him, so she's stopped panicking." Raissa frowned. "There was something strange, though."

"What's that?"

"Maryse said when she went back to Hank's room to check on Helena after talking to the nurse, that she ran into the woman, Lila, Hank's boss that I told you about. Lila was standing outside Hank's room and said she didn't want to go in because there was a woman already in there. But the only woman who could have been in Hank's room was Helena."

Zach stared at her, eyebrows raised. "Maryse thinks Lila saw Helena?"

Raissa shrugged. "She can't think of any other explanation."

"The whole thing is just weird. So Luc used to see her but can't now? What's that about?"

"Luc's a different story than the rest of us. Helena's not the only dead person he's seen. He's part Native American, and apparently ghost-seeing runs in the family. But after Maryse was out of danger, he ceased being able to see or hear Helena."

Zach shook his head in dismay. "Now that's a hell of a thing to inherit. Maybe he and Maryse should consider adopting."

Raissa froze at Zach's words, her mind racing.

"Oh, hey," Zach said, apparently noticing her lack of response. "I didn't mean that seriously. They can have a dozen kids if that's what they want."

"No. I have an idea." She jumped up from her chair and pointed at the files. "Grab those files. We have to get to the hospital. I need to check something."

Zach gathered the files and grabbed his car keys. "What are you thinking?"

"It's only an idea, but I think I can get proof."

"Of what?"

"What those girls had in common. And why Hank Henry was abducted."

Chapter Twenty-one

"Why the hospital?" Zach asked as he drove out of Mudbug toward the hospital. "Do you need to talk to Hank?"

"No. The hospital has a weak security system. It's easy to hack their Internet access. And I'll be less likely to be caught hacking medical records at other hospitals if the signal is coming from this hospital."

"You want me to help you hack medical records?"

"Trust me, Zach. If I'm right, I'm going to blow the lid off all of this."

Zach shook his head, knowing he was making a big mistake. A career-ending, prison-sentence sort of mistake. But if Raissa was right . . . if she really could wrap this up with a couple of pieces of paper, Zach was almost to the point of risking it. He'd figure out a way to get to that point before he pulled into the hospital parking lot.

The lot was sparsely populated, but then, it was eleven at night. This was it, he thought as he parked in front of the building and turned off the car. He either followed Raissa into the hospital because he had no doubt she'd go in with or without his help, or he backed out of the parking lot and kept his record clean. Sort of.

Raissa hopped out of the car, then looked back inside when he didn't follow her. "Are you going to sit here and wait to be discovered by security?"

Zach pointed through the glass front of the hospital to the security guard, flirting with the nurse at the front desk. "Do you have a plan?" Zach asked. "Or are you just going to hijack the front-desk computer when they're not looking?"

Raissa laughed. "I have a plan, but I need to find Helena. I'm hoping she's still here."

It was crazy—a plan to help an FBI fugitive hack a hospital's computer system, with a ghost as the primary advantage. And it was a plan that he'd never, ever be able to tell to anyone else. Essentially, if he was caught, there was no way out of this. No rational justification for his actions. But it was also the last option they had, and time was running out.

He hopped out of the car and flashed his badge at the security guard, who nodded. With all the traffic in and out of Hank Henry's room, the security guard wouldn't suspect anything was out of order. Raissa pointed at the hallway to Hank's room, and they headed down it. They were halfway down the hall, when Raissa stopped short. Zach looked back, wondering what was going on.

"What's wrong?" he asked.

"Nothing," Raissa said. "Helena's right here. She's leaving Hank's room." Raissa quickly explained to Helena that she needed to get into the medical records of several hospitals, then turned to Zach. "She knows just how to help us."

Zach squinted, staring at the air in front of Raissa, wishing he could make out something . . . anything . . . that would prove he wasn't crazy for believing in ghosts. "Help us do what?"

"Break into the medical-records room. Listen, if you'd rather stay out of this, I understand. It's not exactly the sort of thing you want on your record."

"Of course I'd rather stay out of this, but it's too

late now. Worst case, I'll say you're a suspect in an investigation, and I followed you into the hospital to apprehend you. I will have to arrest you, though, if we get caught." *And no one's likely to believe it, but what the hell.*

"Fine by me. C'mon. Helena says the medical-records room is this way."

"Why medical records?" Zach asked as they walked. "Can't you use a computer somewhere else?"

"Yes, but the IP address of every computer is unique, so when I dial into another hospital asking for medical-records information, the security system is going to see the request coming from a medical-records-department computer at this hospital. I'm hoping it's enough to avoid setting off alarms. At least long enough for me to get what I came for."

"Which is? You still haven't covered that part."

Raissa turned down another hallway and stopped in front of the door to the medical-records room. A couple of seconds later, Zach heard the door unlock from the inside and it opened. He looked inside, but couldn't see a thing.

"Hurry up before someone sees you," Raissa whispered, motioning him inside.

Zach hurried into the room and shut the door behind him. Raissa had already slipped behind a desk in the far corner of the room. "Sorry," Zach said, "but that ghost shit still gets to me."

"As soon as I solve the mystery of Melissa Franco, I'm going to help Helena leave."

Raissa motioned for the folders, and Zach handed over the stack. "Help her leave?"

"Yeah, didn't I tell you? Helena was murdered. We're pretty sure that's why she's still hanging around.

So the general consensus is that if we can figure out who murdered her and why, she'll be able to cross over."

Zach shook his head, trying to absorb all of that into anything that resembled rationalality.

Raissa picked up the first file and handed it to Zach. "You read. I'll type. That will be faster. Give me the town the first girl lives in."

"Orlando, Florida." Zach pulled a chair next to Raissa and watched the screen flicker as she worked her magic. Finally, the screen stopped whirling and Zach looked at the header at the top left. "I hope I don't regret this."

Raissa laughed. "Don't worry. I've been doing this for years for my fortune-telling clients. Why do you think I'm so accurate?"

Zach placed his hands over his ears and hummed. "I am not hearing this."

Raissa swatted at him. "Give me the first girl's name with exact spelling. Middle name, too."

Zach read from the file and Raissa typed the girl's information into the hospital medical-records database. "All the girls came from families with moderate incomes and lived in outlying areas of small towns, sorta like Mudbug. I'm hoping they used a local doctor who worked out of the hospital."

"Is that common?"

"Yeah. It cuts out the doctor's office overhead and gives the hospital a doctor on-site a great majority of the day."

"So you're thinking their medical records would be at the hospital?"

"Yeah. Worst case, I'll get the emergency records, which might still tell me what I need."

"Okay." Zach didn't even pretend to understand where Raissa was going with this and apparently she was a show, not tell, kind of person.

"Bingo!" Raissa said. "Her records are here."

He leaned in to watch as Raissa opened the first girl's medical records. "Stomachache, vomiting, fever," he read. "Twice in the four months preceding her abduction." He looked over at Raissa. "So what? She ate something bad . . . had a virus . . . nothing that screams 'kidnap me.'"

"Not yet," Raissa said, and reduced the record to her desktop and opened another search. "Next name."

Zach shook his head and read off the name from the next file, wondering how one bridged the gap between a tummy ache and a kidnapping.

"Look," Raissa said, excited as she pointed to the next girl's record. "Stomach trouble three times in the six months preceding the kidnapping."

"Okay. So kids get sick. Maybe there was some big strain of the flu going around that year."

Raissa turned from the screen and stared at him. "I'll bet you twenty bucks that every single one of those girls went to the hospital complaining of stomach problems within six months of abduction."

Zach shrugged. "You're on. That's too big of an anomaly."

Raissa lifted the files from his lap and started typing. One by one she pulled up the girls' records, and one by one, the facts were right there for Zach to see. When she finished, Raissa looked at him.

"Okay," Zach said, still bewildered by the similarities in the records and the time line to abduction. "I owe you twenty bucks. Now, would you like to tell me what's going on? Obviously this proves your theory."

"I think every one of those girls was sick. I think the reason they were abducted has something to do with what was wrong with them."

Zach frowned. "But after they were returned, there's no record of illness."

"Exactly! And there was no record of illness earlier than six months before they disappeared."

Zach stared at Raissa, amazed. "Seriously? I didn't even notice. What the hell?"

Raissa jumped up from her chair and began to pace back and forth across the room. "Don't you see how extraordinary that would be? The oldest victim is seventeen. I know from my other research that she still lives with her family, in the same home, and they are still in the same income bracket, yet she's never visited the doctor again after her abduction."

Zach struggled to wrap his mind around what Raissa was saying. "So you think . . . what? They cured her?"

"Not then. Remember, they weren't sick until right before the abductions."

Zach ran one hand through his hair. "Jesus, Raissa. That sounds a little crazy, even for you. Even for this case, which is anything but normal."

"Melissa Franco was the same way. Remember, her dad said she was never sick, but Dr. Spencer said the medication they were giving her had curbed some symptoms that were beginning to form. What do you want to bet those symptoms included stomach problems?"

She slid into her chair again, tapped on the keyboard, then pointed to the screen.

"Cancer. And would you like to take a guess at how cancer usually presents itself in the early stages?" She tapped one fingernail on the monitor. "Take a look."

Zach read the screen that provided a list of the

symptoms of leukemia in children. "Initial symptoms are usually attributed to the common flu," he read. "Damn." His mind whirled with the possibilities of everything Raissa had said. "But why these kids? And how did the abductors know when to take them? I'll admit this is fascinating, but it creates more questions than it answers. And it doesn't prove anything."

"I think someone's been carefully watching these girls since they were born."

"Spencer?"

"Most likely. But I bet there's more."

Raissa pulled up the first record. Her fingers flew across the keyboard, pulling up one record after another until she had three hospital records side-by-side on the screen. "Look." She pointed to the records of the parents of the first girl. "Look at the blood types."

She turned and looked directly at Zach. "Don't you see? There's no way she's their daughter. And I'd be willing to bet that we'll find that's the case with all the girls who went missing, including Melissa Franco."

"Peter Franco said they had trouble conceiving. Could be that Melissa was conceived in vitro."

"And the others? All blue-collar families, but they managed to pay the cost of in vitro while in the military? No way. Every one of those children except Melissa was conceived while the father was stationed at the military base in North Carolina."

"So what? Someone made a mistake with meds, or gave them the wrong babies. I don't know what you think this is, Raissa."

"I'm not sure, either. But let's go over what we know. Someone helped these parents conceive babies that were not biologically their own, and Spencer was present on the base when every one of those babies was conceived."

"You think he gave them in vitro—without them even knowing?"

"Could be. The actual insertion of the egg wouldn't require much more than an extensive exam. Spencer could have said their Pap was irregular in order to do more 'tests,'" Raissa answered. "So, continuing with what we have so far, someone was keeping tabs on the kids and arranged an abduction around the time the girls started showing symptoms of a stomachache."

"A possible precursor to cancer," Zach chimed in.

"Right. The girls are taken for a week, then returned—perfectly healthy and with no memory of what happened."

"Okay, even if I buy that Spencer impregnated these women against their will, where did the eggs come from? They had to be the same person, right? There's no way they'd develop the same disease at the same age otherwise. Wouldn't that imply a genetic similarity?"

Raissa nodded. "I think so."

"But that doesn't explain Melissa Franco. Why start all this again after nine years had passed?"

"My best guess is that when Susannah Franco couldn't get pregnant, she talked about it with her family. I'm certain Monk Marsella is the one who kidnapped those other girls, and he must have known enough about what was going on to convince whoever he was working for to do it for Susannah."

"You think Monk Marsella strong-armed Dr. Spencer into impregnating Susannah with a bionic baby?"

"Monk could've threatened to expose the other girls, so he agreed to the procedure."

"Then why wait almost six years after creating Melissa to kill him?"

"I don't know for sure, but it looks like someone's eliminating all liability associated with this mess.

That would also explain why Dr. Spencer's car has a bullet hole, likely from my gun, in his trunk. He must have seen Melissa going into my shop after the appointments. He knew I could expose his relationship with Melissa and her mother."

"And on the day of the kidnapping, you went to the police station. It must have been Spencer who pushed you in front of the bus." Zach was beginning to think that in a bizarre, out-of-this-world sort of way, things were starting to make sense. "That would explain why Susannah lied about Melissa's medical condition, and why I got the feeling she wasn't as worried as her husband. She already knew where Melissa was and why. She knew they were going to do something that would kill off the cancer. She knew Melissa would return to her, the perfect child."

"Exactly. And I think that treatment involved a blood transfusion from Hank Henry."

"Whoa, you lost me here." Zach shook his head. So much for things making sense. "Why Hank? Because he was abducted?"

"Because he was abducted by an *alien*, like the others, and because he had a needle mark in his arm and was anemic when he was brought into the hospital. They were giving him iron pills, remember?"

"Okay, I'll bite—why Hank Henry?"

"We know Hank couldn't have been Helena's biological son," Raissa explained. "But he's obviously tied up in this mess, because Monk mentioned his name to Sonny in connection with the kidnapping—Sonny just didn't know why. And from everything Maryse told me, the man's never been sick a day in his life. I think Hank is the original version of the bionic baby, and a successful one. He supposedly had periodic problems with anemia, but what if it was because they were harvesting blood from him? Doing a transfusion to save the other girls?"

"But Hank's never been kidnapped before."

"No. Because he's always been available, and I think that's why Helena was impregnated. So they could keep an eye on their work. Until the last couple of years, at least, when Hank pulled a disappearing act."

"But the only person who could have gotten that much blood from him without anyone suspecting something is—"

"Yes," a voice sounded behind them. Raissa and Zach whirled around to find Dr. Breaux standing in the doorway, a 9-millimeter in his hand.

"I'm really sorry you had to push the issue," Dr. Breaux said. "We'd stopped our work here because it was too dangerous, but then Monk insisted we start again. I knew impregnating Susannah would be a mistake, but we couldn't afford to kill her. We weren't sure how much her cousin had told her, and with her husband's connections . . ."

He motioned to both of them with his gun. "Put your hands up and step out from behind that desk."

Raissa glanced at Zach, who barely shook his head. There was no way to get to their weapons in time. They stepped out from behind the desk and walked toward the doctor until he told them to stop, about ten feet in front of him. "You"—Dr. Breaux waved his gun at Zach—"take out your gun. Slowly, or I shoot her right now. Slide it across the floor to me."

Zach slid his pistol out of his hip holster and pushed it across the floor toward the doctor.

"Now you," Dr. Breaux said, and motioned to Raissa.

Raissa removed her pistol from the back of her jeans and slid it across the floor. She made no move at all for her ankle holster and hoped the doctor had no idea she always doubled up on weapons.

Dr. Breaux shook his head. "I was hoping I was wrong about you, Raissa, but some things just never added up. And when Dr. Spencer told me you went to the police after the abduction, I was afraid my worst fears were right. You have a certain way of moving, of watching people, that's familiar to me from my war days. You're a well-trained machine."

"How long has this been going on?" Raissa asked.

Dr. Breaux kicked both of their guns into a corner, then studied her for a moment. "I guess it doesn't matter if I tell you. You'll be the only people left who will know everything, except me, and that will all change in another couple of minutes.

"It started after the war . . . during the war, if you want the real beginning," Dr. Breaux said. "I was captured in a village in Vietnam. There was an outbreak of influenza. Thousands of sick people and one doctor. When they found out I was a doctor, they put me to work in their makeshift clinic."

"This wasn't about the flu," Raissa said.

"No. We cared for flu patients all day long and well into the evening, but at night, a Vietnamese doctor worked his own magic in nothing more than a pop-up tent and not even five thousand dollars' worth of medical equipment. Pretty impressive, when you consider he made the first huge theoretical strides in building a superhuman race. He'd barely started work on human embryos, but if he'd had the equipment and more time, he might have been successful. His theories were mostly sound, and decades ahead of anything I'd ever seen."

"So you and Dr. Spencer re-created his research in the States after you were rescued and returned."

Dr. Breaux laughed. "I killed him for his research

and escaped with all of it. Do you really think I was going to let someone beat me to this discovery?"

"You impregnated women without their permission. You genetically altered the embryos before implanting. You knew what you were doing was illegal on so many levels, not to mention morally reprehensible."

"We needed a test sample, and we couldn't afford for all the children to be raised in the same location or someone might clue in on complications. Mothers wanted children. And I had several potential investors lining up to make me a *very* wealthy man."

"I thought Hank was a success. You could've cut and run," Raissa said.

"Yes, Hank was a success, but no matter how hard I tried, I couldn't duplicate the results with girls. No girls, no deal with investors. With Melissa, I'd finally isolated the problem and was ready to move forward with a new round of babies, when Helena got cancer."

Raissa felt the blood drain from her head. "Oh, my God. It was *you* who killed Helena."

"I could hardly have her asking Hank for a bone-marrow transplant, then finding out he wasn't her son. She would've made things very messy."

"And then you kidnapped Hank," Raissa said.

"Of course. I knew where Monk had kept an extra alien suit, but never figured on having to use it. It was quite a bit of fun, though, the look on Hank's face."

"And Melissa?"

"She'll be safely home tomorrow—just like the others."

"Why kill Dr. Spencer?"

"He was a liability. He was in a panic, ready to confess everything, and had forgotten entirely what a crack shot I was in the military. I've always kept in practice. You never know when you might need to kill something."

Raissa stared at Dr. Breaux, his eyes cold and calculating, and realized this was the end. This man had been working toward a single-minded purpose for over half of his life. He believed he was God and wasn't going to let anything get in his way.

She reached for Zach's hand and held it tightly in her own, regret washing over her. "I am so sorry," she said.

Zach shook his head. "I'm not."

"Touching," Dr. Breaux said. His finger tightened on the trigger, and Raissa closed her eyes, waiting for the end.

Suddenly, the door to the records room flew open and Sonny Hebert burst in. Sonny fired one shot at Dr. Breaux and caught him in the leg, but the doctor managed to squeeze off one of his own and caught the mobster in his arm. Sonny dropped his gun and launched behind a bookshelf to protect himself from more fire. Raissa and Zach hesitated for only a moment, then dove behind the computer desk.

Raissa pulled her pistol from her ankle holster and fired off a shot at the doctor, who slipped behind a set of bookcases just in time to avoid her shot. "Checkmate," she whispered to Zach. "Two of us and two of them." Raissa had no doubt that Sonny would only delay coming after her long enough to kill the doctor.

Raissa peeked around the side of the desk and gasped in surprise. Helena Henry was dangling from a ventilation pipe, pushing as hard as she could against the bookcase Dr. Breaux was hiding behind. The bookcase rocked back and forth, almost to the tipping point. Raissa tugged at Zach and pointed to the bookcase. "Helena," she whispered.

Zach nodded and perched on the other side of the

desk, prepared to dive for his weapon as soon as the bookcase toppled. Raissa held her breath as the bookcase tipped forward, then backward, then forward, and seemed to almost pause before it crashed into the bookcase in front of it, setting them off like dominos all the way to the front of the office.

The fallout was immediate. Sonny popped up from behind the desk, dove for his gun, and opened fire at the doctor, who in turn had opened fire at everything in the room. Zach grabbed his weapon and ran for the emergency exit at the opposite corner of the room, Raissa close behind.

She heard Helena yelling at her to hurry, when she felt the bullet rip through her thigh. She stumbled and tried to brace herself, but her head hit the side of a metal filing cabinet. The last thing she remembered seeing was Zach's horrified expression as he looked back at her, and then everything went black.

Chapter Twenty-two

Raissa awakened to a burning pain in her leg and voices arguing above her. She opened her eyes, but everything was blurry. Finally, things sharpened a bit, and she saw Helena hovering right over her face, looking down anxiously at her.

"Are you all right?" Helena asked. "Say something if you are. Anything."

"I think so," Raissa said, a whisper all she could manage with her aching head.

"The emergency-room staff is on their way, although I have no idea how Zach is going to explain this mess." Helena said. "And those two have been going at it ever since Sonny dropped Dr. Breaux." Helena moved to the side and Raissa looked up at Sonny and Zach, squared off and equally pissed.

"I didn't shoot her," Sonny argued. "I was only firing at the doctor. And I'm not going to apologize for killing the bastard who messes with kids."

"*Your* guy kidnapped those kids," Zach pointed out.

"I suspected Monk was up to something, but I could never prove it until Raissa blew her cover. I got all over Monk and he told me some of it, but he said he didn't do another job for them after I found out. I didn't figure out the rest until today, after talking with Susannah Franco. Those doctor assholes convinced him to take that first girl by telling him she was going to die and they could save her. Monk said if they didn't return the girl to her parents, he'd blow the lid off everything. Monk thought he was helping the girls, the dumb son-of-a-bitch. He never should have gotten involved, and he damn sure shouldn't have gotten his cousin involved, especially after he'd been out of it for years."

Raissa sucked in a breath. Finally, things were making sense. After the years spent trying to heal his dying daughter, Sonny would be the last man alive to intentionally hurt a child, despite his many other destructive ways.

"What are you even doing here, Sonny?" Zach asked.

"I came to talk to Hank, then saw you two and figured you were here for the same reason. You went off a different direction, so I waited a bit, then saw that doctor go the same way. I could see the outline of his pistol in his pocket, so I followed. I heard everything that sick fucker said."

Zach shook his head. "This whole thing is unbelievable. Why in the world would Susannah Franco want to have a baby she knew would get cancer?"

"Monk told me the doctors said they'd fixed the problem," Sonny said. "My guess is that Monk never even told Susannah about the illness. I think they were just using Melissa as a last test case before cutting out to another country. When Melissa got sick, Monk knew they'd lied. He confronted Spencer and Breaux, and they killed him."

"You expect me to believe that?" Zach asked.

"I don't give a shit what you believe. I know what I know. I just couldn't do anything about it until I knew for sure Melissa was going to be all right. I've waited years to finally understand this, but it's over. Melissa is the last of them, so there's no longer a use for Dr. Mengele. Besides, he shot at me first."

"He barely nicked you. It's not even bleeding anymore."

"Yeah, well, he didn't just nick your girlfriend. I'd think you'd be thanking me instead of complaining."

Raissa struggled up to a sitting position, distracting the two men from their conversation.

Zach dropped down beside her. "Don't move. You hit your head and we need to make sure there's no damage. The nurse is coming with a gurney."

Raissa looked at Zach, his expression filled with worry and anger and love, and she felt her chest constrict. He really cared for her, and as much as she'd tried not to, she'd fallen for the surly detective in a big way.

The door to the office flew open and two nurses rushed in with a gurney. Zach barked orders, and the nurses made quick work of securing her to the gurney. As they wheeled her out of the office, Raissa looked back at the man who wanted to protect her, then at the other man, the one who wanted to kill her, and was suddenly overwhelmed with the hopelessness of it all.

Zach pulled out his cell phone and dialed Captain Saucier. This was one time his boss wouldn't mind having to get out of bed. He told the captain everything he and Raissa had discovered about the girls, and the captain started making things happen. A quick real-estate search turned up a warehouse in New Orleans owned by Dr. Breaux, and thirty minutes later, Zach got word that Melissa was alive and well and on her way to a hospital.

Susannah Franco broke down when questioned by the police and gave up everything she knew about Monk, the experiment, and the other kidnappings. The mayor had caught her in a lie the day of the kidnapping and she'd confessed everything to him. In a typical move, the mayor had kept it all quiet in the guise of protecting his son and granddaughter, but Zach suspected he just wanted to increase his popularity.

Zach, Sonny, and the two policemen the captain had sent relocated to an exam room just off the lobby of the hospital. The police officers were trying to get everything Sonny knew on record, but kept doublechecking with Zach. Not that he blamed them. Sonny's story sounded more far-fetched than a Hollywood movie.

After ten minutes of disbelief from the officers and swearing and hand gesturing from Sonny, Zach stepped across the hall to the visitor's lounge to pour himself a cup of coffee. What a night. What a mess. Raissa had blown the lid off of one of the most bizarre and corrupt things he'd ever heard of in his life. And she'd taken a bullet for her trouble.

His heart clutched when he thought about how close he'd come to losing her. And as much as he knew that Sonny Hebert belonged behind bars, he couldn't hate the man who'd saved the woman he loved.

Holy shit.

He set his coffee down on the table and the liquid sloshed over the rim of the cup, burning his hand. He shook the coffee off his hand and grabbed a napkin from the counter to wipe off the rest.

You've really done it now, Blanchard.

He stepped up to a window and stared out into the darkness. How the hell had he allowed this to happen? He'd fallen for a woman who was going to disappear like the wind as soon as she checked out of the hospital, and the worst part was, there wasn't a damn thing he could do about it. Raissa would never be safe with Sonny still gunning for her. She'd move off and become a bank teller in Idaho or a waitress in Seattle, and he'd never see her again.

He'd just go on the same way he always had.

No. He shook his head. Things would never be the same again.

Raissa sat propped up against the pillows of her hospital bed, her head still throbbing. The only good part was, the pain in her head had caused her to completely forget the pain in her leg. Maryse and Mildred had arrived earlier, and Raissa had filled them in on everything. Now they sat at the side of the bed, listening to Helena, who was perched on the bed, telling them everything that had happened when the New Orleans police arrived after Raissa had been taken away.

"The police were confused as hell, but the long and short of the immediate situation is that the only bad guy in the mix was Dr. Breaux, who is dead."

Mildred shook her head, the dismay on her face clear as day. "I still just can't believe it. How could we have been so wrong? We never noticed anything at all."

Maryse patted her hand. "It's not our fault. Obviously he'd been at this for a long time. We had no way of knowing that he was someone completely different. How could we?"

"I'm dead proof of that," Helena said. "He admitted to Raissa that he killed me."

Mildred gasped. "Oh, my God. Raissa, is that true?"

"Yes," Raissa confirmed. "I'm sorry. With everything else going on, I left that part out. I accused him, and he said he couldn't afford Helena finding out Hank wasn't her biological son."

"And if she found out about the leukemia," Maryse

finished, "then she'd have asked for a donor match and found out then. Shit."

"But he didn't say how he did it," Helena said, "so I still don't know."

Maryse frowned. "I have an idea, but we'll never be able to prove it."

"I don't care if you can prove it," Helena said. "Just tell me something that makes sense."

"When we were planting that listening device at Sonny's you said you hadn't paid for medicine in years—that you'd gotten samples."

"That's right," Helena said. "Damned pharmacy was always out of my inhaler."

"And Dr. Breaux gave you samples from his office."

"Yeah."

"I think the poison was in the inhaler. Try to remember, Helena. Did you use your inhaler before you drank the brandy?"

Helena's eyes widened. "Holy shit, I did. That must be it."

Raissa shook her head. "Genius. It evaporates into her system, and there's no record of where she got it even if anyone asked. It was the golden opportunity. I think you're right, Maryse."

"It makes sense, as much as anything does," Helena said, then sighed. "I want you all to know that I really appreciate everything you've done . . . for me and for everyone else. I can't believe this is finally over."

"Not quite over," Maryse said, "or you wouldn't still be here. But I have an idea about that, and I'm going to run it by Sabine tomorrow. I'll fill you in as soon as I know more."

"Thanks."

"So, Helena," Raissa said, "finish telling us what

happened when the police got here. Did they arrest Sonny?"

"Oh, right," Helena said, growing animated again. "They didn't arrest Sonny for killing Dr. Breaux, because Zach backs his story that Dr. Breaux was holding you two hostage with the intent to kill when Sonny burst in, and that Dr. Breaux fired the first shot. Probably good for Sonny that Dr. Breaux at least grazed him with that shot."

Raissa nodded, then flinched as her head throbbed more. "Makes him more sympathetic."

"Exactly. And Sonny Hebert needs all the sympathy he can manage. Then the FBI showed up, all mad and everything. They told Sonny they want to question him, but I'm not sure if they can make anything stick, as he wasn't actually the one kidnapping the girls."

"Probably not," Raissa said. "Sonny can always claim he didn't know about the kidnappings until after the doctors killed Monk and he found the alien suit."

"Which he has in his closet," Helena pointed out.

Raissa shrugged. "Doesn't prove anything. Besides, I have a feeling that suit is long gone by now anyway."

Helena shook her head. "Sonny put himself in the middle of a big fat mess. How do you think he'll get out of it?"

"There had to have been other people in on this—doctors, nurses . . . Someone else knows what they were doing, and the cops are going to want their heads on a platter big-time, especially since Dr. Breaux is dead. They'll need Sonny to testify about what Monk told him of the kidnappings and Dr. Breaux's confession, so the cops will deal. That ought to kill them."

Helena blew out a breath and looked at Raissa. "But that means you're still on the hook as far as testifying for Sonny's other crimes goes. Shit. I was hoping the FBI could get Sonny on something else so you could live normally. I guess there's no chance of that, is there?"

"No. If the FBI can't get Sonny on the kidnappings, they're going to want me to testify on the racketeering. The time on that case is almost up."

"So you'll be gone again."

Raissa looked at their expressions, hoping there was another answer but not believing there was. "Gone or dead. There's really no other way. I'm sorry, guys."

"That's bullshit!" Helena said. "I know Sonny's a bad guy, but he was only trying to help those girls, and he told you where Hank was. It's not fair that the FBI leaves you in a position of having no life, and no future but running from Sonny and his family."

"I agree," Maryse said. "Surely something can be done."

Raissa shook her head. "I'm the only witness who can testify to the things I saw and did. No one else is qualified to provide that testimony. I'm all they have."

"Makes me wish you weren't so good at your job," Mildred said. "If you didn't know anything, you could marry Zach and live in New Orleans, or maybe even in Mudbug with Maryse and Sabine." Mildred sighed. "I guess that's just wishful thinking, huh?"

Raissa stared at Mildred, an idea forming in the back of her mind. It was risky in all sorts of ways. In fact, it was the biggest risk she'd ever taken, and that was saying a lot. But it just might work.

Her thoughts were interrupted by a knock on the door. Raissa looked up in time to see the doctor who had examined her earlier, Agent Fields, and Zach enter her room, followed by Sonny and two NOPD officers. Zach went straight to Raissa and kissed her on the lips. "How are you feeling?"

"My head hurts, but I think I'm okay."

The doctor gave her a critical look. "These people insisted on seeing you and asking some questions. I am totally against putting any more strain on you, given your head injury, but I was forced to give you an option." The doctor shot a dirty look at the police and Agent Fields. "If you aren't up to talking, just say the word, and I'll clear the whole lot of them out of here."

"It's okay," Raissa said.

"You're certain? I don't like to think you're being intimidated."

Raissa smiled. "I promise, if any of them get out of line, I'll ask them to leave myself."

The doctor nodded, but didn't look convinced. He gave all of the men a frown and left the room.

Agent Fields stepped forward, followed by the two cops. "First off, we need to hear from you who shot you."

"I have no idea," Raissa said.

Agent Fields frowned. "You came to the hospital to get evidence against Dr. Breaux, and then Sonny showed up. Shots were fired, but you can't say who hit you?"

Raissa frowned. "I came to the hospital?"

Zach looked over at Mildred and Maryse, his face filled with worry. "What's wrong with her? Has she been talking to you?"

Maryse looked over at Raissa, her eyes wide. Raissa looked her in the eye, willing her to understand. Mildred started to speak, but Maryse took her hand and squeezed. "She's been talking," Maryse said, "but mostly about stuff we did months ago." Maryse bit her lower lip and shot a worried look at Raissa. "We were just about to call for the doctor when you guys walked in."

Raissa managed to look confused and made a mental note to talk to Maryse later about her superb ability to lie on command. The woman was a pro.

"I think maybe you should call the doctor now." Zach leaned in close. "Do you know who I am?"

Raissa laughed. "No, I let strange men kiss me all the time. Of course I know who you are."

Zach nodded. "We met because you were trying to figure out why those girls were kidnapped, remember? You figured it all out by looking at girls' records."

"Kidnapped . . . Melissa Franco. She was kidnapped." Raissa sat up straight. "Is she okay? Did they find her? She always made her mom buy blue candles."

"Melissa's mother confessed to her part in everything, and they found Melissa at a warehouse Dr. Breaux rented in New Orleans. All his notes are there—decades worth of testing. We'll be able to figure out everything he did. Melissa's on her way to the hospital but appears to be fine."

"Thank God. I'm glad to hear that."

"There were other girls . . . from years ago. Do you remember?"

Raissa frowned. "I don't know any other girls. Only Melissa."

"You investigated the cases when you were undercover in Sonny Hebert's organization." Zach nodded toward Sonny, who cocked his head to one side and studied her, a confused look on his face.

Raissa stared at Sonny for several seconds, then gave Zach a bewildered look. "I don't know that man."

"That's Sonny Hebert," Zach explained. "You were undercover in his organization when you were in the FBI."

"The FBI?" Raissa widened her eyes and looked from Zach to Sonny to the cops.

Zach sucked in a breath. "You left protective custody over nine years ago and have been pretending to be a psychic in New Orleans."

Raissa laughed. "Pretending? I'm not pretending. I have a lot of clients. You guys are kidding me, right? Really, what's all this about, Zach?"

The room went instantly silent, and Raissa was fairly sure no one was breathing. The doctor walked into the room and immediately checked Raissa's vitals. "Do you want me to remove your visitors, Ms. Bordeaux?"

"No," Raissa said. "They're trying to pull a prank on me."

Zach looked over at the doctor, his face panicked. "She doesn't remember things. Some recent events and anything from about ten years ago." He pointed at Sonny. "She worked for this man for two years, but doesn't know him. I don't understand."

The doctor shone a light in Raissa's eyes and felt her scalp. "The injury was to the section of the brain that stores memory. Memory loss is always a possibility, and long-term memory is the most likely to go."

"But it will come back, right?" Agent Fields asked.

"There's no way to know," the doctor said. "I think it's better if you all let Ms. Bordeaux rest, and no more questioning until *I* say she's ready. Is that clear?"

Agent Fields and the New Orleans cops didn't look happy, but they couldn't exactly argue with the doctor, so they trailed out of the office. Sonny, following behind them, looked the most confused of the lot. At the doorway, he paused and looked back at Raissa.

Raissa stared at him, held his gaze. Sonny's eyes widened and he barely nodded, then left the room.

Maryse hopped up from her chair, pulling Mildred with her. "I think we ought to give you two some time," Maryse said. "We'll go get some coffee. Call if you need anything."

Helena hopped off the end of the bed and trailed behind them, giving Raissa a wink and a thumbs-up on her way out the door.

"Thanks," Raissa said. She lay back against the pillows and looked over at Zach, who was frowning at her.

"You're faking," he said. "Holy shit, Raissa! This is not a game. Why are you faking memory loss?"

"Between my undercover work and hiding because of my undercover work, I've lost eleven years of my life to Sonny Hebert. And the ironic thing is, if it weren't for him, I wouldn't have another eleven years to make things different. He saved my life, Zach. And probably Hank's, too."

"But the racketeering case—"

"I know Sonny's done some bad things, but he did help us find out who was taking those girls, and he found Hank. If the FBI has to have me to make a case against him, then it wasn't much of a case to begin with, was it?"

Zach nodded. "You know what? You're right. You've given more than your share. Let someone else take up the slack. I'm sure Sonny's not going legitimate anytime soon. They'll get him, eventually."

"Maybe, or maybe not. If they didn't make a case in the nine years I was hiding, I can only guess that Sonny's gotten a whole lot better at his job."

"And what about you?" Zach asked.

"What do you mean?"

"What are you going to do, now that you're free?"

Raissa smiled. "Well, I'm not going back to the FBI,

that's for sure. Honestly, I don't know what I'll do. I haven't had the freedom to choose anything in a long, long time." She leaned toward Zach and whispered in his ear, "But I hear there's this detective who needs someone to keep him in line."

Zach smiled. "And just what makes you think you can do the job?"

Raissa softly kissed his neck once, then again, then his earlobe. He groaned and turned to her, crushing her lips with his. He gathered her in his arms, and in an instant, Raissa knew she'd made the right decision.

She'd seen the future, and it was very bright, indeed.

Epilogue

One week later

The party started at five that evening. Maryse had worked her magic with the historical society, one of the recipient's of Helena's massive estate, and they all gathered in Helena Henry's mansion, now a historical landmark. Maryse, Sabine, Mildred, and Raissa had done all the prepping and planning, baking, collecting premade trays from a caterer in New Orleans, and stocking the refrigerator with enough booze for New Year's Eve at a fraternity house. Helena, of course, was there to sample everything before it was deemed worthy of the festivities.

They joked and laughed and swapped tasks, helping each other that entire afternoon. Helena spent a lot of time just watching. It was beautiful, those girls and Mildred. Like a mother and her daughters. They'd endured so much to be here today. More than any thousand people would likely endure in a lifetime, and they'd persevered through it all. There was so much strength, so much love, that Helena got misty just thinking about it.

The men started arriving around five. Luc, with his big smile and enormous charm. Beau, with his big heart and quiet strength. Zach, with his brashness and fierce loyalty. So very different, but all so perfectly suited for the women they'd chosen to make a life with.

When the doorbell rang thirty minutes later, Helena peeked around the kitchen wall to see whom Raissa was letting in. She almost dropped her plate of nachos when she saw Hank walk through the door, holding the hand of that lovely girl Lila she'd seen at the hospital. She watched as Maryse crossed the room and gave the girl a hug. Then she said something to Hank, kissed him on the cheek, and gave him a hug.

Maryse pulled Hank and the girl into the huge, open living area and started introducing them to the people they hadn't met. Hank looked shy at first, but finally relaxed with the warm greetings he received from everyone. Lila watched him every second, her smile radiant.

Luc handed Hank a beer and Lila a glass of wine and waved his hand at the buffet along the wall. They filled plates and joined the others laughing and chatting . . . like a family. Helena rubbed away a tear and smiled. Finally, she took her plate and her drink and went up the back staircase to the second floor. The big spiral staircase in the main living area had a huge landing with a great view of the room. She took a seat above the action and enjoyed the interplay.

After an hour or so of festivities, Maryse directed the others to help her light candles that she'd placed all around the room. Maryse walked over to Hank, took his hand, and spoke to him. Hank nodded, his expression anxious and hopeful. Helena wondered what was up, but before she could sneak down and ask, Maryse looked up at her and waved her down.

"Get the lights," Maryse said, and Mildred turned off the lights to the room, leaving it doused in candlelight.

Helena rose from her seat and started down the spiral stairway. When she stepped into an area lit up by the candles, she heard a gasp. She looked over in the living room, and realized Hank was staring directly at her, as was Lila. "Oh, my God," Hank said. "I can see her. Mother?"

Hank took a step toward the stairway, and Helena hurried down. She stood just inches in front of Hank, his amazement clear. "I can't believe it," he said. "I mean, I knew Maryse wouldn't lie, but I never thought . . . Can you hear me?"

"Yes," Helena said. "I can hear and see everyone. It just doesn't always work the other way. Can you hear me?"

Hank nodded, his eyes filling with tears. "I am so sorry, Mom, about everything—being a lousy son, running off and leaving you to be murdered. I want you to know that it wasn't your fault. You gave me the advantages I needed to be successful. I threw them all away."

Tears formed in Helena's eyes as she looked at the man that wasn't her son, according to biology, but had been in every other way. "I wasn't a great mother. I know that. I didn't trust myself to show my love completely, not even with you. But I always loved you."

"And I always loved you," Hank said. He reached up with one hand to touch her face, and Helena was amazed when she could actually feel his fingertips gently brush her cheek.

"I feel your skin," Hank said, his eyes wide. "I didn't think . . ."

"I wondered," Maryse said, and stepped forward. "When you were in the hospital, Lila saw a woman in your room, singing. I thought she'd seen Helena, but I didn't understand why, as Lila wasn't in any danger." Maryse looked over at Luc and Zach, who nodded.

"Everyone can see you, Helena," Maryse said. "Something's changing, and I thought maybe tonight would be the height of whatever was happening."

"Why tonight?" Helena asked.

Maryse laughed. "Do you mean to tell me you've

been so distracted that you forgot your birthday? Why do you think we bought six cheesecakes?"

Helena stared. "My birthday. My God. I had forgotten."

Helena walked with Maryse and Hank to the center of the living room. Helena stared down at her feet and hands. "It's almost like I feel the floor beneath my feet." She reached out with a hand to touch Hank's shoulder and gasped. "I can feel him. Without concentrating, I mean. Just like when I was . . . alive."

Helena looked around the room, all of them looking at her with love on their faces and tears in their eyes, and she felt her heart swell. No woman deserved this, especially her. "My family," she said, and began to cry.

She hugged them all, one at a time, taking care to whisper to them her thoughts, her hopes for their futures. Something big was about to happen. She could feel it coursing through her body like an electrical charge. Finally, when she'd given her last hug, whispered her last thoughts, she stood in the center of the room and clutched Hank's hand with one of her hands and Maryse's with the other.

"Seems only fitting," she said, and smiled at the two of them. "Since this is how it all started."

As soon as the words left her mouth, a light began to form above them. It was small at first, like a candle on the ceiling of the room, but then it began to grow wider, and it dipped down, lower, lower, until it was past the second-floor landing and entering the first floor. Helena stared at the light, amazed by its beauty, by the warmth inside, and she squeezed Maryse's and Hank's hands as it began to pour over her body.

"I love you all. Be happy and well," she said, then slowly faded away.

INTERACT WITH DORCHESTER ONLINE!

Want to learn more about your favorite books and authors?
Want to talk with other readers that like to read the same books as you?
Want to see up-to-the-minute Dorchester news?

VISIT DORCHESTER AT:
DorchesterPub.com
Twitter.com/DorchesterPub
Facebook.com (Search Pages)

DISCUSS DORCHESTER'S NOVELS AT:
Dorchester Forums at DorchesterPub.com
GoodReads.com
LibraryThing.com
Myspace.com/books
Shelfari.com
WeRead.com

✂ ☐ **YES!**

Sign me up for the Love Spell Book Club and send my
FREE BOOKS! If I choose to stay in the club, I will pay
only $8.50* each month, a savings of $6.48!

NAME: _____

ADDRESS: _____

TELEPHONE: _____

EMAIL: _____

☐ I want to pay by credit card.

☐ VISA   ☐ MasterCard   ☐ DISCOVER

ACCOUNT #: _____

EXPIRATION DATE: _____

SIGNATURE: _____

Mail this page along with $2.00 shipping and handling to:
Love Spell Book Club
PO Box 6640
Wayne, PA 19087
Or fax (must include credit card information) to:
610-995-9274
You can also sign up online at **www.dorchesterpub.com**.
*Plus $2.00 for shipping. Offer open to residents of the U.S. and Canada only.
Canadian residents please call 1-800-481-9191 for pricing information.
If under 18, a parent or guardian must sign. Terms, prices and conditions subject to
change. Subscription subject to acceptance. Dorchester Publishing reserves the right
to reject any order or cancel any subscription.